THE WONDERFUL FRIENDSHIP

D1518627

BY

DAVID SWINDELL

ISBN 978-1-68570-191-8 (paperback)
ISBN 978-1-68570-192-5 (digital)

Christian Faith Publishing
832 Park Avenue
Meadville, PA 16335
www.christianfaithpublishing.com

Artwork by Vanya Cimino and Others

Printed in the United States of America

This book is dedicated to the loving
memory of Ida Swindell.
She touched the lives of so many people.

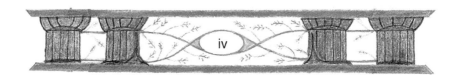

ACKNOWLEDGMENTS

A special thanks to the following people who helped with this book and encouraged me while crafting this story: to Jacinta, my niece, who edited my early manuscripts; to Mason, who always encouraged me to push on and finish the book; to Theresa, one of my coworkers, who always had faith in my talents and who believed in the goodness of this story; to the nuns of the monastery, who shared with me the incredible story of Frankie the Frog; and to John, my special friend and coworker, who gave me insight and direction into the mystery and nobility of ancient peoples and their cultures. Also a special thanks to Margie, who let me take pictures of her tractor, and to my kids on bus 62, who taught me so much about the true nature of the human spirit. From these incredible kids came the insight to see things more clearly from a child's point of view. My observation and interaction with the kids gave me some of the inspiration for this book.

Also a thank-you to my former employer and the staff at Auburn Washburn USD 437 Transportation in Topeka, Kansas. These amazing individuals gave me a

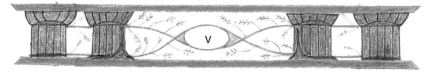

new start after Ida May's passing and the confidence to start my life over. They endured all the trials of dealing with someone like me who has a learning disability. For this reason, they deserve special praise.

CONTENTS

Chapter 1: Bear's Great Adventure 3
Chapter 2: Davie Must Face the Consequences
           of His Actions 18
Chapter 3: The Town Hero......................................28
Chapter 4: A Big Journey for Bear 60
Chapter 5: The Trappers Try to Get Revenge 102
Chapter 6: A Sad Ending for a Great Lady...............118
Chapter 7: Aunt Mimi to the Rescue 181

Chapter 8: New Friends...216
Chapter 9: Davie's Awakening 233
Chapter 10: A Bully Moves to Town.......................258
Chapter 11: Growing Up Together 282
Chapter 12: Conclusion and Epilogue....................288
Chapter 13: Readers Guide......................................308
A Special Note from Davie......................................317
Some Final Thoughts from the Author...................319
Biographical Sketches..321

Friendship is a gift that soothes out the troubles and hardships one often encounters in life. The act of friendship is a giving of oneself without expecting anything in return or expecting praise for actions that are helpful to others. The start of a friendship is often a mystery that involves a chance meeting or an event that draws people together for a common good, an assigned task, or a shared experience. Once the spirit of friendship is released, a new beginning comes into being that reshapes one's attitude and relationships with the people we meet through encounters.

For our younger readers, let me explain friendship in this way. When a teacher assigns you and a new member of your class a shared project, you are forced to work together to complete your assignment and receive a good grade. Putting the two of you together helped each of you to learn something about each other and respect the other person more. Often this new respect and the sharing the same interests and hobbies can lead to a lifelong friendship. The same is true with those who participate in team sports. By working together toward winning the game, each member of a team gives of himself or herself for a victory. The shared experience of winning and losing, of playing with all your heart and strength for your team or school, helps build the team through a shared unity and purpose. Thus, a friendship may develop that lasts beyond school years.

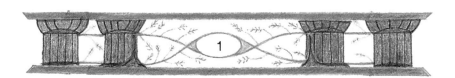

In our story, we find a coming together of animals and humans to overcome sadness, fear, and the jealousy of others. Our little group of friends gives all they have toward helping their fellow travelers on a great journey. Their shared experience and adventure help form a lasting friendship, bringing forth a love that carries them through some of the difficulties in our story. As our tale now unfolds, I hope you are prepared to learn from our friends the true value of friendship and reach out to your schoolmates and neighbors with a new spirit of giving.

Vanya Cimino & David Swindell

1

Bear's Great Adventure

B ear slowly emerged from his cave. He had spent the whole winter napping as the snow blew and thick ice appeared on the streams and lakes. How spring had begun as the last signs of winter vanished. The wildflowers were blooming, and birds were making nests in the pine trees for the new baby birds that would soon come. Bear stuck his big nose in the air, hoping to get a scent of food nearby. The long winter's nap had left Bear hungry. The extra weight he put on last fall from berries and nut picking were now a distant memory.

Now Bear suddenly remembered how delicious one of Ida May's pies had been last summer. In her effort to cool down a pie for expected visitors, she placed a blueberry pie just inside her kitchen window on a small table. Bear just happened to be strolling by and picked up the scent of that pie. He came right up to the window and boldly reached inside to grab his prize when Ida May caught the sight of Bear's big paw enter her kitchen. Bear took off with the pie, but not before Ida May caught up to him with a broom in hand. Although Bear enjoyed his sweet treat later, he had to suffer the shame of an old lady wildly swinging a broom after him, that Ida May chased Bear through the woods and across the meadow before she finally gave up. The other animals in the forest chuckled at Bear's troubles. Now looking back on what had happened last summer, Bear said to himself "You know, I don't think it's such a good idea to venture over to Ida May's house, pie or no pie."

With Bear's hunger still not satisfied, he decided to go fishing. Bear reached down into the water with his massive paws and grabbed a fish for a tasty meal. Now as it turned out, Bear had a favorite fishing place just on the edge of Ida May's farm. The clear running stream had wonderful-tasting brook trout. Grabbing and eating many trout, Bear decided to find a soft sunny spot to take an afternoon nap. Mr. Olson's meadow offered soft green grass and a lot of open sky to warm Bear's massive body. To reach the Olson place, Bear had to walk along the stream where he had gone fishing and find the best way through the thick pine forest that grew in such great abundance in this region of Northern Michigan. (If you look on a map, Upper Michigan resembles a large slice of land nestled between three of the Great Lakes. The people of this region refer to this place as the Upper Peninsula.) The path that Bear took that day would forever change his life and that of his neighbors, in that peaceful land to the North.

As Bear slowly made his way toward the Olsons' farm, he became sleepy and began to daydream about his good luck while fishing. He also thought about the other food that awaited him as spring would turn into the lazy summer months with its rich supply of good things to eat. While thinking on the joys of upcoming days, Bear failed to take notice of a changes on the trail he found himself on. Some trees had just recently been cut down, and many pine branches seemed thrown about. Bear's feelings tried to tell him something was wrong, but the thought of a waiting nap made him pay no attention to the coming danger. Suddenly, Bear heard a sharp snap and felt a strong pain in one of his rear legs. A huge bear trap had closed in on him, leaving him feeling helpless and with no one to help him. (A trap is a steel tool that has two jaws that spring shut when an animal steps in.)

Bear's first reaction to the trap seamed automatic—he tried with all his might to pull himself free of his captivity. The harder he pulled, the stronger the pain became. Bear even let out a big roar in anger, somehow hoping to find a way out of his state. The harder Bear worked at freeing himself, the more pain he felt. After several hours, Bear almost reached the end of his power and will to live. Becoming very weak, Bear fell to ground.

Now as it happened, Floppy the rabbit had heard a great uproar outside his burrow. Floppy stuck his head outside his home and saw the massive shadow of Bear's body. Since Floppy had been chased by Bear on many occasions, he remained fearful and stayed close to the burrow's entrance. Seeing Bear lying on the ground, Floppy thought to himself, *Surely something is wrong.* Floppy carefully came out of his home but kept a safe distance should Bear try to hurt him. Bear, for his part, paid little attention to Floppy's presence but instead quietly moaned as his pain became more intense and the evening shadows began to appear in the forest. Bear, for his part, felt that his end was near.

Seeing the situation Bear was in, Floppy knew that time was running out for one of his fellow animals in the forest. Although Bear had been unfriendly toward Floppy in the past, this brave rabbit knew that he must help anyone in need. Floppy thought to himself, *Who could help this creature of the forest without hurting him further?* From experience Floppy knew that trappers would check their traps every few days, and if they found Bear, it would be all over for him. While going over Bear's troubles in his mind, Floppy had a sudden idea. *Let's get Davie, the farm boy who lives with Ida May, and maybe, just maybe, he can free Bear and help him to regain his health back.* Floppy slowly crept up to Bear and whispered in his ear. He explained to Bear his idea for a rescue, but Bear suddenly stopped him and exclaimed in a soft voice, "No, and absolutely no."

Floppy then said to Bear, "Why?"

"Because Davie is a human, and most humans want to hurt and take advantage of animals for their own gain. Just look what happened to me."

Nevertheless, Floppy held his ground and said, "It's unfair to put all humans into the same lump of clay. I happen to know that Davie is a fine boy and never has hurt even a fly. He will help you if you give him a chance." Finally, Bear gave in, and Floppy's plan was put into action.

It was almost evening, but Floppy knew the way to Ida May's house despite the growing darkness. Since it had been a rather warm day for spring, Davie decided to do his homework with his bedroom window open. The light from his room cast a shadow deep into the side yard as moths danced to the strains of illumination. Floppy wasted no time and boldly hopped up on Davie's windowsill. Davie was caught up with his studies and did not notice Floppy at first. As Floppy cleared his throat, Davie looked up with amazement and a degree of surprise to see a rabbit that close to his window. Looking into his deep-brown eyes, Davie said, "How is it going, little fellow, and what brings you to me on this fine evening?" At about that time, Davie heard off in the distance the cry of an animal deeply in distress.

Now Floppy, unafraid, stated in a clear voice, "Davie, now everyone in these parts knows that you have a deep love for animals, the woods, and the streams of our region. If you had a chance to save one of the creatures of the forest, would you do it without delay?"

Davie scratched his head for a few seconds and then stated, "Well, I suppose so."

Floppy then said to Davie, "Bear stepped into a trap on the path down by the stream and is about to die. Will you help him?"

Looking quite concerned, Davie replied to Floppy with these words: "You see, little fellow, a wild bear is extremely dangerous and, in his state of pain and confusion, could hurt me very seriously. And secondly, Ida May would have an absolute fit if she knew her son was involved with such danger." However, despite Davie's objections, Floppy would take no for an answer. Davie finally agreed to help Bear, but the situation required quick thinking and planning on his part.

Davie knew he had no time to waste. Quickly he grabbed the first aid kit from the kitchen cupboard and some spices from Ida May's shelf above the stove. He also ran to the closet and got a clean white sheet from the neatly stacked linens arranged on the shelf. Before leaving the house, Davie wrote a quick note to Ida May, telling her that he had gone over to the Olson's and not to worry. You see, Ida May had gone over to visit Gretchen, a nice lady from the neighboring farm, and had strictly told Davie to finish his homework before doing anything else. Knowing full well Ida May would demand an account of his time, Davie threw caution to the wind and set off to help a hurt animal in the forest.

After reaching the barn, Davie fired up their old Farmall tractor and attached the farm trailer. Thinking to himself, he wondered how he was going to get a heavy bear back to the farm for care and feeding. Suddenly it dawned on Davie a plan for the rescue. Taking down a pulley from the barn wall, Davie carefully placed it in the trailer. He also pulled down a small cloth tarp from the loft in the barn and a spade and shovel from the toolshed. Knowing he would need something to pry the trap apart, Davie brought a come-along two log chains and a strong rope. (By the way, a come-along is a device that has a ratchet in the middle and two cables with hooks. It is used to tighten and loosen items and secure loads.) Placing all these items in the wagon, Davie also remembering the lanterns hanging from pegs in the barn plus some strong wooden planks that were also needed. Closing the gate on the trailer, Davie quickly jumped up on the tractor and started down the path and the injured animal that awaited him. What Davie failed to realize as he made his way from home that evening was what a great adventure that laid ahead.

Floppy ran ahead of Davie and reached Bear quickly. He whispered softly into his ear, "Davie on the way he's come to help you. Don't worry."

In a deep, soft voice, Bear replied, "I am scared that Davie cannot help me, and I will die here in the forest, my home. How can one so small and only a boy rescue me from my confinement?" Now Floppy marveled at his friend's lack of faith. He then reconfirmed his faith in individuals like Davie that want to do the right thing towards animals and the forest. Floppy reassured Bear that most humans wanted to protect animals and the environment. However, sometimes other people are careless and irresponsible when visiting the forest. He went on to say that only a few humans sought outright to deliberately profit from the killing of wild animals outside the law. As he finished his statement, Floppy and Bear heard the approaching sounds of a barking dog and the tractor. The moment of the great rescue had arrived.

Following his dog Buddy through the back roads and deep forest at night proved difficult. Being a farm boy and knowing the terrain thoroughly helped Davie move more confidently through the rugged back roads leading to Bear. As the tractor approached a clearing in the forest, Davie suddenly caught sight of a large shadowy figure lying on the ground. Buddy began barking and snarling as he neared the motionless figure. Suddenly Bear sprung up and let out an ear-shattering roar that pierced the surrounding forest. Freighted by his encounter with this massive creature, Buddy took off into the forest at a high speed. Now as it turned out, Buddy's quick exit proved quite lucky since Davie had to work calmly but dangerously with a wounded animal of that size and strength.

Jumping down off the tractor, Davie went right to work with his plan to save Bear. He knew that speed was needed to save his life before this massive giant bled to death. He also knew that it was a matter of time before the trappers who placed the trap would return and claim their prize. To make things worse, Bear was losing his will to live. Taking the lanterns from the back of the trailer, Davie struck a match and lit their wicks. He took one of the lanterns and placed it near the tree stump just a few feet from the trap. Looking down on bear's position, Davie thought to himself, *Blasted poachers, they will stop at nothing just to make a few extra dollars.* Now a poacher is someone who hunts or traps out of season or in restricted areas.

In order for him to get Bear out of the trap, Davie knew that some sort of sedative was required to first relax and calm this massive creature. While rummaging through Ida May's kitchen cabinets, Davie came upon several bottles of apricot brandy. Ida May always kept brandy on hand for her delicious mince pies that she prepared at Christmas. Taking the brandy was easy, but explaining the loss of this liquor to Ida May remained a more challenging task. Nevertheless, the situation at hand needed immediate attention; explanations would come latter. Spotting Floppy, Davie said to his new friend, "I need your help to successfully liberate our friend. He needs to drink this liquid to help him sleep and avoid feeling some of the discomforts that lie ahead."

Floppy went straight up to Bear and softly whispered in his ear, "Drink this and it will make you feel better." Luckily, he was already drowsy, but as soon as Davie came closer, he let out a soft, low growl. Showing no fear, Davie approached with a tin pan full of honey and brandy from Ida May's pantry. Smelling this bearish delight, our friend quickly licked it up. More liquid was brought until Bear became very sleepy.

Now Davie knew that removing the trap required great skill. He had to find a way to pry open this massive device without hurting its victim any further or harming himself. To accomplish this feat, Davie retrieved the logs chains and the come-along from the wagon. Taking one of the log chains, Davie wrapped one end around a tree stump and securely hooked it back on the chain. He then hooked the other end of the chain to one side of the steel jaws holding Bear's leg. Another chain was placed around another tree stump opposite the first chain. Then the come-along was secured both to the other side of the trap's jaw and the second chain attached to the second stump. As he stretched the chains taut with the aid of the come-along, the process of freeing Bear had begun.

With real effort, Davie began pulling apart the trap. The sound of the ratchet on the come-along penetrated the stillness of the forest. All you could hear was the *click, click, click* as the jaws of the trap grudgingly gave up their prey. Suddenly the trap sprung open, and Bear awoke from his slumber. Davie, sensing the danger, ran quickly for the wagon. He yelled out to Floppy in a frightened voice, "Calm him down quickly before he hurts himself or one of us."

Floppy ran up to Bear and encouraged him with these words: "My friend, it's okay. You're finally free, and Davie and I will see to your care. Just trust us, and everything will come out all right." With these words, Bear quickly gave in and put his head down on the soft grass of the forest floor.

The next step in Bear's rescue would prove even more difficult. Using the sheet from Ida May's linen closet, Davie cut strips of cloth for bandages. He also mixed olive oil and thyme to make a special antiseptic. Davie attempted to prevent infection from setting in by pouring the mixture of spice and oil over the wounded leg. He next tied bandages over and around the injured leg.

The next challenge was how to get Bear into the wagon for the trip back to the farm. Placing a strap on the ground next to Bear, Davie secured one end of it to a stake in the ground near his rear feet. Davie then stretched the strap tight. Floppy then whispered in Bear's ear, "My friend, please help us by rolling back and forth." Although very drowsy, Bear complied with this request even though it hurt him. Slowly, Davie was able to work the strap underneath the great creature. The same process was repeated under the front legs. Davie then placed the two ends of each strap together; he secured them with a fastening hook. He also made sure that the straps were not too tight so Bear could breathe. The next step in the rescue required attaching the two sides together and connecting them to a single line. The rope was next connected to a pulley block that resembled a wooden block with a wheel in its center. This action made a cradle to hoist Bear onto the trailer. The fact he weighed around eight hundred pounds only worsened the challenge facing Davie.

The tractor was then unhitched and brought alongside the wagon. In addition, planks were placed on the back edge of the wagon and the ground below. Using the planks as a ramp was something Davie had learned in school while studying how the ancient Egyptians had built the great pyramids. In addition, blocks were put underneath the trailer wheels to keep them from moving. Coming alongside the trailer, Davie attached the rope to the back of the tractor. Slowly moving the Farmall forward, he edged Bear forward onto the planks. Floppy climbed upon Bear to calm him in case he stirred. The rope strained under the weight. Finally, Bear slid safely into the wagon. Davie quickly placed all the tools and the lanterns back into the wagon and hitched the trailer. He called out to Buddy, and his dog came running out of the woods. With that, Davie started the tractor and headed back to the farm. Despite the successful rescue of Bear, Davie wondered what kind of reception awaited him back at the farm. As they made their way through the darkness, a nagging feeling ate away in Davie's stomach. He thought, *How in the world am I going to explain all that happened?*

WHAT SHOULD WE LEARN FROM CHAPTER 1?

F ear is an important human emotion. At times it protects us from taking actions that are harmful or dangerous to ourselves or others. However, fear can often keep us from doing what is right or learning new things or meeting new people. In our story, Davie knew the danger of rescuing a wild animal deep in the woods at night. Despite this, he chose not to trust others in helping him make a rescue attempt. Davie was fearful that others would not come to Bear's help, or they would simply want the animal destroyed. For Bear's part, trusting a human proved difficult. Although Bear wanted and needed help, his fears and animal instinct made treatment much more challenging. From Bear's perspective, all humans are not worthy of trust, since many of bear's encounters with humans proved less than favorable.

Now taking what we learned from Bear and Davie, let's compare these emotions within the area of human experiences. For example, how many times have we taken negative attitudes toward others of different races or cultures? It is so easy to distrust newcomers and people with customs different from our own. Sometimes we feel threatened by outsiders, thinking they will take away jobs and our own social position. If there is simply one thing we can discover from our friends in the story, it is that it is always wiser and more rewarding to offer a hand of friendship than shut others out because of fear and mistrust.

2

Davie Must Face the Consequences of His Actions

The road home seemed extremely long for Davie as the tractor and wagon made its way through the forest and into the clearing next to Ida May's house. As the little party made its way down the lane,

Davie could sense a great commotion going on in front of the house. There were cars lined up along the road, and people were talking together in small groups. Mr. Olson spotted Davie right off and came running up to the wagon. Davie shut down the motor on the tractor and got down off the seat. In a loud voice, Mr. Olson addressed Davie with some very prying questions.

"Boy, where have you been? We got half the county out looking for you. Son, you better have a good explanation for your sudden disappearance." About that time, Ida May came running up from the house. She grabbed Davie and held him as she let out great tears of joy. For Davie all this fuss and emotion was unnecessary, but he knew the fewer words spoken, the better. For now, his story and the rescue of Bear would have to wait until later. He just had to keep his peace until the grown-ups were ready to listen. However, their happiness upon Davie's return soon turned serious as inquiries and explanations were now required.

Just as the happy reunion was going on at Ida May's house, the little party heard the approach of a patrol car. Now as it turned out, Sheriff Hanson had just finished his sweep of the area, hoping to spot Davie and his dog. The boy appearing seemed to relieve some of the sheriff's concerns, but this public defender was eager to get to the bottom of Davie's disappearance. Strolling up to the wagon, the good sheriff consoled Ida May and stated he would halt the current search still underway. Then turning to Davie, Sheriff Hanson asked the boy why he left home. Davie knew he would face the wrath of the sheriff and his own community if he told a lie. Speaking to the sheriff directly, Davie told Mr. Hanson his version of the events that unfolded.

"Sir, I was doing my homework when the sound on an animal in distress reached my ears. After following that sound, I discovered a bear in a trap and rescued him from his terrible distress."

Now Davie's story sounded a little far-fetched for a hard, practical man like Sheriff Hanson.

"Now, son, tell me the truth," retorted Sheriff Hanson in a rather gruff voice. Despite the sheriff's urgings, Davie held to his story. As it happened, at about that time, Bear woke up from his brandy-induced sleep and let out a big growl. He was hungry and scared, finding himself in a strange place outside the friendly confines of his beloved forest. As he stuck his big head out of the wagon, the residents of the town now jumped into their cars while others took off running down the fence rows, scared half out of their wits. Even the brave Sheriff Hanson climbed atop his own patrol car. The sheriff even pulled out his revolver and began swinging it widely in the air. It seemed like a whole lot of folks panicked over the sight of this big old bear.

Fearful that Sheriff Hanson might shoot bear, Davie stepped between the sheriff and Bear. Davie spoke to the sheriff Hanson with these words: "Sir, this old bear is injured, and I realize the danger of treating and caring for a wounded animal. But this is one of God's creatures, and he deserves a chance to live as nature intended him to be. Please, sir, let me try and tend to him and help him return to the wild where he truly belongs." Seeing the boy begin to cry, Sheriff Hanson climbed down off the car. He went and got his flashlight. As he shone the light in the back of the wagon, Bear seemed oblivious to what had transpired, his endurance finally diminished after his long ordeal. Sheriff Hanson then said to Davie, "Will get old Doc Wilson to come over and look at him in the morning. In the meantime, the boys and I will help you get him unloaded." So as it finally turned out, Bear was placed on some soft hay in the barn and out of danger. The events that unfolded that day would now bring Davie and Bear into a new friendship that would endure for many years to come.

By morning Bear woke from his sleep and began to feel some hunger pains. Now about that time, Davie had just finished milking the cows. He brought bear some fresh milk and placed it in a pan near bear's head. For the first-time, Bear made no fuss as Davie approached. It seemed that Bear was beginning to get over some of his distrust of humans. About that time, Floppy emerged from his hiding place in the barn. With all the commotion from the previous night, that shy old rabbit had slipped out of the wagon and waited until the coast was clear and quietly tiptoed into the barn. Seeing Floppy pop his head out of the straw, Davie looked surprised and expressed his astonishment.

"Wow, what a night. We sure gave the good folks of Wakefield something to talk about." As Davie and Floppy continued to talk about the events of the previous evening, they heard an approaching automobile. Looking through a knot hole in the barn door, Davie spotted old Doc Wilson, the local veterinarian. Turning to Floppy, Davie motioned with his hand and said, "Be quiet and go back into hiding." As for Bear, his situation was yet to be determined.

About the time Doc Wilson drove up in his car, Ida May dropped her load of laundry and headed toward the good doctor.

"Good morning, Doc. Thanks for coming over on such short notice."

"Ida May, I am always at your service. After all, you and I have treated a whole lot of sick calves and farm animals through the years. By the way, how in the world did you folks end up with a wounded bear?"

"Well, Doc, Davie heard the cry of that wild animal and went to his rescue."

Scratching his head, old Doc Wilson thought for a bit and then said, "It is incredible that someone of his age could manage an animal so large and heavy."

"You know, Doc," Ida May stated, "that boy sometimes amazes me. When you look at the bear, do not be afraid to tell Davie the truth concerning his condition."

He needs to know the truth concerning the health of his new pal. Also, Doc, Davie and that bear have bonded. He's really attached to the animal now, so make sure you explain your treatment carefully to him." With this, Ida May and Doc Wilson made their way toward the barn. The question now remained: Would Bear recover to return to the deep woods he loved so deeply, or would he gradually succumb to his injuries? This question weighed heavily on all the folks out on the farm.

As old Doc Wilson and Ida May entered the barn, Davie stood beside Bear with a look of concern on his face. Davie addressed Doc Wilson, saying, "Be easy with him, Doc. He's had a rough time the last day or so."

"Do not worry, Davie," replied Doc Wilson. "In my day, I have treated all kinds of animals, both wild and tame. One or more wounded bear will do nothing to shake my ability as either a professional or caregiver to animals." With this reassurance, Davie breathed a sigh of relief. Speaking to Davie in a rather rough voice, old Doc Wilson stated, "Now, Davie, our real challenge is to keep this animal quiet so that an examination of his condition is possible and no one gets hurt in the process. Will you help me with this task?"

"Sure, Doc, no problem," Davie replied.

Old Doc Wilson first went into Ida May's kitchen and washed his hands very intensely. He put on some latex gloves and headed back to the barn. Reaching into his deep old bag the good doctor pulled out a rather large syringe and a vile of some dark-looking liquid. Inserting the tip of the needle into the vial, Doc Wilson drew what looked like a massive amount of fluid. Looking toward Davie, Doc said, "It takes a lot of sedative to put a bear under. Now, Davie, you need to distract him while I give him his shot." Davie went into the stall were Bear was lying. He gently touched and reassured Bear that everything was okay through his gentle touch and calm voice. Then suddenly old Doc Wilson sprung from his position and quickly shot Bear in his rump with his prepared sleeping drug. All this happened in a flash of a second.

With Bear under the influence of a powerful sedative, Doc removed the dressing Davie had placed on Bear earlier and peered deeply into the wound on his leg.

"Well, Davie, it looks like our friend has a little infection, and the cut on his leg goes through to the bone. I am going to sew him up. It is important that you keep him quiet and give his leg a chance to heal. Also place these drops in his milk, and it will help him sleep. This will make your bear more comfortable during his recovery. In the meantime, I will come over every other day and change the dressing on his leg." Hearing these words of encouragement, Davie felt better. Feeling more relieved, Davie asked Doc what he thought Bear's chances were for a complete recovery. "Well, Davie, that depends on a lot of factors. First and foremost is the care he receives from you. If you take good care of him, his chances improve a great deal. Now do not worry. Your mom is one of the best handlers of farm animals in the county. She has nursed back to health many sick farm animals. Son, Ida May will do all she can to help you get this bear back on his feet." With these words, Davie just knew that Bear had a fighting chance. From that moment on, Davie did everything in his power to ensure Bear's recovery. With Doc's positive outlook on Bear's improvement, they became more positive out on the farm.

After Doc left the farm, Ida May called Davie into the house for some discussion concerning the past day's events.

"First and foremost, let me say how profoundly proud I am of you for rescuing that old bear. It took a great deal of courage to trudge off into the night and face a wounded animal. However, despite your bravery, you exercised some faulty judgment. First and foremost, you lied to me about where you had gone. And second, you put your life in danger handling an animal of that size alone. Son, in my estimation, had you called on one of our neighbors for help, then it may have proved less dangerous. And in addition, you ransacked the house and took many items of importance without my permission. Despite these facts, I realize that sometimes the situation requires some hasty actions. Overall, I believe most of your deeds were honorable. Therefore, I am going to punish you less severely for what you did. For the next month, you will not be able to stay up late on the week-ends, or go bowling with your buddies in Ironwood. Is that understood, young man?"

"Yes, Mom," Davie replied. In the end, Davie took his punishment in stride. He had to help his mom with additional projects around the house. All in all, Davie accepted what had happened to him in stride and kept a positive outlook. Besides, now Davie had a new responsibility that would require most of his attention in the coming days.

WHAT SHOULD WE LEARN FROM CHAPTER 2?

Human pride is clearly a double-edged sword. We all need to experience a sense of accomplishment for a job well-done or achievement accomplished. However, pride can also keep us from growing by allowing self-importance to shut out humility and true concern for others. In chapter 2 of our story, Davie had to swallow his pride in rescuing Bear and admit his own miscues through a lie and taking property that did not belong to him. Saying we're sorry and asking for forgiveness is never a sign of weakness. By humbling ourselves, we acknowledge the respect and dignity of the person we have offended. But if we stand on false pride, then we only hurt ourselves in the process.

3

The Town Hero

On his way back to town, Doc Wilson decided to stop at the Main Street Café in downtown Wakefield for lunch. Upon entering the café, Doc Wilson was greeted by some of the local boys who always frequented the place.

"Hey, Doc, what is going on up at Ida May's place? We've heard some wild rumors about those folks having a wounded bear on their property. Is that true?" Doc Wilson pondered for a few seconds while he scratched his nearly bald head.

"Well, boys, it is like this. Ida May's son, Davie, found a wounded bear in a trap up by their place. Without any help from anyone, he managed to singlehandedly load that bear into that dilapidated old wagon of theirs. What really amazes me is how someone so small could pull off a stunt like that. Why, it is a wonder that a wounded animal of that size did not tear that boy to shreds." After making his statement, Doc Wilson tried to retreat to his table for one of the many tasty specialties served at the café. However, before Doc had only moved a few feet, Jim Hanson, the leader of that little group, made a rather direct demand of the good doctor.

"Do you suppose that the boys and I could go up to Ida May's place and look over that bear of theirs?" Jim's inquisitive request made Doc Wilson a little bit uncomfortable.

"I do not want any sightseers up on Ida May's farm. They got their hands full the way it is. You fellers best keep out of their way." Doc then proceeded to order up some of the best cooking found in town.

Now it did not take long for news to spread around Wakefield concerning Davie's exciting rescue of Bear. As it always happens in a small town, news travels fast, and without exception, word quickly spread through the town quicker than a lightning bolt out of a thunderstorm. Why, even Bob Urban over at the Wakefield News wrote a short piece for the weekly edition about Davie and Bear's exploits. In addition, the local television station ran a small story concerning Davie's adventure for their local viewers. Soon people began to call on Ida May and Davie out on the farm. They all wanted to see this mysterious bear that everyone was talking about. With all the attention Davie and Bear were getting, Ida May became a little perturbed. It was not that Ida May was envious of her son, but her concerns were simply for his schoolwork and chores out on the farm.

As for Bear, his recovery continued at a remarkable rate. Floppy stayed in the barn with Bear and would go out into the forest and bring back some of Bear's favorite food. He would gather berries and wild honey for Bear to feast on while Davie brought huge dishes of fresh milk and leftovers from Ida May's table. Old Doc Wilson came over every other day as he promised. All this special care and attention perked up Bear and made him more accustomed to being around humans. And over time, Bear gradually let down his guard and began to enjoy and trust his human hosts.

Now through their hardships together, Bear and Davie formed a special relationship. The old saying that time heals all wounds fit this pair most accurately. Davie would take Bear for short walks in the meadow nearby. The two of them would wrestle in the tall grass as the sun gently poured out its golden rays on the last days of spring. As for these great wrestling matches, Bear had a sizable weight and strength advantage. He could pin Davie very quickly. Nevertheless, they both enjoyed these tussles on numerous occasions. Bear never intentionally hurt Davie and instinctively knew how much force to use. Occasionally bear would scratch Davie with one of his claws, but Davie never seemed to mind. While these great matches were underway, Bear would make soft growling sounds while Davie would growl back and make menacing gestures. All this playful interaction made the encounter between these two more enjoyable.

Often after putting Bear back in the barn, Davie had to spend considerable time picking grass and leaves from his hair and clothing. He would always stop outside the back door of the farmhouse and wash his face and hands with Ida May's homemade soap and plenty of fresh water from the well. To bring the water up from the ground, the family used a rusty old pump that required quite a bit of physical exertion to operate. No matter where you were on the farm, you could hear the squeaking and chattering of that old pump. Ida May would stick her head out the door and say, "After cleaning up for supper, pump me some more, water and bring some wood in for the stove." As you can see, even though Davie and Ida May had a special guest to look after, life on the farm always meant special tasks and work that required attention.

One Sunday afternoon, after coming home from church, Ida May and Davie saw a strange car come up the tiny lane leading to the farmhouse. As the vehicle came closer, the two of them noticed a rather distinguished-looking gentleman at the wheel. As the car stopped and the man got out, Ida May and Davie realized that this was no ordinary visitor to the farm. Tilting his hat in a polite gesture, the man spoke in a rather direct fashion.

"Well, good afternoon, folks. My name is Brian Jones, and I am with the TGN Television Network. Our local affiliate ran a recent story concerning Davie's discovery and rescue of the bear he found in the woods. The folks over at our organization want to run an in-depth television article concerning the event with a possible appearance on *The Big Night Show* with Jimmy Vick. Have you folks ever watched *The Big Night Show* and heard our motto, '*The Big Night Show*, where the stars of Hollywood come out to play'?"

Now Ida May was never a person lost for words, but this news seemed to take the wind completely out of her sails. Saying nothing at first, Davie had to pat his mother on the back and encourage her to speak. Speaking softly at first, Ida May showed great astonishment on her face.

"Mr. Jones, is what you are saying true?"

"Ma'am, let me reassure you, the offer is completely legitimate. In addition, TGN will provide you and the boy with all the travel arrangements to and from Los Angeles plus a small amount for Davie's appearance on *The Big Night Show*. You could use the money from the show for a college fund for your son."

At the news of a possible trip to California, Davie began jumping up and down with great delight. He said to Ida May in an excited voice, "Can I go, Mom? Please let me go." For Ida May, all this fuss seamed a waste of time and effort. She turned and looked Mr. Jones straight in the face.

"For the sake of my son, I will give this matter some consideration." Giving Ida May his business card, Mr. Jones turned and drove away in his sleek and shiny car. Davie watched the car make its way down the lane. He wondered if the events of this day would ever come true.

The news of a possible appearance on *The Big Night Show* spread quickly throughout Wakefield and the surrounding communities. It seems that no one from that sleepy little hamlet had ever achieved this type of notoriety before. In fact, most of the townspeople and farmers of that area were quiet folks who took great pride in their work and raised their families with respect for others, the forest, and wildlife. The thought of having someone from their community on national TV seemed unbelievable to them. However, the local townsfolk were split in their opinions whether having one of their own appear on national TV was such a good idea. Some thought the appearance of Davie on TV would bring curiosity seekers to their town, disrupting their peace and quiet, while others in the area thought more visitors to Wakefield provided greater income and tourism for the local economy.

That night at supper, Ida May had prepared chicken fried chicken, new potatoes in a white sauce, her special coleslaw, and plenty of fresh lemonade. She also made up one of her famous lemon meringue pies that Davie liked so well. As they both sat down at the dinner table, Ida May composed her thoughts on how to break the news to Davie that they were not going on the trip. After all, she thought about who would manage the farm with them gone plus a sick bear to look after. At about that time, Ida May's thoughts were broken by the sound of a knocking on the front door of the farmhouse.

Going to see who had come calling at this hour of the day, she swung the front door open to find Mr. and Mrs. Olson smiling from ear to ear. Mr. Olson spoke first in his usual Scandinavian accent, "Mama and I heard the good news about the television show and wanted to be the first to offer our congratulations. And by the way, do not worry about the farmwork while you are gone. We will take care of everything for you, including that big old bear out in the barn." Now Ida May tried to speak, but Mr. Olson's said in a rather stern tone, "Ida May, we've have been friends for many years. This is a great opportunity for you and the boy. We will take care of everything. After all, what are neighbors for?"

Mrs. Olson spoke next, "I made one of my special strudels to help celebrate this special moment." At about that time, the phone began ringing in the parlor. It was the neighbor down the road, congratulating Davie on his prospective television appearance. As all this commotion was going on, Ida May slowly came to the realization that a trip to Los Angeles seemed certain. Her original objection to the trip seamed to melt away as easily as one of Mrs. Olson's strudels did on a person's palate.

The night before the big trip to LA, Davie found it terribly difficult to sleep. He was so excited about the prospect of going to the city of angels and seeing the television studio where *The Big Night Show* was televised. In addition, a staff member from the show had promised to take Davie and Ida May on a sightseeing tour of Hollywood plus a trip to Galactical Universe (Your Keyway Park to the Stars) and trips to famous restaurants. For Davie, the possibility of experiencing all these places seemed like a dream come true. For many a night, Davie sat in front of the TV, watching comedies and dramas that drew him into a wonderful fantasy world. He truly wondered what life really was like in California as many of the shows he watched centered on the beauty and lifestyle of the state. As the morning drew closer, Davie could hardly wait to see if the California dream portrayed on television really lived up to the billing it received.

The trip on the bus down to Detroit seemed almost unreal to Davie. After all, this was his first big trip away from the farm. As the miles rolled on and the bus traveled farther and farther from Wakefield, Davie's thoughts turned back to his special friends back on the farm. Davie took comfort in the knowledge that the Olsons were caring for Floppy and Bear. Nevertheless, the events concerning Bear's rescue had built a special bond between them. As his thoughts drifted farther and farther away,

Davie was suddenly brought back to reality by a tapping on his shoulder. It was Ida May saying in a clear, sure voice, "Son, a penny for your thoughts." At first Davie had no response, still somewhat immersed in the emotion of the moment. Before he could reply, Ida May said, "Son, I bet you're worried about your buddy back on the farm. Don't let these doubts overcome you. Bear is perfectly fine. His care is assured through our good neighbors and old Doc Wilson." At about that time, the bus reached Detroit International Airport. The bus driver opened the door, and a flurry of people reached for their bags and personal possessions. For Ida May and Davie, the trip of a lifetime had begun.

The flight took off down the runway at breathtaking speed. This was, after all, Ida May's and Davie's first airplane flight, and everything happened quite fast for these new air travelers. When they boarded the airplane, Davie had offered the window seat to his mom out of respect. However, Ida May would take no part in this kind gesture, repeating the old saying, "If God had intended man to fly, he surely would have given him wings." Davie took his seat near the window and watched in utter amazement as the earth got more distant. To Davie everything on the ground seemed so small. As the plane punched through the clouds, Davie's thoughts returned to the farm where he grew up. He reflected on the glorious Michigan summers he had known from his earliest recollections. He especially remembered lying down in the tall grass in the meadow, watching the wonder and glory of both sky and earth. Now he was soaring higher than any bird could fly and defying the very laws of nature.

When the plane landed in Los Angeles, Mr. Jones of TGN met Ida May and Davie at their gate. He greeted the pair in a friendly manner and arranged for a porter to pick up the bags. Ushering Ida May and Davie to his car, Mr. Jones spoke candidly with Davie about his upcoming appearance on *The Big Night Show*.

"We at TGN want to make you and your mom completely at home while you are with us. If, for any reason, you do not feel up to going on the show, please let us know. There will be a lot of bright lights and people looking at you, son. Does this situation bother you?"

"Well, to be truthful, Mr. Jones, the thought of going on national TV scares me a little bit, but you know, Mom always told me not to worry over things that cannot hurt you." With this response, Davie smiled while Mr. Jones patted him on the head.

"Way to go, Davie. That is the kind of confidence we like to hear from our guests."

The drive to the hotel took only thirty minutes, but to Davie and Ida May, the drive felt like being shot out of a rifle. For these new visitors to LA, the fast-paced driving and freeway system proved almost too much for simple folks from the back country of Upper Michigan. Ida May whispered in Davie's ear, "These folks are in an awful hurry to get somewhere." For Davie, this ebb and flow of the Southern California highway system heightened his interest. He paid special attention to the snazzy convertibles and hot rods that defined the California street culture. Davie was glued to the window as the limo made its way down Sunset Boulevard to their hotel. As the limo pulled into the driveway, many thoughts ran through the minds of Davie and Ida May. They both had second thoughts as to whether they had made the right decision in coming to Los Angeles. They both thought about what lay ahead them. Fortunately, for our travelers, all these fears and doubts passed quickly as the excitement and drama of the moment began to sink in.

Checking in at the hotel proceeded with lighting speed. Mr. Jones snapped his fingers, and the desk clerk sprang into action.

"Is the suite ready for our guests?"

"Why yes, Mr. Jones, just as you requested."

"Then make them as comfortable as possible, and see to all their wishes. Remember, these folks are here at the request of TGN, so treat them with the utmost respect."

The desk clerk ran a bell, and a bellhop quickly gathered up their bags, and they proceeded to their suite. Entering the elevator, the bellhop pressed for the fourteenth floor. After a quick jolt, that elevator shot up with amazing speed. Ida May held on to her hat and explained in a rather startled voice, "This is almost too much for an old lady."

On the other hand, Davie expressed great delight in their rapid ascent. He exclaimed with one word his great satisfaction: "Wow."

On the fourteenth floor, the elevator doors flew open, and the bellhop took his guests down to room 1428. As he took out his keys and opened their room, both Davie and Ida May were startled by the size and beauty of their new surroundings. Why, there was this massive living room with all the amenities and two adjoining sleeping rooms. The staff at the hotel had also provided an array of fresh fruits and cheeses and all the beverages anyone could ever want. On his way out of the room, the bellhop told his guests, "Remember, ring for room service when you get hungry. And the swimming pool is on the ground floor next to the lobby." Finally, after a long ordeal, Davie and Ida May were left alone. Excited by the day's events, Davie wanted to do everything and explore his new surroundings while Ida May needed her quality rest time after the trip. For our travelers, this new adventure opened both a world of discovery and amazement.

After a few hours of rest, Ida May and Davie put on their swimming suits and headed for the pool. Now Davie, having no fear of the water, plunged right into the deep end of the pool while Ida May stuck her big toe in to check for the water temperature. After the pair was in the water for a while, they were overtaken by the warm sensation on their bodies and the almost mystical way the light was reflected on the surface of the pool. To make things even better, a waiter came and took their drink order. Davie had a root beer while Ida May sampled a glass of wine from one of the California vineyards that populated the Napa Valley to the north.

Ida May and Davie's California experience that day made a big impression on them. For his part, Davie loved swimming in the big pool, especially jumping off the diving board. For Ida May, enjoying all the dishes and having someone wait on you hand and foot proved to her liking. Ida May and Davie just loved their new surroundings and wanted to stay for a long time. However, the call of Michigan, their home state, and the farm overshadowed the glamor and glitz of the big city.

The next day, a driver and limo appeared at the front of the hotel. Sam, the limo driver, quickly opened the back door to the car and gently urged his two passengers inside. Then Sam quickly took his position at the driver's position. The limo speed off, and Sam turned back and addressed his riders.

"The schedule for today is to go to Galactical Universe." With that, the pair headed off to that enchanted destination that intrigued young and old alike. Upon their arrival at the park, Davie became so excited and jumped up and down at the prospect of riding on all the special attractions that awaited them. Ida May calmly placed her hand on Davie's shoulder and spoke in a rather loud voice, "Now calm down, son. We have all day to see the sights." With this hope, Davie and his mom headed for the main gate of the park while Sam met the pair and presented them with complementary tickets.

Little did Davie know that day that the TGN team had made special arrangements for the two of them to be in the Rocket parade. After entering the gates, both Ida May and Davie were met by none other than Oliver Rocket, Lucy Lunar, and Freddie Comet. Speaking in a rather low-pitched voice, Oliver said to Davie, "Welcome to Galactical Universe, young man. We're your official ambassadors for the day. We hope you enjoy the park and partake in all its activities and attractions." At about that time, Alvin Asteroid appeared and introduced himself to the pair.

"How are things going?" said Alvin in an excited voice.

"We are fine," replied Davie and Ida May. Then without hesitation, Alvin pointed to a golf cart, and the whole group of characters and visitors sped off into the heart of the park. In addition, Davie was presented with his very own space suite which he wore with great pride that day.

The day at the park proved an unforgettable experience for both Davie and Ida May. Davie and Ida May were treated like royalty. They never had to stand in line for the rides or attractions. Of course, Davie wanted to see and ride everything. They went over and rode the roller coaster named the Black Hole as it twisted and turned many times before descending into the bowels of the earth. The fast and furious rides delighted Davie but did little to please Ida May. At one of these attractions, Ida May turned to their hosts and said in a rather distressed voice, "Do you have anything slower for an old lady?" However, Alvin reassured Ida May that she was doing great and that youngsters like her regularly rode these rides in the park. On one occasion, Ida May's hat blew off as the pair whirled about. A park employee quickly recovered Ida May's prized hat, and our guests were quickly transported off to the next attraction.

By the end of the day, Davie and Ida May had visited just about everything at Galactical Universe. They were given a splendid lunch and dinner and rode on a rocket in the parade. In fact, several people recognized Davie from his earlier television appearances and asked him for his autograph. By the end of the day, our pair of travelers were all in. On the way back to the hotel, both Davie and Ida May fell asleep in the car. Although the events of that day passed quickly, these two adventurers found a new fantasy world different from anything they had ever known.

That evening our pair of travelers retired early, for tomorrow Sam had promised to pick them up early for a trip to the beach. What Davie did not realize was that arrangements had already been made for surfing lessons with two of the top female surfers in California. The very next day, Sam drove the limo up to the hotel and quickly picked up Ida May and Davie for the next journey. Sam pointed his sleek, shiny limo north on California highway 1 toward Malibu. The scenic journey took our travelers past beautiful white-sand beaches and slender mountains that hugged the coast for many miles. Both Davie and Ida May were struck by the beauty and appeal of the California coastline. The journey up to Malibu appeared dreamlike and different for people accustomed to the deep woods and lakes of the north country. As the limo slowed down and entered the parking lot at Malibu Beach or pair of travelers were awakened to the reality of wind, sun, and surf.

As our pair of northerners got out of the limo, they were greeted by a beautiful pair of ladies all attired in wet-suits. The ladies introduced themselves as lifeguards and surfing instructors. These attractive ladies were key members of a new generation of California surfers. Ladies like these had changed the sport into an activity that appealed to everyone. At first Davie did not know what to say, but Ida May gave her son a gentle nudge in the back before he finally opened his mouth. In a rather soft voice, Davie said, "Nice to meet you." The ladies replied in a pleasant tone and explained their purpose for meeting the two of them.

"We have come today to teach you the proper way to surf and really get to know and love this sport."

Taking Davie down to the water, the ladies gave this young man his first surfing lesson. The wetsuit and other equipment seemed rather strange at first, but Davie slowly got the hang of the sport while Ida May sat on the beach and watched events unfold. Davie was a little wobbly at first on the surfboard. In fact, he waved to his mom then quickly fell into the ocean. The day turned into a real delight for them. Up on the beach, Sam brought a picnic hamper full of good things to eat and an ice chest full of cold sodas and juices. Why, they had wonderful deli sandwiches, potato salad, baked beans, and MoonPies for dessert. In the meantime, the ladies told about their surfer accomplishments and doing stunts for movies. The drive back to Sunset Strip seemed almost sad after the many wonderful events of the day. Ida May and Davie watched the last rays of light disappear as their limo sped through the picture-perfect mountains along California's Pacific Coast highway. What had taken place that day is the stuff that dreams are made of.

By the next morning, Ida May and Davie were exhausted from their travels and exciting explorations. The good California life had agreed with these mild-mannered visitors. The pair slept in that morning until a sharp knock at the door awoke their peaceful slumber. As Davie opened the door, Mr. Jones and his secretary entered the room at a rather fast pace. Mr. Jones began speaking quickly.

"Well, folks, this is our big night. Davie, tonight you will appear on *The Big Night Show* with Mr. Jimmy Vick, and the rest will be history. Son, are you ready to go on the show this evening?"

Without hesitation, Davie replied confidently, "Sure thing, Mr. Jones."

Then Mr. Jones went on to say, "Preparations are currently underway for your arrival at the studio. We will send Sam and the limo around three this afternoon to pick you up. Sam will take you to Oceanside. There are a lot of things to do before we go on air. You will meet the staff, talk with our director, and go through makeup. The whole process will take a few hours before we go live."

With that said, Mr. Jones and his secretary made a mad dash for the door. After they left, Ida May scratched her head and looked rather confused. She said, "That man is headed for a heart attack if he doesn't slow down. I think that he would enjoy life more if he only took time to smell the roses."

Davie shook his head in agreement. Then he said, "Things really move fast out here." With that said, Ida May and Davie got ready for one of the biggest nights of their lives.

Davie's appearance on *The Big Night Show* began with Sam picking them both up promptly at 3:00 p.m., as arranged by Mr. Jones. They were driven to Oceanside Studio, where the staff of the show quickly went to work directing and prompting Davie on the do and don'ts of live TV. The suit Davie wore for the occasion did not meet the expectations of the director, so staff members took measurements, and a new suit appeared in less than an hour. After dressing, Davie was directed to the makeup artist for special touch-ups. He put up a fuss at first, saying, "Nobody's going to put girl stuff on me." After reassurance from Ida May and the staff, Davie consented to the coloring and lipstick that is used for television appearance.

The makeup artist told Davie, "You want to look good on TV, don't you?"

"Well, sure," replied Davie.

"Then you need the coloring in your complexion to reduce the bleaching effects of strong television lighting."

After makeup, Davie and Ida May were directed to a waiting lounge, where they were to stay until it was time for Davie to go on the show. The lounge had a television so Ida May could watch her son's performance since she was not appearing. While they waited, a staff member burst into the lounge and told Davie not to mess up his new clothes. In the meantime, a hairstylist came in and touched up Davie's hair while a manicurist (that's someone who does peoples nails) came in and filed and buffed Davie's fingernails.

All this primping and fidgeting with Davie's appearance made him a bit uneasy. Davie took the fuss they made over him in stride. However, the time before the show ticked down ever so slowly. For Davie this was his big night, and he did not want to blow his opportunity on national television. Then finally a staff member came in and said, "You're up next." Suddenly it was as if a time bomb went off in the pit of Davie's stomach. Despite his last-minute jitters, Davie managed to pull himself together and waited for his introduction. This night would forever change how he viewed the world and how others perceived him; his monument in the spotlight had finally come.

Then without fanfare, the TV lights went up, and Jimmy Vick introduced Davie as the band played a quick little musical piece. Davie walked a little slow toward the desk and his waiting hosts. The camera lights were very bright, and it took a little getting used to for him to adjust. Despite all the hoopla and applause from the audience, Davie waved to the crowd with a self-reliance knowing that everything was going to work out okay. As the music died down, Davie shook hands with Mr. Vick and Aiden O'Connor, the cohost, and then turned and waved at the orchestra, saying, "Great sound, guys." Davie then plopped down into one of the big chairs provided for the guests on the program.

As everybody settled in on the program, Mr. Vick then turned to Davie and said, "You've become quite a national sensation since you rescued that bear up in Northern Michigan. Now tell us a little of what happened for you to take such a risk."

"You see, Mr. Vick," Davie replied, "I've been taught that we all must take care of the forests and streams and all the creatures that inhabit our good earth. That bear was one of God's creations, and letting it suffer in that trap was more than I could endure. I had no one to turn to, being alone at home, so I determined that saving that bear alone was my only option. However, getting Bear out of that trap required some fast thinking and later some personal regret because of the punishment I received from my mom. You see, she wasn't too happy with the danger involved with the rescue and whopper of a lie I told."

At that Jimmy Vick smiled, and the audience let out a chuckle. Mr. Vick then asked Davie, "Are you telling us she took away all your fun stuff?"

"If you mean grounding sir, you bet she did." With that statement, the whole studio audience erupted into laughter. As the interview went on, Davie became more relaxed and related more of his experiences.

Little did Davie know, *The Big Night Show* staff had secretly arranged with a prominent zoologist to appear on the show. As it turned out, a few months earlier, one of female black bears at the local zoo had given birth to two cubs, one male and one female. The zoo arranged for the cubs to appear on the show with Davie. As the interview continued, Mr. Vick suddenly turned to Davie and asked if he would like to meet a couple of visitors who were waiting backstage.

"Why sure, Mr. Vick." With that the band struck up a tune, and to Davie's surprise, out came a trainer with the two cubs on a leash.

Now those bears cubs made a straight dash toward Davie if they had known him his entire life. My friends, it was quite a sight as Davie got down on the floor and wrestled around and played with the animals. He and Mr. Vick fed the bears. The trainer talked about the cubs, but the real show was the interaction going on between Davie and the bears. One of the bears climbed up into Mr. Vick's lap, and he held the cub as it settled in for a nap. Davie took one of the bears and gently lifted its front paws and danced around as the band struck up a lively polka tune. The whole segment of the show turned into a real free for all, with both host and guests having great fun. During the show, Davie and the bear cubs captured the hearts of their television viewers. Right after Davie left the set, the switchboard at TGN Broadcasting lit up with calls of praise. The viewers just loved the performance.

On their way out of the studio, a staff member from *The Big Night Show* came running down the hall and finally caught up with Ida May and Davie as they were about to leave. Excitedly and somewhat out of breath, a young lady in her early twenties made this startling remark: "Mr. Vick wants you to come over to his house, Davie, and meet his three sons. They have a big swimming pool and will provide lunch. We realize that you are to return home tomorrow, but if you want to stay over another day, Mr. Jones from our office will make all the arrangements for you." With this new development, Ida May looked at Davie with a puzzled expression.

"What do you think, Davie? Should we accept Mr. Vick's invitation?" Without hesitation, Davie blurted out a resounding yes.

"Okay, we'll set everything up for you tomorrow. Have fun and leave everything to us."

When Ida May and Davie returned to the hotel, excitement seemed to be all around. Sam, the limo driver, gave Davie a high five as he let them out of the car. When they got back to their room, Mr. Jones from TGN called and stated that early ratings for the show were one of the highest on record. Mr. Jones also indicated that he would send Sam around at 10:00 a.m. for their morning and afternoon with the Vicks. In the meantime, the Olsons from back home called and could hardly speak because of their excitement. Almost everyone back in Wakefield could hardly believe that one of their own appeared on national television. Old Doc Wilson and some of the local boys had run through Wakefield's rather small downtown, carrying on till the wee hours of the morning. Why, the whole town was talking about the events that transpired that evening. Even with all the excitement, Davie wanted to know how Bear was getting along from his injuries. The Olsons reassured Davie that his bear was doing fine and even wandered off for a brief time in the woods. However, Bear always seemed to find his way back to the farm; it seemed that he was looking for his friend, but Mrs. Olson's wonderful cooking caused his speedy return.

The next morning, Sam pulled the limo up to the hotel entrance, ready to pick up his two guests. Ida May and Davie were waiting inside the hotel lobby. Sam took their belongings, which included their swimsuits and towels and a bag full of personal items such as suntan lotion and other assorted items. They all piled into the car, and Sam sped them away out toward the ocean and the Vick home. When they arrived, Mrs. Vick greeted them with a big smile and showed them around their beachfront house. She apologized that Jimmy was not there to meet them. It seemed that some of Jimmy's old friends had dropped by the house the previous night after the show, and they stayed up quite late.

"Jimmy sends his regrets and will spend some time with you as soon as he gets up."

At about that time, from out on the patio came three energy-filled boys who seemed highly spirited and full of playful curiosity. Mrs. Vick introduced her three sons, Edward, John, and Warren, to Ida May and Davie. Warren, the youngest of the Vick children, went straight up to Davie and welcomed him with a firm handshake while putting his arm around Davie's neck. It seemed that they became instant buddies. Edward and John stuck out their hands in friendship and said loudly, "Wow, that's really cool, what you did with the bears on the show last night. Why, practically everyone around here is talking about it."

Now Davie, not wanting to seem to self-import-ant, said in a mild manner, "Ah shucks, it wasn't any-thing special. I've got what some folk call a special talent with animals." Then Davie looked at the Vick boys and said, "I hear you got a great view of the ocean from your house and, even better, a killer swimming pool." With that said, the boys took Davie and rushed out the patio doors quicker than a race car down the final stretch of a race. The boys' rapid disappearance left Mrs. Vick and Ida May standing alone together in the living room of the house. The two ladies looked at each other and smiled, pausing only slightly to laugh, then Ida May replied with some of her fine country humor by saying, "I guess boys will be boys." Mrs. Vick took Ida May by the hand as the women entered the kitchen for some girl chat.

When Jimmy got up later in the day, the kids were having a great time in the pool, and Mrs. Vick and Ida May were exchanging practical tidbits about life and raising children. Ida May jotted down a couple of her famous recipes for Mrs. Vick while the boys ran into the kitchen several times to get drinks and sandwiches. Everyone seemed to be having a great time. Jimmy shook Ida May's hand as he entered the kitchen. Jimmy said to Ida May in his showman-like fashion, "You folks from the Upper Peninsula are really special, especially that son of yours."

"Why, thank you, Mr. Vick," replied Ida May. "Davie really has a generous quality about him. He seems to love everybody and especially animals. I know that is the reason he did so well on the show last night." Jimmy nodded in agreement as the Vicks and Ida May slowly made their way out to patio. The afternoon California sun glimmered brightly as the adults retired to the comfortable seating around the pool. The cheerful sound of children playing in the water only added to what had become a perfect day.

As the Vicks and Ida May were exchanging small talk, Jimmy asked Ida May a direct question.

"How come everyday folks like you seem to have such success in raising children? As you know, I have been married several times, and show business has taken a toll on me and my family. What is your secret for having such a stable relationship with your son?"

Ida May paused for a few seconds and then looked Jimmy straight in the eyes.

"Well, Mr. Vick, it's like this: Just love your children with your whole hart, and make them feel special and wanted. Use discipline only when necessary, and protect and nurture them in a way that is unmistakably genuine. Jimmy, those boys of yours love you very much. I can see it in their eyes. And they want to be closer with you. Just be strong and take the first step, reach out to them, hold them, and never let them go." After making that statement, Ida May turned to Jimmy and said, "Mr. Vick, forgive the ranting of an old lady."

With that statement, both Mr. and Mrs. Vick turned to Ida May and said, "Your words contain more wisdom that anything we've heard from the so-called experts in the field of child psychology. We'll take your profound words and put them to work with our relationships with our sons. Thank you so much."

The next day proved very tiring for our two travelers. Sam brought the limo by the hotel at 6:00 a.m. to pick up Ida May and Davie. They arrived at LAX after a short drive and found Mr. Jones and his assistant from the TGN network waiting at the terminal. Mr. Jones greeted the pair and personally thanked them for coming out to California and appearing on the show. He then wished them a pleasant journey. Mr. Jones then turned and paused for a few seconds.

"You know, we would like to come out to the farm and take some footage of you Davie and your friend Bear. Would that work for you folks?"

Ida May looked at Davie and then asked, "Is that okay with you, son?"

"Why sure," replied Davie with a big grin on his face.

Then Ida May said, "You folks are always welcome. Why, I'll fix you one of the best farm suppers you've ever tasted."

At that suggestion, Mr. Jones said, "I look forward to some of your fine cooking, Ida May."

The trip back home to Wakefield was both pleasant and relaxing for Ida May and Davie. Ida May took a nap on the plane while Davie looked through some of the magazines purchased from the news stand at the airport. The bus ride from Detroit to Wakefield proved uneventful since there were only a few other passengers traveling in that direction. However, the real shock for Ida May and Davie came as the bus rounded the corner on Main

Street of downtown Wakefield. To their surprise, a large crowd had gathered to greet the returning heroes. The local high school band was playing a stirring march. Why, it felt like all the inhabitants of Wakefield had gathered to greet two of their own. Mr. and Mrs. Olson were the first to greet Davie and Ida May as they stepped off the bus. The town mayor, Mr. Thompson, shook Davie's and Ida May's hands, and some of the residents slapped Davie on the shoulder. They shouted, "Way to go, Davie. Great job!" and all sorts of good wishes. It also turned out the local church ladies had cooked a special supper for their returning townsfolk, and all enjoyed the special evening together. By the time Ida May and Davie got back to the farm, it was after midnight. It had been a wonderful day and one not forgotten by the good folks of Wakefield and by the returning travelers.

The next morning, Davie got up and hoped he would find his buddy Bear. He fixed his own breakfast and quickly took off for the woods. While Davie was out in California, old Doc Wilson and Mr. Olson had released Bear back into the forest. His leg had gotten better, and he could walk on all fours without too much discomfort. Hunting far and wide, Davie had great difficulty locating his friend. Remembering the little rabbit that had assisted him during Bear's rescue, Davie headed over to the burrow next to the meadow. Searching around, he found the opening just as Floppy had stuck his head out of the hole. Davie said to Floppy excitedly, "Why, there you are." I was hoping to find you today in hopes you could lead me to Bear." Floppy was so excited to see Davie that he jumped for joy right into Davie's lap.

"You see, Davie, Bear has looked all over for you and was so disappointed that you did not come."

"Well, Floppy, I have been away for a while but am home to stay now." With that announcement, Floppy grinned from ear to ear. Then Davie said urgently, "Now let us find Bear."

As it happened, Floppy knew all of Bear's favorite places.

"All we have to do is show patience and wait!" exclaimed Floppy. Now Floppy knew that Bear always liked to cross the meadow on the farm at about mid-morning. Both Davie and Floppy staked out a good spot to watch from underneath the branches of a big oak tree. It did not take long for Bear to come slowly lumbering through the trail that led through the tall grass. From their concealed hiding place, Floppy whispered to Davie, "Let me go first. After all, we do not want to surprise our friend." Floppy emerged from his hiding place and caught up with Bear on the trail. Bear seemed happy to meet up with his old friend.

Bear said in a surprised voice, "What brings you out this way on such a fine day?"

"Well, Bear," exclaimed Floppy, "I just happened to run into an old friend of ours, and he wants to say hello." With that introduction, Davie came walking down the trail toward his two friends. From that moment on, the happy reunion began. Bear stood up on his hind legs and thumped his chest in wild excitement.

He then turned to Davie and said loudly, "Why, Davie, where have you been?" With that Davie told his friend all about the events that unfolded over the last two weeks. The happy trio spent the rest of the morning and afternoon wandering about in the forest and backcountry. The sun shone brightly on a warm Michigan day as the three renewed and strengthened their friendship.

WHAT SHOULD WE LEARN FROM CHAPTER 3?

The ability to seek out trusted and worthy mentors in our lives is a sign of great wisdom. We must seek knowledge at times from those who have fought the good fight and rely on our own inner voice that reside in each of us. In our story, Ida May gave her best insights to the Vicks on child-rearing. We must, likewise, develop good traits that enhance our own knowledge while exercising good listening skills. Usually in any conversation, the opportunity exists for us to learn and retain what is good and then toss out what is hurtful or unimportant. This insightful process can help us enrich and strengthen our decision-making. Thus, by exercising good judgment, we strengthen our inner selves while building a value system that helps ourselves and the greater community that we all serve.

Likewise, to build ourselves up and make good decisions, we must build on a foundation that strengthens us both physically and mentally. To accomplish this, we need to keep our grades up and keep our body strong and free from drugs and substances that weaken us. We must also prepare ourselves against the challenges of loneliness, frustration, loss, and despair that everyone suffers during their lifetimes. By taking on the qualities of a sound life, we allow wisdom to grow within us. And lastly, a person must never fear failure. From a human perspective, one must realize that fear is part of a person's emotional makeup. However, we must never let fear rule us to the point that it prevents opportunities for us to grow and reach our full potential. As we learned from Davie and Ida May, the trip to Los Angeles had its fearful moments. However, the new experiences they obtained outweighed all their doubts and concerns.

One additional thing to remember about the decision-making process in life is that careful thought and soul-searching is always required. To see if your life has true meaning, you must ask these questions of yourself. Is my career path and personal activities uplifting in service to my fellow man, or is the path I have chosen primarily about satisfying my own needs? Is what I am doing producing good fruit? Or do my personal accomplishments mean more to me than anything else? Do I have inner peace about what I am doing that guides me through the roughest of storms? Additionally, are doors and circumstances opening to me that never seemed possible before? If the answer to these questions is yes in a positive way, then you are well on your way to a committed and purpose-driven life. A power and grace will flow through you that never existed before. And with this new positive energy, you will go on to do incredible things.

Vanya Cimino

4

A Big Journey for Bear

Later that summer before school started, the film crew from TGN came out to film Bear and Davie. This proved an exciting time on the farm. The film crew brought with it a whole moving van of equipment. Why, they brought lights and special close-up cameras to get some great film footage of Bear and his pals. Mr. Jones from the network coordinated the whole operation. Mr. Jones talked over with Davie how to approach and get the best film footage of Bear. Davie came right out and told about the difficulty of getting Bear to come out of the woods, especially if he felt the presence of strangers. Davie went on to say, "You know, the best way to handle this situation is for you to build concealed shelters all around the meadow where Bears often comes. You need to camouflage your positions so Bear will not see, smell, or hear you. A number of tree stands and hidden positions around the area assures the best results. If you make a number of filming stations on his upwind side, then Bear won't pick up your sent. As a matter of fact, our friend will not come out of the forest easily since he's already had one bad encounter with humans. My best advice is simply to set everything up and wait. I'll do everything possible to draw him out." Mr. Jones then made all the preparations for what was to come.

That evening Ida May and some local ladies from their church set out a supper for the entire film crew. Those city folks had a real surprise awaiting them since most of them had never experienced good down-home cooking. They all commented how good everything looked and tasted plus the freshness of the food set before then. Why, these folks acted like they had not eaten in weeks. They just scarfed down the food, and Ida May then quickly brought out new platters for the crew to enjoy. By the time supper was over, these city folks had experienced at least one of the pleasures of country living. In fact, they all complained that they had eaten too much and had to retire early to bed. The hospitality shown by Ida May and Davie left a lasting impression on their visitors.

Early the next morning, the film crew was out on the farm and prepared to shoot footage of Davie and Bear. The sun began to peak through the trees of the forest as everything was readied for a morning filming. In the meantime, Davie slipped away from the farm and went over to Floppy's burrow to see if he was home. Davie called out to his friend in a loud voice, "Hey, Floppy, come out. I have got something of importance to tell you." Well, let me tell you, it was quite a sight as Floppy emerged from his burrow and wiped the sleep from his eyes.

Floppy said, "Davie, what's all the excitement about?"

Then he replied, "My friend, the film crew from TGN are here today to film Bear and me. You know, it seems to me that some of the other animals in the forest need their story told as well."

Floppy then told Davie, "That's a fantastic idea."

Now Floppy agreed to help Davie and the crew. He quickly went to work rounding up all the other animals that lived nearby. Floppy told Mr. and Mrs. Beaver and the deer from down the way. Soon the word got around, and many of the other animals of the forest converged on that clearing. Davie then made his way back to the farm and set everything up with Mr. Jones. However, it was strictly up to Bear if he showed up for his grand introduction to the world.

Vanja Cimino

Everything was ready for the film crew to begin shooting. The camera crew were all in place, and the weather was perfect with little wind for Bear to pick up the scent of strangers nearby. Preparations were so complete that almost every trace of the film crew was camou-flaged. Mr. Jones had the heavy-equipment truck and all the other cars and vehicles moved away from the farm. In addition, the film crew was instructed not to use any personal products that were perfumed or scented. The crew also received instruction to keep completely still and not to move around once in place. All was now in place as Davie calmly waked out into the meadow near the big tree where he usually met Bear. Davie called out his buddy, but there was no response. He called out a second time but no response.

Davie then thought to himself, *I wonder where Bear is today. Well, maybe he went in search of food like fish down by the stream or went looking for a honey tree as all bears like to do.* After several minutes, Davie began to pace back and forth. Then he heard the snap of a tree branch. Davie then thought, *Now we're getting someplace.* Going up close to the edge of the forest, our young man called out again, but his friend made no response. Then it came to Davie what to do. He took out of his back pocket and unwrapped a candy bar and held it up. At that very instant, a slight breeze blew the scent of that candy bar into the forest. And you know what? That was all it took for Davie's friend to lose his shyness. You see, Bear loved candy bars. Why, that bear came charging out of the for-est and practically took off Davie's arm to get at that bar. As all this was happening, the cameras were rolling. Bear then became the most celebrated animal star in the world.

What happened next turned into quite a show. After scarfing down that candy, Bear went over to Davie to see if he had more treats. That big old bear stood up as if to beg for more. He gently stuck his massive paw on Davie's shoulder as if to ask for more candy. All this time, the cameras caught this amazing footage. As time went on, Davie and Bear began their usual play. They both got down and rolled around in the grass with all kinds of giggles and snorts. Then Davie grabbed Bear by the ear and whispered something to him. This massive creature of the forest stood up and let out a deep growl that was heard all over the farm and surrounding area. Next these two pals played a game of hide and seek. Davie could disappear out of sight, but Bear always found him given his ability to smell and track his friend. After considerable time at play, the two went down by the stream that ran nearby and lay on some flat rocks to rest. Davie and Bear listened to the trickle of the stream and felt the warm rays of the sun on their faces. For these two, it was a beautiful day that neither of them forgot.

What happened next was a complete surprise to Bear. The beavers came splashing down the stream and said hello to the pair. Next a fawn and its mother came and took sips from the stream. The two paid their respects and quietly retreated into the forest. Surprising everyone, an eagle swooped down and landed on the tree branches overlapping the streambed. The eagle made loud screeching sounds while flapping its wings. And then without warning, their old friend Floppy appeared and hopped up on the rocks next to those two after the eagle left the area. Davie reached down and picked up Floppy, saying, "Welcome, my old friend." As the morning rolled on, other animal friends came over and showed themselves to the cameras. Then they heard down in the streambed the splashing of water and a low, soft call that sounded like this: *rivet, rivet, rivet.* Floppy then said, "I wonder who's come to visit us." Then a big green frog hopped up on the rocks. Then later that morning, Mr. Owl, the great night hunter swooped down and greeted them with screeches. It is so unusual to see an owl during the day. As for the camera crew, the footage they took turned into a real jackpot. Why they got close-up pictures of animals that are difficult to discover and film.

As the morning rolled on to early afternoon and the sun became high in the sky, Davie, Floppy, and Bear became a bit hungry. Davie then told his buddies, "Let's see if mom's got anything cooked up for dinner." At that they all trotted off to the farmhouse. On the way home, they heard the dinner bell being rung by Ida May, and they all took off at a fast pace. The camera crew was left stressed as this little party flew by their positions. As usual Ida May had prepared some wonderful things to eat. Seeing that she had visitors, Ida May gave Bear a huge platter of food and some milk to drink, and she pulled some fresh vegetables from her garden for Davie's furry little friend Floppy. By this time, Mr. Jones and the film crew came over to the farm, and they all marveled at the ease these wild creatures felt at home at Ida May's place. As for Bear, he loved the newfound attention he received from the camera crew. Many of the crew members fed Bear candy, which he ate with great zeal. When the day ended, Mr. Jones and the film crew left the farm. What Davie and Ida May did not know was how deep Bear's newfound fame affected his future.

The film footage taken by Mr. Jones and the crew found its way on to a special presentation aired on the TGN network. Highlighted in the film was Bear and the other wildlife that occupied the Upper Peninsula of Michigan. As it turned out, the film was a huge success. Well, Bear's charm and personality won the day. For their efforts in creating the film, the Trans Global Network received a special award for excellence in presenting animal life in a natural setting.

Bear's newfound celebrity posed a bit of a problem for Davie and Ida May on the farm. Many visitors came out to their place, looking for Bear. Davie and Ida May had a schedule that kept them busy during the day. When you run a dairy operation, there is always a lot of work every day. Why, those cows of theirs required milking twice a day, and there was always the cleanup and feeding of the farm animals.

Then out of the blue one day, Davie and Ida May noticed a huge circus truck running up and down the road past their house. Ida May called the Olsons to see if they had any news about a circus coming to town. The Olsons told Ida May that no circus was scheduled for Wakefield. In fact, they told Ida May that there had not been a circus in this area for years. Well, Ida May just scratched her head in confusion as she hung up the phone. She thought to herself, *I wonder what this all means, having these folks come way up here.* However, as the days wore on, it became clear what had happened and the reason for the out-of-town circus visitors in their big truck.

One lazy Sunday afternoon, Davie took a walk over to the meadow where he usually met his old buddy Bear. As he reached the place, something seemed different than normal. Davie called out to his old friend, but there was no response. Davie then tried hand signals that Bear knew and most often responded to. However, this time nothing. For Davie something was out of order. Now it was not unusual for Bear to go off on hunting and foraging expeditions. Sometimes Bear disappeared for days. Then thinking to himself, he thought maybe Floppy knew where Bear went off to.

Reaching Floppy's burrow, Davie called out to his friend. Floppy had just finished his afternoon nap, so he was a little sleepy when Davie came to visit. Then Floppy asked his young friend what brought him out this way. Then Davie said worriedly, "I am concerned about Bear. In fact, I've not seen him for quite some time." Floppy reassured Davie not to fret.

"Why, he's probably out looking for food or getting his bear cave ready for hibernation this winter. Davie, do not feel bad. I will ask around and see what is going on." With that Davie left for home with a heavy heart. In a few short hours, the animals of the forest and those on the farm got an answer to the question of Bear's disappearance. The reality of that situation startled them all.

In the early evening, just at dusk, Floppy made his way up to the farmhouse to see Davie. He went over to the big water pump near the house and waited. It was not long before Davie came out to milk the cows. As Floppy spied Davie leaving the house, he said softly, "Hey, Davie, over here." After getting Davie's attention, Floppy went on to say, "The circus people captured Bear and took off with him. They set huge nets and waited for Bear to wander by. According to Mr. Owl, Bear fought with all his might, but the nets were too strong for him. Well, they got him, all right."

Upon hearing this news, Davie was greatly troubled. Looking Floppy straight in the eyes, Davie said, "We need a plan of action to get Bear back. Have Mr. Owl go and do a recon mission and locate Bear. Have him fly back as soon as a sighting is made. In the meantime, we will have Mom contact Sheriff Hansom to see if anything is possible from a legal standpoint." As they all waited for Owl's return, the hours seemed like days.

Mr. Barnes, the traveling manager for the circus, delighted in capturing Bear. In his mind, he saw nothing but dollar signs gently floating above his head. Despite that nostalgic feeling, he realized that it was going to take a long time to train Bear for his new role as a performer in his show. The circus was now in a real bind since they had taken a protected species of animals without permission and had broken the law concerning private property rights. In addition, Bear's shoulder was damaged because of the free for all during his capture. However, despite these obstacles, Mr. Barnes was determined to forge ahead regardless of the cost or danger. His purpose was driven by greed rather than logic and farness.

Mr. Owl had no problem in finding Bear. His superior sight and flying ability led him to the circus's current stop located in Ironwood, Michigan. That brave old bird just swooped down that night and located Bear in a big cage near the opening of a huge circus tent. The circus had someone to watch Bear throughout the day but no one assigned at night. This made it easy for Owl to land directly atop Bear's cage. Why, that cagy old bird sat there and hooted a soft call that finally woke up Bear. Seeing Owl, Bear quickly sat up and paid attention. Now Bear was so glad to see a friend from the forest but was saddened by his current state of confinement.

Owl tried to cheer Bear up and calm his fears by saying, "My friend, everything is being done to get you released."

Then Bear said sadly, "These people are at times really mean to me. Why, they are trying to train me for their show, and they don't display much patience toward me or my injury. Furthermore, they say the circus is moving into Wisconsin in two days. They'll take me away forever, and I'll never get home."

Despite Bear's gloomy outlook, Owl had these words of encouragement for his friend: "You know, Bear, it's not as dark as it seems. Now you got yourself in this mess, then you can surely find a way out. After all, Bear, you can use the intelligence and gifts that you have to make an escape." With those words, Bear felt better and secretly thought out his next steps to reach freedom.

Back at the farm, Ida May and Davie were called on by old Doc Wilson and Sheriff Hanson. Doc got there first and gave them the recent news about Bear.

"The circus people called me and said they had a bear that needed attention. When I got there, it was apparent that this was the same bear treated out here on the farm. The scar on his leg told the whole story. The good news is that he's okay. His shoulder is sore, but it's healing just fine. The strange thing about this whole situation is that when I asked to see the animal's paperwork, they produced some phony document."

Now about that time, Sheriff Hanson rolled up in his squad car. He got out and addressed everyone.

"Those circus folks are trying to pull a fast one on us. Went over today and looked at their paperwork. It's obvious to me that something's not right. The problem for us right now is that we can't get a restraining order."

(A restraining order is a piece of paper that requires a person or group to stop actions or set aside work until a court of law reviews the protest.) "Since Judge Scott is out of town this week on his annual vacation, this leaves us with few choices. The circus leaves Ironwood tomorrow after their last performance and crosses the state line. Well, it looks like this case will end up in court or be taken over by the feds since bears are protected animals." Well, this news from the sherriff bothered Davie quite a lot. He wondered deep down if he would ever get to see his buddy again.

Feeling that his situation was improving, Bear became incredibly hopeful. Then out of the blue, Bear got this great idea. He thought, *Somehow, someway, maybe I can put forward a plan that will get me out of this mess.* With that inspiration, Bear started to think more positively. However, first this cagy old king of the forest needed events to fall into place and a little bit of luck to help him on his way. It also dawned on him that he had special talents and gifts that provided an advantage over his foes. For now, it was the time for Bear to overcome his fears and proceed with total force of heart and mind.

For Bear to escape, he needed to totally put his captors at ease and then fool them with a bit of trickery. To accomplish this feat, Bear began to show obedience to his trainers and handlers. In his heart, Bear disliked the circus people for what they had done to him, but he knew he had to outsmart them. So he wisely cooperated with his captors long enough for them let their guard down and get away. That day when the trainers came to teach Bear, he did everything right and without resistance. In fact, Mr. Barnes was so delighted with Bear's performance that he ordered extra food for his new circus sensation.

While Bear was delighting the circus people, his thoughts returned to his beloved forest and his many friends back home. Then Bear ate his food and settled down for what appeared as a nap. Keeping one eye open and listening to every sound nearby, our friend waited for his chance to spring into action and at last reach freedom. For Bear the wait was not long.

As events were unfolding at the circus, things back on the farm were proceeding at a different pace. It was hard for Davie to accept the loss of his good buddy Bear. Whatever Davie did, he always thought of his friend and mourned his loss. Since this was the last day for the circus in Ironwood, Davie thought, *Maybe we should all go down and say goodbye to our dear old friend.* Davie then asked Ida May if there was any way of traveling to the circus that day despite the short notice and distance involved. At first Ida May was reluctant to say yes, but she knew deep in her heart how much Davie missed his old friend. As Ida May and Davie jumped into that old truck of theirs and headed down Route 2 toward Ironwood, little did they know how fortunate this trip was going to be.

Now as it happened that day, young Mason and Carrie had gone to the circus with their mom. This pair of twins were by nature very curious and carefree. In fact, they were always getting into trouble, and this day this was no exception. As you see, our pair wandered off on their own after their mom had stopped to buy ride tickets. Being so excited with all the sights and sounds of the big top, these two found no obstacle too large or small to overcome. In fact, these two were highly creative and had a unique talent for going over and under things and into restricted areas. As Bear found himself face-to-face with these two children of extreme energy and playfulness, he thought to himself, *This is the opportunity I've been waiting for.* Wasting no time, Bear went straight to work on regaining his freedom.

Mason and Carrie were overjoyed to see all the animals up close in their cages. As they passed by Bear's cage, that slick old fellow stuck his paw past the bars and motioned for the twins to come closer. Of course, Mason and Carrie were drawn near because of the lure of a big old bear. As the children got closer to the cage, Bear said, "Hey, you kids come over here. Come closer. I've got something to show you." For the kids, a talking bear seemed more interesting that anything they had ever seen. Pressing up closer to the cage, these young visitors were spellbound as they listened closely to Bear's every word. What happened next raised the level of excitement at the circus to an unbelievable height.

Now no one at the circus knew that Bear talked. You see, he always kept his ability to speak a secret. The only time Bear spoke was to children and trusted friends plus his fellow creatures in the forest. Pressing forward to the outside of the cage, Bear looked at his two visitors and said, "Would you like me to do some circus tricks for you?" Mason and Carrie clapped their hands with great excitement. With the approval and encouragement of his new friends, Bear went straight into his circus performance. He balanced a ball on his nose, got up on his back legs, and acted like he was dancing. Bear's circus act met with wild excitement by the kids. It was now time for Bear to make his final move and win the complete trust of his young fans.

Gaining the confidence of his two admiring guests, Bear said, "My friends, I can do even more tricks for you if you let me out of this cage." Mason and Carrie were a little bit frightened of setting loose such a big animal, but Bear's soft and reassuring voice calmed their fears. Bear then said coolly to the children, "Do you see that big ball over there? I can do a handstand on it and keep my balance. I can do that trick if you want me to." Both children shook their heads in agreement as Bear stuck his paws up against the cage in a sign of affection. Then Bear reassured the children by saying, "Letting me loose won't hurt anybody. Also remember this—I won't harm you." From that point on, the children were eager to help their newfound friend.

The moment of Bear's final release was about to happen. Bear then said to Mason and Carrie, "See that set of keys over on the table? Bring them over here." Then Mason, the more adventurous of the kids, boldly went over and grabbed the keys. Then Bear told him, "Do you see the big brass-colored key in the center of the ring? That's the key you place in the padlock to my cage." Doing as Bear had told him, Mason was about to turn the key when Carrie reached out and grabbed Mason's hand. She looked at her brother and said, "We're headed for deep trouble if we let this bear loose." However, just at that moment, Bear reached out of his cage and tapped Mason on the shoulder. Bear wasted no time and softly said to Mason, "Please help me to get back home." With that Mason turned the key until the lock made a clicking sound. The lock opened, and Mason removed it and opened the door to Bear's cage.

Now Bear kept true to his word and preformed all kinds of tricks and acrobatics for the kids. It was about that time that Bear heard the trainers and animal caretakers returning from lunch. Before leaving, Bear gave both Carrie and Mason a pat on the head and then took off in a mad dash for freedom. That big old bear headed down the circus midway with all his strength and might. In the meantime, Mason and Carrie had some deep explaining to do. For these two youngsters, their punishment was lessoned by the fact they had given freedom to one of the earth's noblest creatures.

The circus people sounded the alarm as the animal handlers raced around with nets and capture sticks. While

Bear was running down the circus midway, he was greatly distracted by the smell of cotton candy. Now Bear loved cotton candy, so it was no surprise when he stopped at some vendor's stand and tore through the wrappers, trying to get at that delicious candy. The man selling this wondrous confectionary ran off in terror as this eight-hundred-pound eating machine descended on his product. Bear kept eating until he saw his captors closing in on him. With that, Bear took off again, and the chase continued. In the meantime, law enforcement was notified, and the local TV station did a special story about the escaped bear from the circus. The television story also issued a law enforcement report advising everyone to stay indoors while this bear was still loose. The news of the escaped bear spread very quickly as the whole county went into an uproar.

Bear took off and headed North as the circus people chased him with trucks that sped down the roads out of Ironwood. A helicopter from the Ironwood Police Department joined in the search. Bear did his best to evade his captors. Keeping off the roads and out of the populated areas, that crafty master of the forest slowly made his way toward home. However, if Bear was going to make it, he needed a little bit of luck to assist his efforts. As it so happened that day, a stroke of good fortune came his way.

The trip down to Ironwood proved incredibly sad for Davie and Ida May. Neither one of them said much in the way of conversation. These two travelers had, in many ways, reflected on the many happy memories they had with Bear. The trip that day seemed longer than normal as traffic was heavy because of the circus in town. As they arrived on the outskirts of Ironwood, Davie and Ida May spotted a bear up ahead crossing the road. Now seeing wildlife in certain parts of Michigan is not unusual. However, seeing a bear this close to town got their immediate attention. Looking intently on this creature, Davie sensed something familiar. As they pulled up closer, Davie recognized his old pal right off. He then shouted at Ida May to stop the truck. Ida May pulled over to the shoulder of the highway, but Davie stood on the running board of the pickup and jumped off in a mad dash after his old friend. At first Bear did not hear or recognize Davie because of his intense effort to avoid capture and the sound of the traffic noise. Then Davie decided to use his special call to get Bear's attention. Davie whistled for his friend, and Bear instantly remembered that sound. At that moment, Bear knew that things were about to get better.

After Bear heard the whistle, he thought to himself, *How could this be? Why, that's the sound that Davie uses.*

Well about that time, Mr. Owl had gone to check on Bear. He spotted his friend and swooped down next to him. Owl said to Bear, "Glad to see you made it out. Bear, do you know that Davie is standing right behind you."

With Owl's reassurance, Bear turned around and saw his buddy grinning from ear to ear. Davie then flew into Bear's arms, and they all cried tears of joy. For now, things were much better, but deep in his heart, Davie knew that darker forces were closing in on Bear. For now, the real challenge was to get him back home.

The journey back to the farm seemed simple enough, but on this day, events were about to challenge the rescue team in a big way. Davie had Bear hop in the back of the pickup truck, and they all took off. Just about that time, the Ironwood chief of police and officers with the circus descended upon Ida May, Davie, and Bear. Ida May pulled north onto Route 2, and the chase was on. Trying to avoid capture, Ida May poured on the gas while Bear's captors stayed hot on her heels. What followed was an epic chase that involved half the law enforcement agencies in the county. In fact, to this day, folks still marvel at how Ida May outwitted those Ironwood folks. Why, she managed to face down a whole lot of folks with far greater resources and talent plus managed to get a bear and a boy home without hurting anyone.

The little old pickup truck of Ida May's was no match for the big circus trucks and the patrol car of the police. But you know what? Ida May had a secret weapon. That clever woman had in fact an incredible knowledge of the area between Wakefield and Ironwood. She knew almost all the back roads and the special features of the region. From a practical standpoint, it was impossible for Ida

May to outrun her pursuers. However, that savvy lady just had the gumption to outwit her opponents, and that is just what she did.

Seeing an opportunity ahead, Ida May swung that little pickup down a gravel side road and really took off. Why, that woman did more twisting and turning down roads than a carrousel at the county fair. The circus truck simply dropped back while the police car managed to stay about a half mile back. For Ida May, that was all the time she needed to put the next phase of her plan into motion.

As the chase continued, the police chief from Ironwood became more frustrated at the lack of progress. To aid in the pursuit, he made a radio call for the helicopter to give the exact location of the truck and thus protect a possible escape. Well, it did not take long for the helicopter to locate a truck with a big bear in the back. Sensing fear, Davie said to Ida May, "Mom, it's only a matter of time before they close in on us and take Bear back to the circus."

Ida May then said to Davie loudly, "Look, son. Everything's going to come out okay. Just trust in me." With that reassuring statement from his mom, Davie felt better, but as the helicopter flew overhead and the red flashing lights on the squad car got closer, this young man certainly had his doubts.

What Ida May did next was a real stroke of genius. She remembered a lonely stretch of back road that was heavily covered by the trees on each side of the road. The trees formed a thick dome of vegetation over the road that was not visible from the helicopter. Entering under the trees, Ida May slammed on the brakes as the truck skidded sideways for a moment. Ida May then told Davie to take Bear from the back and head for the woods.

"And, Davie, meet me at Foster's clearing down by the old oak tree in two hours. Also, son, stay out of the open fields where they can spot you." Ida May then took off like a bat out of hell. When she came out into the open only a short distance down the road, the helicopter was there to radio her new position to the police following. For the moment, Ida May and Davie had given their pursuers the slip. What happened next surprised even those who had known this spunky country woman for many years.

The next part of Ida May's plan was to give Davie and Bear a head start. To accomplish this end, Ida May deployed a bit of deception. She raced down that country road with speeds unseen in those parts. Coming to a junction in the road, she brought the truck to a sudden halt. The dust from the road came rolling up like a great cloud, covering everything. The police car and the circus trucks came rolling up behind in a matter of seconds. Ida May kept the truck running as a patrolman came up and asked her to shut the motor off and see her driver's license. Then as they were checking the information on the license, the police commissioner came up and asked Ida May what she had done with the bear.

Now Ida May's response was quite amazing. She said, "Commissioner, if you are seeing bears these days out of passing trucks, then I think you had way too much alcohol today." Ida May went on to say, "Commissioner, I am just an old lady out for a weekend drive. Now what is the harm in that?"

The commissioner replied, "What's wrong with that? How about speeding, for a start, and failure to stop for an officer of the law? You better know this, sister. Come Monday I expect to see you in court, where I am going to throw the book at you." Well, in the end, the police gave back Ida May her driver's license and issued her several tickets. The commissioner also told Ida May he would have her arrested if it weren't so important to recapture that bear for the circus. In the end, he placed an officer to follow her just in case she had any ideas of helping Bear.

Davie knew that making the right decisions and avoiding detection was the only way to make an escape. Since Davie was a country boy, he knew exactly what to do. Unfortunately, his skills as a woodsman were not on an even keel with modern technology. Therefore, it was going to take every bit of his efforts to outwit those tracking them down and prevent Bear's recapture. Keeping to the forested areas, these two fugitives made their way toward the pickup point. Coming to a clearing in the forest, Davie and Bear paused for moment, not knowing how to move forward. As all this was taking place, Davie and Bear heard barking dogs approaching that were sent out by the police. From the noise of the dogs, Davie knew that they were only a half mile behind them. The dogs were in fact closing in for the kill. At this point, these two knew they had to do something fast. However, was the decision they were about to make the right one? With that in mind, Davie and Bear stepped into the clearing. This leap of faith had the possibility of hurting or helping Bear's chance for lasting freedom.

As Bear and Davie made their way across the open meadow, they were immediately spotted by the helicopter as it made an aerial sweep. Running as if their lives depended on it, Davie and Bear shot through the tall grass and entered another stretch of deep woods on the other side. They tumbled and twisted down a steep embankment until they came upon a small stream. The stream was partially filled with water from a storm on the previous night. Trying to lose the scent of the dogs, our fugitives followed the twists and bends in that depression until they came upon a huge tree that had fallen across the stream. For our two travelers, this was the opportunity they needed. Davie had Bear climb up on the log, and they both crossed the stream and proceeded up a steep incline of rocks until they reached the top. Running with all their strength, the two ran through the woods on the other side until they broke through and found themselves in a hayfield. For now, these two were safe, but they were still only steps ahead of the dogs.

As it happened that day, Farmer Brown was just finished loading his trailer with hay bales. Davie waved to the farmer as he drove by. Not believing his own eyes, Farmer Brown quickly turned the tractor and trailer around and shut off the motor next to the boy. Judging from the expression on the farmer's face, Davie quickly surmised that the man was somewhat confused and bewildered at the sight of a boy and bear together in such a remote place. Davie took the first step by introducing himself and his buddy. Then he went on to say, "Those are some nice bales you've got there. Do you need some help getting them into your barn?" With that statement, farmer Brown knew he was dealing with someone brought up on the farm.

The farmer spoke up next, saying, "What are you and that bear doing all alone way out here?" Now Davie put Mr. Brown to ease by saying that this was his pet bear and they had gotten lost in the woods and needed to get home. Davie further reassured farmer Brown by having Bear do some of the tricks he had taught him. Next, Davie asked a favor of his new acquaintance.

"Is it possible for you to take the bear and myself back to your farm? We'll catch a ride from your place back to our own home." The request was granted by Mr. Brown as he pushed aside some of the bales for Davie and Bear to climb up into the wagon. The trip back to farmer Brown's house was uneventful. As for Davie and Bear, this experience taught them a valuable lesson about the goodness of rural people and their generosity toward others.

When the police and the tracking team with the dog handlers arrived at farmer Brown's hayfield, they were highly agitated. As it turned out, there was no sign of the boy or the bear. The trackers were disappointed because they had made good time, and it looked like the end of the chase was almost certain. Once the dogs got to the place where Davie and Bear had jumped on the hay wagon, the dogs lost the scent. For now, the work of these canine wonders was complete. To resume the chase, the police commissioner turned completely to the helicopter for further reports and sightings of these two runaways.

Anticipating that their presence may become known, Davie told Mr. Brown that some of the bales had shifted in the load and needed adjusting. Mr. Brown was not surprised with this outcome because lightly secured loads sometimes shifted while going off road on the farm. As he stopped the tractor and started to climb up on the trailer, Davie hollered down and said everything was okay and that he had fixed the problem. Well, in fact, what really happened was that Davie had Bear climb under some bails to avoid detection. Trusting Davie, the good farmer got back up in the tractor seat, and they all proceeded down the road to his farmhouse. When the helicopter flew over sometime later, all they saw was a load of hay and what looked like a farmer and his son. In fact, Farmer Brown and Davie waved at the helicopter as it flew directly overhead. This bit of trickery fooled the searchers as they flew on without batting an eye. As for Davie and Bear, this little event helped seal their fate and made escape more possible.

Farmer Brown pulled up into his barnyard, turned off the tractor, and called up for Davie and Bear to come down off the trailer. Turning toward Davie, Mr. Brown said, "Son, why don't you let me drop you off someplace. You know it's a long way out here and even farther to town." Davie was quite surprised at the offer and quickly agreed. With that Farmer Brown brought up his old International pickup truck. Why, that old pickup had more rust on it than a sunken ship, but you know what? It still ran and served as the main workhorse on the farm. When Davie and Bear got in the back of the truck, Mr. Brown said to his riders, "We'd better put a tarp over the two of you, just so folks don't get the wrong ideas and become alarmed about seeing a full-grown bear in the back of my truck."

Davie agreed, and both he and bear slipped under the tarp. Before they got underway, Mr. Brown asked Davie where he wanted to go, and without hesitation, he said, "Foster's Clearing." As they took off down the road, the adventure of a lifetime awaited these two travelers.

The trip over to Foster's Clearing seemed exceptionally long for Davie and Bear. Farmer Brown's pickup moved across the Michigan countryside as if laboring on its last journey. Davie peaked out the tarp from time to time to witness the glory of a beautiful day. The sun was high in the sky, and the birds were chirping their approval. For the first time that day, Davie began to breath a bit easier. Then just at that moment, farmer Brown slowed down the pickup and tapped on the back of the cab. He said in a low muffled voice, "Roadblock up ahead." Bringing the truck to a complete stop, they waited for what seemed like hours. What happened next brought terror into the hearts of Davie and Bear.

Davie and Bear waited in complete silence as the situation in the truck got increasingly tenser by the minute. Davie put his hand next to Bear's mouth, trying to keep his friend quiet. As the pickup slowly went forward and then came to a complete stop, Davie and Bear heard farmer Brown talk with a police officer just outside. By chance, that day Mr. Brown happened to know the officer. The officer said, "Why, Fred Brown, what brings you all the way out here today?"

"Well, Tom, just had some business in town and wanted to check on one of my fields that I just recently leased from Ms. Penelope." As their conversation continued, the officer asked Fred if he had heard about the escaped bear in Ironwood. You know we have a bear hunt spread over three counties, looking for that critter."

Now farmer Brown showed no alarm or any concern after hearing the news. At this point he said, "You know me, Tom. I am way too occupied with my farm to keep track of all the news. By the way, thanks for the information." With that, Officer Tom turned his attention to the cargo in the back of the truck. For that brief instant, farmer Brown and those in back panicked; it was almost like time stood still. The terror of that moment signaled either a lifetime of freedom or confinement for their friend Bear. Now which of these realities was about to take place?

Now sometimes in life, you get a lucky break, and for our three travelers, that is what happened. Officer Tom asked Fred, "What you got in back under the tarp?"

"Well, Tom, just go and check it out for yourself."

With that the officer proceeded to pull the tarp up. However, before Officer Tom got a clear view of what was inside, this incredibly bad odor came wafting out of the back. The stench from that pickup was all that was needed for Officer Tom to drop the tarp and look no further. In fact, he said in a loud voice, "PU, that stuff really stinks."

At that point, Farmer Brown was laughing his head off. He said to Tom while he was still snickering, "I see you discovered my load of manure for the Bates sisters. You know, Tom, they grow some of the best strawberries in the county."

Still trying to get his breath, Officer Tom said, "Fred, I am just going to take your word on that recommendation." Well, as it turned out, the odorous episode with Farmer Brown's truck served as an effective check on Officer Tom's curiosity. He then quickly motioned for

Fred to proceed. As Davie and Bear felt the truck move forward and the wind sweep over the tarp, they knew that they had cleared another obstacle toward Bear's final liberation. Nevertheless, there were many new obstacles that lay ahead.

As Davie and Bear were experiencing the adventure of a lifetime, Ida May was trying to ditch the officer who was trailing her. Using every opportunity presented to her, this shrewd country lady led the officer trailing behind through some of the most difficult and narrow roads in the area. Coming to the top of the hill, she sped up and shot down the other side in a flash. Seeing an opening up ahead, Ida May flew off the road through a break in the fence line. She next drove superfast through a farmer's field while skidding and sliding, throwing up dust everywhere. She next parked the truck undetected behind a hedge row. As the trailing officer came over the same hill, there was no sight of Ida May and only a cloud of dust. Whizzing by, the officer lost complete visual contact with his suspect.

That amazing daredevil of a women Ida May had put on a driving demonstration that few NASCAR drivers ever thought of doing. For the moment, she was safe in her concealed location. Waiting for about half an hour, she started back up and used extreme caution to reach Foster's Clearing. To get to her destination, every trick in the book was used, including taking all the backroads. Making the pickup point before Davie and Bear arrived now seemed difficult because of the extra time it took for her to get free. Her only thought at this point was whether Davie and Bear had made the journey okay.

Farmer Brown made his way over to Foster's Clearing as the sun was high in the sky. Pulling his truck into what looked like a big ocean of tall grass, the good farmer strained to see if anyone else was around. Pounding on the back of the truck cab, the driver gave the signal for Davie and Bear to come out from under the tarp. These two travelers emerged rubbing their eyes as the brightness of the midday sun poured in upon them. Since no one was around, Davie and Bear became worried about Ida May. They thought to themselves about what had kept her from making the connection. At about this time, they all heard a vehicle start up in the distance. In a flash, Davie knew it was his mom because he recognized the distinct sound of the glass-pack mufflers on the truck. Letting out a big smile, Davie said to Bear, "It's okay. Ida May is coming."

And sure enough, in a few seconds, they saw their little farm truck come barreling through the high grass to reach them. Now Davie and Bear jumped down out of farmer Brown's truck and started jumping for joy. At that instant, they knew they were free and almost home. As they all thanked farmer Brown for his help and support, the trip home seemed uneventful except for one thing. Ida May made Davie and Bear ride in the back of the truck. In Ida May's typical forward fashion, she said,

"Some feed lots smell better than you guys." Taking no chance, Ida May managed to guide them all back to farm without incident. However, despite the optimism of the moment, one large dark cloud hovered over them all.

By nightfall they all made it home safely. The first thing Davie did was take a bath while Ida May hosed off Bear with a garden hose. That night Ida May cooked up a celebration supper fit for a king. Davie and Ida May retired early, and Bear stayed in the barn with a big bowl of honey and warm milk. As they all settled in that night, each of them thought about the day's events. Davie and Ida May were so happy to have Bear home safe. On the farm, things seemed complete, at least for now.

The very next afternoon, Ida May suggested that they take Bear over to the ice cream parlor in Wakefield for a special treat. You see, Davie and Ida May were so happy to have Bear home that they wanted to do something special for him. They all piled into the truck and picked up Floppy along the way. Arriving in no time at all, Davie went in to order while Ida May stayed out at the truck. Now when it came to ice cream, Bear was the king and found no difficulty in consuming great quantities. Therefore, it was a great surprise to everyone in the store when Davie ordered eight large ice cream cones. The clerk taking Davie's order was somewhat taken back by this rather large request. He said, "All for you?"

"No, sir," said Davie with a smile on his face, "one cone for my mom, one for me, and six for my bear."

After hearing Davie's request, the store clerk came out from behind the counter and looked out the front window. He said in total amazement, "Well, I'll be darned."

All the customers in the store strained their necks to witness a big bear in town. Then Davie took the ice cream cones outside, but Bear grabbed some of the goodies before he reached the cab of the truck. After taking two cones from the tray, Davie fed bear the rest of the ice cream. Why, that old bear slurped up those ice cream cones one after another until they were all gone. After they all had eaten their ice cream, it seemed like a great time to lie back and enjoy the rays of the sun beating softly down. For everyone at the store, this was a perfect day. However, soon this illusion was shattered by a different reality.

The calm of that wonderful afternoon was suddenly shattered by the noise of approaching cars and large trucks rumbling into the heart of Wakefield. As this grim caravan go close, Davie recognized the circus decals on the sides of the trucks. The police chief from Ironwood led the way in his squad car. Once this group spotted Bear in the back of the truck, they all descended around him like a plague of locusts. Why, they dragged out of their trucks all kinds of capture sticks and nets to take back Bear. Seeing this all take place, Ida May told Davie to stall for time. Then she quietly slipped away, going into the store, and placed calls to Sheriff Hanson and old Doc Wilson. In the meantime, Davie stepped in front of

Bear and let no one near him. Floppy, for his part, also stood up on top of the truck and showed his fighting pose. Bear snapped and growled at the men from the circus as they tried to get closer. At this point, a real standoff was underway. The real question now was whether truth and freedom prevailed. Or did the forces of greed and power win?

The struggle between the circus people and those protecting Bear became a real war. The police chief continued to yell at Davie to step aside, but he refused. Some of the circus men tried to slip a rope around Bear's neck, but he quickly batted them away. Bear fought hard because he did not want to lose his freedom again and live the rest of his life in a cage. At about this time, Ida May managed to slip up next to Davie, and she started yelling and screaming at the circus people. The battle waged on for some time as residents from the town came to the defense of Ida May and Davie. These folks pushed and yelled at the circus people as they tried to do their jobs. What happened next surprised even the most casual observer.

Just as things had got almost completely out of hand, Sheriff Hanson and old Doc Wilson came charging up with lights and sirens blazing. The two of them jumped out of the squad car and stood over by Ida May and Davie. Then raising his hand, Sheriff Hanson told everyone to stop and settle down. Then without much effort, it became so quiet that you could almost hear a pin drop. Now the real problem began for Sheriff Hanson on how to sort this entire mess out. Without hesitation, the sheriff went straight to work. As he was an old veteran at settling conflicts, it did not take long for the truth to come out.

The old saying that there are always two sides to a story or two sides to a coin really played out at the Wakefield standoff. Sheriff Hanson let the circus people and the Ironwood police chief speak first. Speaking in a truly angry and agitated tone of voice, the chief said, "These folks stole this prized circus animal and transported him out of Ironwood. They violated the law regarding receiving stolen property, and this woman broke many laws while speeding and failure to stop for an officer of the law. And you know what, if I get my way, she and the whole lot of you will have much to answer for before our judge."

Then looking over at Ida May, Sheriff Hanson motioned for her explanation of events. However, before Ida May spoke up, Davie said to the sheriff and the crowd directly and loudly, "That's not what happened, and you guys know it." From that point, Davie had everyone's attention. What happened next is what legends are made of.

Davie laid out their case by stating the following: "You know full well we didn't steal this bear. In fact, we were never at the circus and only found him wandering along the highway. We were only helping him get home to his rightful place in the forest. You know, Sheriff Hanson, that this is the same bear that I rescued from those trappers that came on our land sometime back."

With that said, Sheriff Hanson was somewhat at a loss for words. He paused for a few seconds then took off his trooper's hat and said, "What we have here are two conflicting stories. We can solve this mystery without going to court and ruffling anyone's feathers." With that the good sheriff proceeded to bring the truth out to the light of day.

Sheriff Hanson knew how to prove this case. Looking at Davie, he asked to have Bear brought down from the truck. Davie then used one of his hand signals, and Bear jumped down without hesitation. Next Davie gave Bear several commands, which he performed perfectly. Then Davie and Bear preformed one their famous wrestling matches to the total delight of the townspeople and everyone present. Sheriff Hanson interrupted these two and told Davie to put Bear back in the truck. Turning to the circus people, Sheriff Hanson stated the following: "In my mind, you have no case here because this bear is familiar with these folks and has lived in these parts for a long time." After hearing these words, the circus people and police chief from Ironwood were outraged and visibly mad. They were not yet willing to give up their prize without a serious fight. What happened next sealed Bear's fate and his future for the coming years.

Having Old Doc Wilson come over with Sheriff Hanson proved a stroke of luck for Bear. Usually the good doctor was out tending to the animals of the area. Nevertheless, that day things were slow, and Ida May's telephone call found him at home. When they arrived, Doc walked by the pickup truck. Bear being the rascal that he is sometimes reached over and patted Doc on the head. The doctor's scowling facial expression gave away his feelings for this attention. Then wasting no time, Doc went straight to work and examined Bear. Pulling back the fur of the right hind leg, Doc found the scar from the time Bear got caught in the trap. Yelling, Doc Wilson told everybody to come over and see the scar for themselves. After a considerable number of people looked at the scar, old Doc Wilson set the record straight.

Addressing the crowd, Doc Wilson said, "Folks, this scar on the back leg of this animal proves that this animal is not owned by the circus."

Then the circus people all shouted, "That's a lie and you know it. Now this is our bear, and we're not leaving till we get him back." The argument over Bear raged for a considerable time thereafter. But despite the confusion and alarm, old Doc Wilson showed little doubt or fear. For you see, the good doctor had an ace up his sleeve that was certain to settle the identity of Bear.

Having knowledge is a powerful weapon in any fight. Then quieting the crowd, old Doc Wilson reached in his suit jacket and pulled out a white piece of paper. Holding the paper, he told everyone that this was a copy of a permit required to transport large exotic animals through the state, in this case, a bear.

"Now, folks, let me tell you this. The bear listed on this report does not match the same physical characteristics, weight, and markings of the bear before you. Furthermore, I phoned around several states that the circus visited and found out their bear died sometime back in an accident. Judging from the facts I've placed before you, this is the complete and total truth. This bear before us is not the property of the circus and never has been." With this news, the circus people hung their heads down a bit. In fact, deep down they knew they had already lost. With this latest revelation, all those from Wakefield breathed a sigh of relief. Our little group had accomplished a lot in a short time. However, to get Bear completely free required some additional work.

Although the Ironwood police chief and circus people knew they had little to stand on, they tried to make Ida May and Davie pay a price for their actions. Staring at the family, the police commissioner made these rather wild charges. He said sternly, "These folks were part of a conspiracy to steal a valuable circus animal for their own gain and profit." Then sneering at Davie and Ida May, the police chief told everybody present that these folks were dangerous, and the law required him to take them before a judge and receive the full justice they deserved. At that point in the conversation, Sheriff Hanson broke in and set the record straight. Sheriff Hanson signaled for everyone to quiet down. The sheriff stated the fact as they appeared to him.

"If Ida May and Davie are guilty for what they've done, then so are the circus people. In fact, these people captured a wild animal without a permit, on private land. They also trespassed on federal lands since Ida May's property runs next to a federal national forest. The circus people also transported this bear without the proper permit. In my eyes, the circus took an animal only to exploit it for their own use and financial gain." Then looking straight at the police chief, Sheriff Hanson said, "Give me those traffic tickets you have against Ida May, and I will let you folks go home in peace. Otherwise, the circus people will face charges with possible fines and prison." With this impossible stalemate before them, both sides backed down. The police chief handed over Ida May's tickets, and the circus people got in their vehicles and left town. Then taking the tickets over to Ida May, Sheriff Hanson smiled and slowly began tearing up those traffic citations. For Ida May and Davie, this was the end of a long struggle and the final victory for Bear.

Bear's reunion with the other creatures of the forest was a joyful occasion. For the other animals, it meant their king had returned. As Ida May drove the pickup truck into the meadow near the farmhouse, the birds of the air screeched Bear's homecoming. Davie then let down the tailgate of the pickup and Bear quickly jumped down into the soft grass. The sensation of the grass under his feet felt strange to Bear at first. It was like he was uncertain of that feeling in his feet. Then to everyone's surprise, Bear began swaying his head from side to side as if to show his approval. Then Mr. Owl came flying in to show his welcome. Why, even the beaver family came up from the nearby stream to say hello. As the day went on, many of Bear's friends came to greet him. And best yet, Davie and Bear found time again to lie in the grass and soak up the warm rays of the sun. As Ida May and Davie drove away that day, they were proud of their accomplishments. They had saved another creature from a lifetime of captivity, ensuring his freedom forever.

WHAT SHOULD WE LEARN FROM CHAPTER 4?

I f we are to learn anything from Bear's experience, it is that freedom is always worth struggling for. Bear lost his freedom through the greed of others, and Ida May and Davie had to work long and hard to get him back. Now relating our story to a personal level, we must always remember that making good choices in life gives us the freedom to live above fear and worries that can drag us down and make us less of a person. Likewise, choosing a lifestyle that is wholesome and good gives us a sense of joy because it lifts our spirits. We are then able to live above the things that can enslave us. Also remember this: selfishness and disregard for others always make us smaller than we are. Being totally free requires being empowered with a giving nature and the acceptance of just authority. In reaching this step, we become committed toward higher goals and principles that heighten our true potential. Reaching a higher plain requires that we free ourselves from the hold of possessions, embracing values that put us closer to a unity of purpose, action, and works that totally transform our world and those around us.

Relating to our story, when Bear faced the possibility of imprisonment for the rest of his life, he had to reach deep down inside himself and overcome fear. Bear's ability to trust in the sage advice of Mr. Owl helped him summon the courage to act. Bear already had the instincts to outwit his captors, but he needed to listen to his inner voice and finally have the courage to break free. In the same way, we must learn from Bear, knowing that our inner strength is always there to help us. However, none of us can go it alone. At times, we must trust in others who are worthy.

David Swindell

5

The Trappers Try to Get Revenge

As the long summer dragged on into fall, things on the farm seemed to move at a snail's pace. The excitement of the past weeks, the trip to Los Angeles, and the television appearance seemed to fade away like an ice cream cone on a hot summer's day. The seasons that mark life in Upper Peninsula Michigan began to express themselves in vibrant colors as the leaves shed their green faces and took on the beauty that lay below. For now, it seemed like life was standing still.

Nevertheless, events on the farm would soon shatter this illusion.

On one sunny afternoon, as the sun set high in the sky, Davie and his pals Floppy and Bear were playing in the meadow near the farmhouse. They were completely cut off from reality. Bear would act as the aggressor always trying to find Davie as they played hide and seek. Floppy would join in the fun, taking his turn as well. Time seemed to stand still as our trio wound down the hours of the day. Little did our friends know that a huge storm was brewing just beyond the horizon. Soon the peace they had known that day was broken by the approach of unwanted visitors.

As Davie and his friends were playing, two pickup trucks pulled down the lane leading to the farm. Inside were the Bowman brothers, just about the meanest individuals the town of Wakefield had ever known. With the Bowmans were the Woodland boys, some local rowdies that always seemed to hang out at the local bars rather than pursue meaningful work for themselves and their families.

At the sound of the approaching trucks, Davie made his way toward the house to see who was visiting them on this fine day. As it happened, Ida May had gone over to one of the neighboring farms for a social visit, and Davie was left home by himself. Seeing who had pulled up to the farm, Davie made a mad dash for the back door of the house. Unfortunately, one of the Bowman brothers grabbed Davie and threw him to the ground. Then in a very irritated voice, he and the others started taunting Davie with words like these: "You thought you were such a hot shot by freeing that bear trap. What you did, boy, was take our property, property that belonged to us. This time that old bear of yours will not live to tell the tale. Boy, we're here to claim our prize." With that one of the woodland boys reached into the pickup and brought out a high-powered hunting rifle, shouting, "Boy, you better show us where that old bear likes to hang out. If you don't, I will tan your hide."

Davie then stood up to the boys and said in a firm voice, "I'd never lead you to Bear, and furthermore, you're hunting illegally out of season anyway." With that one of the boys slapped Davie on the head. Davie shouted back, "The government of the state of Michigan makes the hunting rules, not you."

Then one of the boys addressed Davie's reply by saying, "You know, son, me and my kin have hunted in these forests for over a hundred years. No blasted government is going to tell us what we can or cannot do."

Now Davie shouted back, "You are entitled to only so much of the bounty from nature, and as caretakers of the land, we need to preserve and manage our natural resources for future generations."

Meanwhile, as the standoff on the farm continued, Floppy slipped away over to the Hansons, where Ida May was visiting. He hopped up on the hood of Ida May's car. Just about that time, Ida May was finishing her visit with Mrs. Hanson and was heading out to her vehicle. Now Ida May seemed surprised to see Floppy so far away from his home. She said in a rather surprised tone, "What brings you out this way, little one?" As it turned out, communicating with Ida May was going to take some serious imagination since Floppy only spoke with children and those he completely trusted. Old Floppy made rapid foot movements and flapped his arms in a wild fashion. He also motioned for Ida May to get in her car. Seeing the urgency of Floppy and using her womanly intuition, Ida May sensed danger. She threw Floppy into the front seat of the car, and off they went.

Not knowing what was happening, Ida May decided to use caution in approaching the farm. Now there was a rather high hill that overlooked the farm from the road where they lived. One of the meadows they owned lay next to farmhouse, so Ida May could gaze down on the farm from her vantage point without being detected. She parked the car on the crest of the hill and, to her surprise, saw the two pickup trucks parked in the long sweeping driveway that led to their house. Scratching her head, Ida May thought to herself who these visitors were. Then suddenly, like a bolt of lightning, she remembered that one of the Bowman brothers drove a ratty old truck like the one sitting in her driveway. At that instant, Ida May knew the danger that faced Davie, and she needed to act quickly to protect her son.

Knowing most of the back roads helped Ida May determine a way into her property without detection. She started her car and slowly backed up out of sight. Ida May then took one of the cross-section roads around the back of the farm. There was an old road that went into her property with a rusty old gate. Ida May slipped out of the car and quickly threw it open. It made a loud screeching sound; fortunately, the sound of that old gate did not attract attention from the farmhouse. The old windy road led to a clearing behind the barn, so Ida May parked the car and slipped to the back door of the house. As she got inside the house, she could hear the commotion going on out front. Davie was holding his own and not backing down while the Bowman brothers were heaping verbal abuse on the lad.

Ida May's next move was sure and swift. Quickly she went into the parlor and took her double-barreled shotgun down from the fireplace mantel. She next retrieved her .32 caliber Smith & Wesson revolver from the hall tree drawer near the front door. She loaded the revolver with ammunition and next broke open the shotgun and placed two double buck cartridges in the magazine and clicked the gun back into position. Removing the safety on the shotgun and placing the revolver in the belt of her dress, this modern-day Annie Oakley was ready for action. Slipping out the back door undetected, she proceeded carefully around the back of the barn and crept down behind the hedges. She held the shotgun firmly and then popped up getting a bead and a clear shot angle on those rowdy boys threatening her son.

Now when it came to protecting her family, Ida May never flinched an inch. She knew that timing was everything when confronting someone of greater strength. When Ida May popped up with her shotgun, one of the Bowman brothers reached for his rifle. She took high aim and let go one barrel of her shotgun. She next motioned for Davie to come over closer to her. Ida May then addressed the Bowmans and their rowdy friends in the following manner: "You boys better not move an inch, or you're going to feel the buckshot of my shotgun." Next, she instructed Davie to go over and pick up the rifles that the Bowmans were toting.

Davie quickly pulled back the bolts of the rifles and removed the cartridges inside. Then he said to his mom, "They're all unloaded." With that, Ida May felt relieved and breathed slightly easier now that things were under her control.

She next turned to the boys and said in an irritated voice, "What in the world were you thinking when you trespassed on my land and treated my son and our property in such a disrespectful manner? Did you think that you could force your way onto my place and get whatever you wanted without a shred of common decency?" With that being said, she motioned for the boys to speak up for themselves. Ida May waited for a reply, but silence and the whispering of the wind through the trees was her only reply. Finally, Ida May shouted; "Well, speak up for yourselves."

Next, one of the Bowman brothers said defiantly, "We were only exercising our rights to make a living and bring home our prize that was stolen by your son."

Judging from the explanation given by the boys, Ida May chuckled a bit and then said, "You boys seemed a bit confused. In the first place, you put your bear trap on my land. And secondly, as Davie already told you, trapping that time of year is illegal. Furthermore, you endangered us and my cows who occasionally stray into that forest clearing. Why, even one of us may have accidentally stepped in that big old trap." Next Ida May gave the boys a moment for their decision. "Now you boys need to make up your minds right here and now. You can apologize to me and my son or suffer the legal consequences when Sheriff Hanson comes out here. He's a personal friend of mine and will not consider your actions today as honorable." However, despite Ida May's urgings, the Bowman brothers and their buddies remained defiant in their attitudes.

What transpired next is still talked about today by the townsfolk of Wakefield. Ida May really did not want to hurt the boys; she only wanted to protect her family and receive respect from all her fellow citizens. However, what happened next only brought justice to Wakefield in its own way. First, she had Davie take the rifles into the house and then carefully removed the keys from the trucks. In a loud voice, she made the following demands: "You boys will never—I repeat, never—get your rifles and trucks back until I receive an apology. In addition, since you boys were so fired up to kill Bear, then it's only fitting that you have that chance. However, this time you won't have the benefit of rifles and traps. Let's say you'll meet Bear to man and man to bear." With that Ida May had Davie give out his special call to bring Bear home to the farm.

As it so happened, Bear had been nibbling on some berries after his nap. Bear heard Davie's voice and raised his massive head in a somewhat surprised look. He thought to himself, *I wonder why our young man is calling me back again. Better go over and see.* Bear slowly lumbered over to the edge of the farm. From the scent in the wind, he determined that strangers were present. Bear thought to himself, *I wonder who came to visit us.* As he drew near, he sensed an uneasiness and fear present. Therefore, he approached the farm with caution and a degree of uncertainty.

Well, the great showdown between Ida May and the poachers had entered what you might call its serious stage. Bear popped his head through the bushes and looked with great surprise at the strange men standing in the driveway. Bear wondered who these people were and what their business was with Davie and Ida May. At about the same time, Davie waved at bear to come over closer to him. Why, Bear just broke through those bushes like a hot knife through butter. Davie grabbed his friend by the ear and whispered softly, "These fellows that came out to the farm were the ones who set the trap for you in the forest. They also came out here to try and kill you today. Why, they've been most unkind to both Ida May and me." Davie went further to tell his pal this: "Ida May wants you to teach these boys a lesson they will not soon forget. Just rough them boys up a bit, and send them running for the hills."

Bear then whispered back, "Davie, that's a great idea."

As you may imagine, those Bowman and Woodland boys were getting a bit nervous staring down the barrel of a loaded shotgun and a huge bear standing before them, fearsome in appearance and size. Finally, one of the boys pulled a hunting knife from its sheath and began waving it at bear. Why, that was all it took for our massive friend to spring into action. Bear stepped forward and took one swipe of his paw and sent that old knife flying. The boys looked on in terror as bear stood up on his back feet and let out a spine-tingling growl. With that introduction, the boys took off across the front lawn like scared rabbits. Bear and Buddy, the farm dog, took off in pursuit. One of the Bowmans tried to take refuge in a tree, which bear also climbed up. This scared visitor to the farm got stuck on a small limb of the tree. The weight of that old boy proved too much for a small tree; he fell to the ground and was fortunately not hurt. Bear did not have time to climb back down before this fellow leaped up and took off through the bushes faster than a lightning bolt. Bear and Buddy kept up their pursuit over several miles. Why, that pair chased those boys halfway to town before old Doc Wilson stopped to pick them up on the road. Meanwhile, back on the farm, Ida May and Davie were rolling with laughter. They had never seen anything so funny in all their lives.

After things settled down a bit, Ida May turned to Davie and said, "I know these boys will try and sneak back tonight and take back their trucks and rifles, so let us not oblige them." Ida May drove the two pickup trucks into the machine shop on the farm and locked the doors. She placed the rifles into her locked gun case in the kitchen. Her next step was to put Buddy on a chain near the house. Well, Ida May's instincts were right because that very night, the boys tried to sneak back to the farm and locate their vehicles. Despite a valid attempt, those fellows came up empty. It did not take them long to figure out that Ida May held most of the cards in this dispute. They faced the possibility of having criminal charges brought against them for a host of crimes that included trespassing, hunting out of season, and threatening a child. All Ida May had to do was wait these boys out until they came around to her way of thinking.

Well, the Bowman and Woodland brothers finally came back to the farm the very next day. However, their appearance was not so good. Why, they had Band-Aids on their faces and scratches all over their arms. It looked as if they had run through every sticker and thorn bush in the area. Old Doc Wilson had brought the boys out in his car since the fellows seemed to lack transportation. The conversation was pleasant at first with the usual greetings. But things turned ugly as both sides restated their cases. Finally, old Doc Wilson stepped in and told the boys, "Look. You fellows could face considerable jail time if you don't step down from your pride and admit you were wrong." As I see it, modern reality and scarcity of wildlife means that humans simply have to make adjustments in the way we hunt and trap. We can no longer take from nature in the same way as before."

Then Doc said, "Humans have to reinvent themselves and learn to manage natural resources better and find new ways to make a living. Just because you boys come from families that have hunted these woods for generations, doesn't mean you can continue to do so. Humans have the ability to change and grow while animals can do only what nature and our Creator intended. Therefore, boys, it's time to give up hunting as a livelihood. Instead, hunt for pleasure." After hearing Doc's little speech, the boys seemed more at ease with what they had to do.

Turning to Ida May, one of the Bowman Brothers said, "Please forgive us for our intrusion on your privacy. I guess we got carried away and overstepped our boundaries by coming on your place without permission and roughing up your son. You see, we have a great passion for hunting and trapping and didn't stop to think that our actions could hurt others." With that statement, the boys went over and shook the hands of Ida May and Davie.

Ida May next said to the boys, "I am a churchgoing woman, and it says in the Good Book that we are not to hold grudges and should forgive our neighbors when they hurt us. Therefore, I am willing to excuse you for what you've done." Those words from Ida May were mighty comforting to the boys as they seemed to relax more.

What happened next was no surprise. Ida May told Davie to go into the house and bring out the rifles and the ammunition they had taken earlier. He handed the boys back their rifles and reached in his pocket and pulled out the unused cartridges. Ida May then took out her keys to the machine shop and opened the doors. Securing the keys to the trucks, she fired one up then the next and drove them out one at a time to the front drive. The boys thanked Ida May and Davie for being hospitable toward them. Then Ida May turned to the boys and said, "Before you go, there's something else you need to do. Please make peace with bear." Davie then made his call out into the woods. Bear was foraging nearby, so it only took a few minutes for our friend to appear on the scene.

Bear did not appear happy to see the Bowmans and their friends back on the farm. In fact, he was almost ready to tear them apart for what they had done to him and Davie. Fortunately, Davie stepped in and talked with his pal first. He said, "Bear, it's time now for us to let go of our feelings toward these fellows."

But hearing this, Bear seemed somewhat mad. He said to Davie in an angry voice, "Why should I let this go? After all, they were the ones that started this whole mess by setting the trap and coming on the farm and starting all that trouble."

Nevertheless, Davie would have no part in Bear's attitude of unforgiveness. He stated to Bear why we need to forgive others when they have harmed us.

"Bear, do you remember the time you stole that blueberry pie from Ida May and the time you raided her strawberry patch? Didn't she forgive you for your conduct? That's why we need to make up with these boys, so they can feel peace in their hearts and have closure." After weighing what Davie had said, Bear came around to forgiving the boys. Bear then went around and gave each of the boys a friendly nuzzle. Buddy, the farm dog, joined in the fun by pressing his paw against the boys one by one. Everyone began to laugh, and the tension between these two parties simply faded away. When the boys drove away, both Davie and Ida May felt a great weight lifted from their lives.

As the Bowman and Woodland boys left the farm, a silence surrounded their departure as they drove back to Wakefield. Then Jim Bowman, the real leader of the group, spoke up and stated these words with great wisdom: "You know, we are all lucky that we didn't go to jail over our actions. If we learn anything from this encounter, it's that the feelings and rights of others are important in how we act towards our fellow man. That Ida May is quite a woman. She's quite active for her age. Let's not get tangled up with her again." With that said, the boys seemed quite relieved that their experience with Ida May, Davie, and Bear had ended. Well, in fact, these young fellows learned quite a lot from their encounter. They later turned into quite respectful citizens in Wakefield and proved their worth through help and support to the community.

WHAT SHOULD WE LEARN FROM CHAPTER 5?

Forgiving others who have harmed us is always difficult. Anger can often speak to us in a powerful way. By our very nature, we want to get even and settle matters with those who have hurt us. Forgiveness requires us to step beyond our emotions and feelings and step into the world of compassion and mercy. We must ask ourselves why forgiveness is necessary. This question lies deep within the inner self of all humans. From a practical standpoint, it is necessary to know that hurt is a process that everyone goes through. The real importance of that fact is how we react to that hurt. Does our hurt overtake us to the point that revenge becomes central to us. By holding on to bitterness and resentments, do we gain anything in return? To answer this question, we must understand the true nature of self-giving and how it affects relationships with others.

A person must further understand that the people we interact with in life are a true gift to us. This includes at times the people we have the hardest time getting along with. To understand this better, we must come to the reality that all people, regardless of their position, ability, physical beauty, or shape, deserve our respect because they are part of the human family. Therefore, squabbles, conflicts, and wars are only extensions of individuals and groups that fail to recognize the true dignity of others. From a practical viewpoint, it makes more sense to build bridges between ourselves and others rather than endure the raging waters that seek to undermine and destroy us all. Additionally, we must understand that the greatest treasures in life are neither possessions nor social status but instead the relationships with our brothers and sisters who walk with us through a common journey.

One additional note concerning relationships: some people feel that they can go it alone and do not need the help of others emotionally. Simply put, these individuals miss so much from life. They can often end up cynical and do not trust others. A self-centered outlook on life often leads to bitterness and frustration. Therefore, it is better to have company along the way and have caring and loving individuals that will support and nurture you. This also includes people that will tell you the truth about yourself and help you grow into a complete individual.

David Swindell

6

A Sad Ending for a Great Lady

S ometimes in life, changes come quickly and without warning. Getting off the school bus one sunny fall afternoon, Davie made his way down the road that led to the farm. A gentle breeze pushed against his forehead and parted his hair. For Davie everything seemed so beautiful. The backdrop of the earth against the blue sky added to his peace as his mind shifted to thoughts of far-off adventures. He thought of warriors and beautiful maidens. He dreamed of battles with the evildoers and slaying the evil dragon. For Davie everything seemed so perfect. Soon Ida May would have supper ready, and he could watch TV with his mom. After evening chores, Davie saw himself settling down with one of his favorite books. The illusion that Davie had brought to his mind came to a sudden end as he turned the corner and headed up the drive towards the house. Something was out of place. There were many cars in the driveway, and an ambulance was parked next to the house. For Davie the pleasant feelings he had experienced turned into something that seemed unreal. Without hesitation he ran up to the door of the house and entered. What happened next would sadden his heart for an awfully long time.

The look on the faces of those gathered in Ida May's living room told the whole story. Davie made eye contact with old Doc Wilson first. Doc Wilson sensed the confusion and surprise on Davie's face. Immediately Doc took Davie by the shoulder and escorted him into the kitchen, away from the small crowed of people gathered in the house. Doc spoke in a soft, sure voice as he gave an account of what happened.

"Davie, as far as we know, your mother died this morning sometime around 10:00 a.m. It looks like she had a sudden heart attack. We found her in her chair with the telephone receiver off the hook. I think she was trying to get help but just passed out. Davie, your mother was a fighter and one tough lady. She would want you to stand up like a man during this difficult time." By now the tears were streaming down Davie's face, and he felt as if his feet and legs had turned to rubber. Turning toward Doc, Davie made this profound statement for someone so young.

"What made my mom special was her inner strength. She always believed in herself and always had faith in others to do the right thing." With that said, Davie now prepared himself for a long journey, a journey that would test who he was and the direction of his future.

Now in a surprise move, Davie turned to Doc Wilson and made this request. Davie said, "Can I spend some time with Mom before you take her away? You see, Doc, Ida May and I were awfully close, and it's only fitting that we have a few minutes together." For Davie, requesting to see his mom was a painful decision. Nevertheless, Davie wanted some time alone with her to say goodbye before the other relatives and friends arrived. Old Doc Wilson turned to Davie and nodded in approval.

"We put her in the back bedroom. Take all the time you need."

Walking down the hallway to the bedroom seemed like a descent into darkness for this young man. Davie got to the door and tried to turn the knob, but something prevented him from doing so. A feeling of fear descended upon Davie as if a sudden wave of water washed him and his mom out into a stormy ocean. In that moment, he pictured in his mind Ida May and himself being torn apart and carried away in different directions. It appeared to him that Ida May was being pulled away into the light while he was drawn toward a huge tree on the shore. At the same time, Davie was undergoing the rage of endless darkness in a dark sea; Ida May was being lifted into a new life. Pulling himself together, Davie tried to overcome this sudden terror and find inner strength. Putting those inner thoughts behind him, Davie turned the doorknob and entered the room. From this moment on, Davie now confronted the full reality of his new life.

Seeing his mom lying lifeless on the bed sent chills down Davie's back. He began to cry again as his tears ran down the side of his face. He managed to gather enough strength to sit beside her in the chair next to the bed. Slowly he placed his hand upon hers. Ida May was no longer warm like she always had been but instead felt cold and lifeless. Her color had changed too. Davie felt an emptiness that he had never experienced before. Ida May was with him in the room, but her presence was somewhere else. Despite this, Davie felt a strong comfort that someone was looking out after him and still cared very much for him. While sitting in that room, Davie's thoughts turned back to all the beautiful memories he and his Mom had had together. The years Ida May and Davie spent on the farm were some of the best years of their lives. As for now, Davie's tomorrow seemed less promising than before. A shadow had overtaken him, leaving only despair with little hope.

While Davie was still in serious thought, old Doc Wilson came into the room. Doc went over to Davie and whispered in his ear, "Davie, come out into the kitchen with me for a while." As they walked down the hall together, old Doc Wilson said, "You know, Davie, it's time for us to make plans. Things are not as dark as they appear at this present moment. Ida May left you in good hands and planned for your future. She established a college fund for you and paid off the debts on the farm last year. The money you earned while appearing on national TV left you with a decent savings account. Now the real question is who you are going to live with until you turn eighteen. At that point, you can legally take over the farm." Then Doc spoke to Davie in a more business-like tone, "Why, Davie, you can even sell the farm if you wish and move away from Wakefield."

Now Doc's words got Davie's attention. Looking directly at Doc Wilson, Davie made a sincere statement.

"Look, Doc. "My whole life centers around this farm. All my memories are tied up with this place. My special friends live in the woods nearby, and all the neighborhood kids I go to school with live next to me. Just how in the blue blazes could a person like me leave this all behind?" Doc shook his head in agreement.

"Well, Davie, this makes things a bit more complicated, but do not worry. We will work something out."

Doc stayed true to his word and did his best to help Davie out during the next few weeks. However, Davie's fate would remain uncertain as others decided his immediate future.

Ida May's funeral came on a beautiful fall day. The sun was out and very bright, and the leaves on the trees showed their wonderful autumn colors. For such a somber occasion, the weather looked almost out of place. Now practically the whole town of Wakefield came out to pay their respects for this great lady. As Mrs. Olson summed it up best, "Our friend was loved and respected by almost everybody in our town." Why, even the Woodland and Bowman boys, those rowdies whom Davie and Ida May had that run in with earlier, showed up to offer support to Davie. While they were all waiting to go into the church, a lady from out of town pulled up in a white Cadillac with two kids in the back. Davie had never seen these folks before and wondered where they came from. Looking at the car's license plate, he noticed that they were from Kansas. Davie then thought, *What brings these folks all the way up here for my Mom's funeral?*

The services for Ida May were simply beautiful according to the report in the *Wakefield New* and by all who attended. The church chorus sang one beautiful song after another. The local minister gave an inspiring account of Ida May's life. Not all the people in the church were downcast with Ida May's passing. In fact, many of these folks talked in great length after the service about the goodness and kindness of their neighbor and friend. They also chuckled and laughed at how Ida May had singlehandedly outwitted the Ironwood Police Department. However, for Davie the passing of Ida May was extremely hard to handle. He struggled with many questions concerning his loss. For him, the real challenges of his mom's passing were ever present and painful to deal with.

After the services were concluded, old Doc Wilson came up to Davie and tried to comfort him. You see, Doc Wilson was never a talkative type of person; he always had a directness about him. His words to Davie were straight and to the point.

"Davie, the loss of Ida May will leave a big hole in your life for a long time. However, it's now time to move on and start a new life for yourself. There is someone you need to meet." Without further introductions, Doc Wilson waved his hand toward an attractive middle-aged woman and the two kids with her. Doc then said, "Davie, this is your aunt Mimi and her children, Jackie and Big Dave." At first Davie seemed rather surprised to see this threesome but suddenly remembered the women and the two kids who had pulled up in the shiny white Cadillac.

As the conversation continued, Davie turned to his aunt and said in a soft voice, "Hey, you got a nice car."

Then Aunt Mimi smiled back at Davie and said, "I am glad you like my car, young man."

After a bit of chitchat, old Doc Wilson spoke up and said to Davie, "Davie, is it okay if your aunt and your two cousins come out to the farm and stay with you for a few days?"

At first Davie did not know what to think. He thought for a few seconds, then said, "Well, I guess it's okay. We have a small house, but we can all manage somehow."

Aunt Mimi then turned toward Davie and said in a most kind tone of voice, "Why not ride out to the farm with us? We really don't know the way to your place." Then they all piled into the car and took out for the farm. The ride for Davie was distant and quiet. He tried to talk with his cousins about the farm and their lives, but his mind always drifted back to the many unanswered questions that lay ahead.

For Davie having relatives visit just after Ida May's passing was both good and bad. He loved the idea of meeting his aunt and cousins for the first time, but he felt a deep sadness that he could not overcome. What Davie needed was some time to himself to sort out his feelings and work through the sorrow. However, events in Davie's life were moving at a fast pace. He was being forced forward whether he was ready or not. As Aunt Mimi drove her car up the lane to the farm, Davie remained deep in thought and focused on the many wonderful memories he and his mom had together. Only the stopping of the car and the opening of the doors brought him back to the present time.

As everybody got out of the car, Aunt Mimi took charge of the situation. She said to Davie in an incredibly soft voice, "Why don't you get changed out of your good clothes and put on something more comfortable. Then you can show Jackie and Big Dave around the farm." At first the thought of showing outsiders around the farm seemed a bit pushy. However, Ida May had trained Davie to respect authority, so he followed the directions of an adult. Davie took his two cousins all around the farm and into the woods. These two city kids were excited and fearful as they encountered many new things, including different plants and animals, for the first time. For Davie taking others into his own space seemed like an invasion of his privacy. After all these were the woods that he loved so much. Because of these feelings, Davie refused to show his visitors his secret places or introduce his cousins to Floppy and Bear.

As the tour of the farm concluded, Davie heard the dinner bell and knew that Aunt Mimi had most likely cooked up something up for them to eat. The sound of the bell brought back memories of how his beloved Ida May had always prepared one of his favorite dishes. Hearing the bell now only saddened his heart as he realized the truth of living without a mother or father.

The next few days out on the farm seemed normal enough since farm chores were always a part of country life. Davie kept himself busy by mending some fences and making sure the cows were milked and had plenty of feed and water. Jackie and Big Dave were lost in this rural setting. These city kids always seemed in the way and asked a thousand silly questions. For Davie, this time in his life remained painful. His only thoughts now centered on the loss of his beloved Ida May. He also wondered deep in his heart what was to become of him. For Davie, the outcome of his future was about to unfold.

That night after supper, Aunt Mimi called Davie into the living room and had him sit down. Jackie and Big Dave came in too, but Aunt Mimi told them to get ready for bed. She had planned to send them all to school the next day, and since the school bus came quite early, Aunt Mimi wanted them ready for tomorrow. Now Aunt Mimi was never a woman long on words; her talks were always carefully chosen and to the point. She offered Davie a chocolate chip cookie she had baked that very afternoon. Davie respectfully declined, saying he simply was not hungry. Then Aunt Mimi got down to the real business at hand.

"Davie, I know that you want to stay out here on the farm. However, you are too young to farm this big place all alone. I am prepared to help you reach your goal. Please allow me and my children to stay with you a few years until you are old enough to manage on your own." Then turning to Davie and looking him straight in the eyes, Aunt Mimi made this truthful statement. "Davie, I am blessed with considerable wealth. In fact, many people consider me a millionaire. Therefore, my place of residence is not tied to a job. I can live anywhere. Young man, does this offer appeal to you?"

Then Aunt Mimi went on to say, "If, for some reason, you don't want to stay here on the farm, we can have the place boarded up, and you can move with me back to my home in Kansas." At the sound of these words, Davie was both lost and confused. He told Aunt Mimi he needed a few days to think things over. Then Davie turned inward with his thoughts. What he did not realize was that his future life depended on his decisions during the next few days. In the meantime, Davie was going to undergo a test, a test that was going measure his own courage and his determination to live.

As the days passed, the weight of Aunt Mimi's offer seemed to weigh more heavily on Davie's heart. He respected his aunt but still thought of her as an outsider. He resented that he was no longer the center of attention in the family and thought of his cousins as competitors. Davie did not like the idea of someone else living on Ida May's farm and sleeping in his house. The whole situation grew tenser as Jackie and Big Dave quickly made friends at school. His cousins quickly adapted in their new school while Davie struggled with his grades and making friends. To make things worse, Aunt Mimi wanted a decision from Davie on the farm. All these issues piled up for Davie and made his life more depressing. He was battling emotions within himself and struggling how to relate to new relatives in a different setting. For this reason, Davie made the decision to run away and escape the perceived mess at home. Davie just wanted to get away and think things out. However, as Davie was about to find out, decisions made quickly and without proper thought are not always the wisest. Davie walked out of the house into the cool air of a Michigan evening. What happened next would mold his character forever.

A full moon shone brightly on the fields and trees as Davie ran toward his secret hiding place on the farm. The tears were running down his cheeks as he made his way toward the big fir tree that stood on the edge of clearing several miles from the farm. In his rush to sneak out without Aunt Mimi hearing him, Davie had forgotten to take a jacket or any supplies for the journey. The emotions of the moment were too much for him to handle. The problem now, as he stood in the forest, was that thick clouds and a heavy mist were settling into the area. The full moon that had shown him the way earlier had disappeared into the darkness. The night animals that prowled through the darkness were coming out to find food, plus off in the distance, Davie could hear the cry of a wolf pack. He could feel the air getting colder and began to panic. For the first time in his young life, Davie realized he was lost and felt great fear. From this moment on, only his determination and survival skills could help him stay alive.

Now Davie found himself in a real mess. He had no place to turn as the night closed in on him. The usual landmarks of trees and rocks that always guided his steps were no longer visible to his sight. Traveling on, Davie stumbled upon a clearing through the trees. As he came into this big open space, nothing seemed the same as usual. Everything appeared out of order, changed, and dim to his sight. Following the clearing for a short distance, Davie found a trail leading back into the woods. For this young man, the trail looked right, but deep within himself, Davie was unsure if this was the right way home. Davie wondered which way to proceed, take the trail or stay in the clearing and try and find another way out.

After thinking about which direction to take, Davie decided he needed to follow the trail. As he traveled along this path, it suddenly occurred to him that his earlier decision was not a good choice. As you see, the trail led Davie deeper into the woods, to a place he had never been before. The branches of the trees seemed to grab at him as he passed along the trail. Davie also fell over the rocks that littered the floor of the forest. This young man found himself battered and bruised as he continued his travel. At this place in his journey, he had little strength to go on, only something higher than himself guided him now.

The trail now became steeper and more difficult as Davie made his way through the forest. Suddenly and without warring, he stepped out of the forest into a huge open space. The high grass that covered this gentle rolling countryside tossed back and forth in the wind. These grass stems thrashing about from right to left then back again.

It was like the movements of the grass were trying to convey some type of warning dance. The grass also seemed to say, "Young man, beware. Young man, watch yourself, because danger is near." Now just at that moment, the wind stopped, and a break in the clouds allowed the moon to shine brightly down on Davie. Davie was able to see through the deep haze the outline of a neighbor's farmhouse. In that instant, Davie breathed a sigh of relief.

Those feelings of relief lasted only a short time. The clouds rolled back in, and the moonlight disappeared almost as quickly as it had appeared. To make things worse, Davie saw off in the distance the movement of dark, shadowy figures coming toward him. He thought to himself, *Why is this happening to me*? As you see, these dark figures began to encircle Davie. He knew from the movement that these creatures were that pack of gray wolves he had heard off in the distance earlier. The wolves moved in ever closer toward Davie and began growling and snarling at him. This young man was their next meal. As for Davie, he did not know what to do. He was faced with trying to stand his ground and fight or run like mad and make a break for safety. Whichever choice Davie decided, his future depended on clear thinking and a great deal of cunning and swiftness.

Before the wolves had completely cut off all escape routes, Davie spotted an opening back toward the forest. Taking off like a bolt of lightning, Davie ran with all his strength and endurance. He crashed through the grass and tall brush on the edge of the clearing. His heart was pumping blood at a rapid rate while his feet and arms moved back and forth, trying to gain extra speed. He knew this was a matter of life or death. If the wolves caught him, they would rip him apart in no time at all. As he kept running, the path took him over dead logs as he scrambled down and over rocks and through ditches. At the same time, the entire wolf pack chased in hot pursuit. The two fastest wolves began to close in on Davie; they drew closer and closer at every step and turn. In fact, these two powerful animals reached within easy striking distance of their prey.

Then suddenly the clouds parted as they had done earlier. This time, however, it was like rays of moonlight showing Davie a clear pathway to a tall tree in the forest. This tree had a grouping of three branches lying low to the ground. Without thinking or wasting a single second, Davie ran toward that tree while the wolves were only a few feet away. Taking a giant leap, Davie managed to land on the lowest branch of the tree. He quickly tried to climb up, but one of the wolves grabbed him on the leg, tearing at his jeans. For a moment, the wolf seemed to have the upper hand, but Davie reached up with his arms and grabbed a tree limb. He pulled with all his might, and suddenly his jeans ripped, and this young man made it to freedom. As for the wolves, they ran around the tree, barking and growling at Davie. Despite not capturing their dinner, the wolves kept a watchful eye on him, hoping he would fall asleep and tumble out of the tree. It was now a standoff between the wolves and Davie; it was only a matter of time before one side would win out.

Now it so happened that Aunt Mimi had awoken out of a sound sleep. As she wiped the sleep from her eyes, a terrible, troubling felling seemed to come over her. Jumping to her feet, she went to check the house and the kids. Knowing that Jackie was still asleep in the girl's room, Mimi searched the rest of the house. On checking Big Dave, she found him asleep on the sofa in the living room. Proceeding to Davie's room, she slowly crept down the hall and opened the door only a tiny bit, trying not to wake him. Despite her best efforts, the hinges on that old door let out a loud creaking sound as she tried to enter farther. Figuring that Davie had awakened by now, Aunt Mimi opened the door as far as possible and turned on the lights in the room. To her surprise, Aunt Mimi found no sign of Davie anywhere. The bedsheets and blankets were all pushed up into the corner of the bed, and the clothes that he wore last night had disappeared. At seeing these developments, Aunt Mimi began to panic as her inner fears began to take hold. Trying to gain courage and stay calm, Mimi thought to herself, *There is some reason or explanation for Davie's disappearance.*

Taking matters quickly into her own hands, Mimi began a search of the farm. She got Jackie and Big Dave up out of bed. Big Dave protested a little bit when forced to get up. He said, "Mom, why do I have to get up and look for that stupid old cousin of mine?" Aunt Mimi would take no excuse from her son and made him get up. All of them began and wide search of the farm. However, despite their best efforts to find Davie, nothing turned up.

Aunt Mimi was never the kind of woman who feared challenges. She immediately got on the phone and called all the neighbors to see if they had seen her nephew. She also called Sheriff Hanson, who searched the area around the farm in his squad car. After he was unable to find Davie, he arranged for a tracking dog. The tracking dog would arrive in the morning to begin a search of the entire area. Sitting at the kitchen table back at the farmhouse, Aunt Mimi sipped on some strong black coffee as she tried to think of a clue to Davie's location. Then suddenly, as the old clock in the kitchen struck four, Aunt Mimi received an inspiration like a bolt out of the blue. It came to her that she needed to find Bear and try and convince him to search for Davie. Now finding a grumpy old bear in the middle of the night is not an easy undertaking, but for Davie's sake, Aunt Mimi knew she had to try. For Aunt Mimi, the road ahead was full of dangers. Only her own purpose and sure grit would guide her way.

Wasting no time, Aunt Mimi went straight to work with her plan to find Davie. She went into the hall closet and got down her heavy coat and slipped on some winter gloves. She also placed a warm scarf on her head. Going out into the barn, she tugged on the heavy doors, but they simply resisted her every move. Finally, after almost exhausting herself, she made the big doors give way and swing open. As she entered the barn, darkness overcome her; she reached out, trying to find her way, when she ran smack-dab into one of the support poles holding up the hay loft. Remembering that a kerosene lamp was on the opposite pole, Aunt Mimi made her way to the other side of the barn. Running her hand up the post, she found the lamp and the box of matches that were on small shelf. She pried open the lamp and struck a match to light it. At that very instant, the wind suddenly gusted and slammed those big barn doors. Mimi jumped almost out of her skin, dropping the lit match and almost losing her balance. Now Mimi was normally a mild person, but on this occasion, she let out a few chosen words. She said loudly, "Oh crap, I could have burned the whole barn down." Now after this little event, Mimi, with great care, lit the lamp and made her way outside. For this brave lady, many challenges lay ahead. She walked off into the darkness and into uncertainty. This was a night she would never forget.

Now Aunt Mimi knew the spot out in the meadow where Davie and Bear liked to play. She carefully followed the path behind the house into the forest. Holding the lantern high, Mimi made her way slowly up and over fallen tree limbs and rocks in her path. After considerable effort and struggle, she made it to the edge in the clearing. Reaching this point proved rather exhausting for this fine lady. Now with all her effort, Aunt Mimi found the strength to go on. She searched over the area but could not recognize any landmarks or features that pointed to Bear's cave. Not knowing what to do next, Mimi stopped in her tracks and waited. At that very moment, the clouds parted, and the moon shone its rays deeply upon the clearing. For the first time, Mimi got a brief view of her surroundings. Out of the corner of her eye, she spotted the big White Pine tree where Davie and Bear loved to go. Getting her directions firmly set in her mind, Aunt Mimi took off in a straight path for that tree. The moonlight that had shown her the way, now suddenly and without warning, simply disappeared. Staying on her course, Mimi managed to find her way across the clearing and get to that tree. As for Mimi, this only represented the first step in an epic journey. She was now determined to reach out to Bear and put all her faith in him.

For Mimi trying to find Bear seemed like trying to find a needle in a haystack. No matter which direction Mimi turned, only darkness and the howling of the wind were present. Calling out for Bear in the darkness seemed so hopeless. At this point in her journey, Aunt Mimi summoned all her strength and let out a call that pierced even the wind. You see, Mimi had wanted Bear to answer her call, but nothing happened. Then suddenly Mimi heard the snapping of branches and wrestling of leaves. Then on the edge of the clearing came running a shadowy large brown figure. It broke into the open and lunged at Mimi with full force. Then suddenly this massive creature stood before Mimi as if frozen in time. The big brown head only inches from her face then paused as if to observe and study this rather small woman with a face solid as stone.

Mimi's was fearless on the outside. However, on the inside, she was nearly scarred out of her wits. Then calmly Aunt Mimi spoke to Bear. As she spoke, the tears began to pour out of her because she loved her nephew so much and wanted him home and safe. She said to Bear, "My dear friend, Davie is lost and left the house this evening without telling anyone, nor did he leave a note to guide us to his whereabouts. As you know, Davie is not himself since the passing of Ida May. Dear Bear, if you can help find him, I just know that you can bring him home safely."

With these courageous words from Aunt Mimi, Bear responded by turning his head from side to side. Then Bear lifted his head toward the night sky and let out a roar that was heard throughout the forest. Next, he ever so gently brushed his nose against Aunt Mimi's face. In an instant, Bear quickly disappeared back into the forest. As for Mimi, her fearful encounter with this massive creature had left her shaken. As she made her way back to the farmhouse, her only hope was that she had gotten through to Davie's pal and true friend. Now only time would tell if Mimi's words had taken effect with Bear and the other animals of the forest.

As for Bear, he knew that time was running out for his good friend. At a reckless full speed and running on all four legs, Bear crashed through the forest. He ran over to Floppy's burrow and began scratching wildly at its entrance. Now our friend Floppy was sound asleep but suddenly woke up to all the commotion outside his humble dwelling place. Finally, after considerable effort, Floppy stuck his head out from below. He rubbed the sleep from his eyes, only to see Bear glaring down at him with a worried look on his face. Bear wasted no time and spoke to Floppy very quickly and with great force. Bear said, "Davie is missing and has wandered off in the woods alone tonight."

Now Floppy knew the dangers of being alone in the woods after dark. As you see, this is the time when the night predators roam at will. Floppy then said to Bear, "We must find Davie quickly."

At that very instant, Floppy and Bear heard the night cry of the wolf pack off in the distance. Then looking skyward toward a hazy moon, Bear spoke these deep words: "Davie's time of darkness has come. We must help him before it's too late."

In an instant, Floppy hopped on Bear's back, and they were off in a flash. These two searchers stopped throughout the forest, asking the other animals if they had seen a young boy come this way. Most of the animals did not notice any human movement or were asleep at the time. Then suddenly, Floppy and Bear heard Mr. Owl just ahead. Following his hooting, they called up to their friend in the tree just ahead. Floppy said to Mr. Owl, "Have you seen a boy pass your way this evening?"

Then in great excitement that old owl flapped his feathers and jumped up and down on the limb he was perched on. Without hesitation, Mr. Owl said, "Why yes. Just a few hours ago, I saw this rather tired and lost boy come this way. He looked like your friend Davie, looking rather beaten up and confused."

Now for Floppy and Bear, the important information given by Mr. Owl was exactly what they wanted to hear.

"Which way did that young man go?" said Bear excitedly.

"Well, my fine friends, your young man stayed on this trail that leads to the clearing ahead. I tell you what," said Mr. Owl. "Let me fly over that way and see if I can find him. My super night-vision eyesight can spot almost anything, and I can direct you to his exact location." Mr. Owl took off and flapped his wings as he went airborne in the night sky. As for Floppy and Bear, the hardest part was waiting on news about Davie. They wondered if Davie was okay or if something sinister had befallen their friend.

It was not long before Mr. Owl returned. Why, that old king of the night skies found Davie without much effort. Upon landing in his tree, Mr. Owl gave a full report to Floppy and Bear below. Mr. Owl said, "My friends, it doesn't look good for your young lad. A wolf pack has got him cornered way up in a tree over by the edge of Hanson's Meadow." Upon hearing this news, Floppy and Bear became very worried. Then Mr. Owl said in a strong voice, "This young man won't last long before the wolves move in for the kill. If I were you, I'd move fast."

Now Floppy turned to Bear and said, "Wolves! You know that wolves eat rabbits."

At that moment, Bear turned to Floppy and said, "Floppy, our friend is in trouble. We must put our own safety aside to help this young man. Have courage, and let us defend and protect him from the evil that's now present." With these encouraging words, Floppy found his inner strength and hopped on bear's back. They were now ready to do battle for the safety, glory, and honor of their friend.

The situation for Davie was growing worse by the minute. His body was tired, and he found it more difficult to fight back sleep. Perched high in that old tree, he was offered temporary safety for now. However, Davie had to use all his strength to keep himself secured to the branches. If he fell out of the tree, the wolves would have a ready meal to satisfy their hunger. It was only a matter of time before tragedy befell Davie. The real question was whether his rescuers had enough time to save him. Or would this young man succumb to weariness and fear, thus reaching his end?

Now few knew it at the time, but one of the biggest battles in Northern Michigan was about to unfold. It did not take Bear long to reach full stride. Floppy did all he could to stay on Bear's back. In a matter of minutes, they broke through the clearing and entered Hanson's Meadow. Stopping quickly, Floppy flew off Bear's back and hit the ground with a thud. Looking around, these two warriors prepared for combat. Not sure which direction to take, they stopped, looked, and listened for signs of Davie's whereabouts. After a short pause, Floppy and Bear heard the barking of the wolf pack ahead.

Now unbeknown to the wolves, Floppy and Bear had worked out a very cleaver battle plan. There first objective was to divide the pack and allow Bear, with his bigger size, to get control of the situation. Bear had the ability to take on several wolves on at a time but not the whole pack. To help distract the pack, Floppy's purpose was to have some of the wolves chase him and, by doing this, give Bear a fighting chance. As Floppy and Bear came nearer the pack, the tension between them reached new heights. Bear stood up on his hind legs and let out a growl that caused the wolves to move back. Likewise, Floppy perched himself on an old tree stump and teased his rivals. Floppy stood up and said, "Why, you mangy mutts, it's about time you faced someone your own size." Floppy went on to say, "Today Bear and I are going to teach you a lesson you're not going to forget." Bear then lunged forward and grabbed the leader of the pack.

Floppy took off at full speed, and three of the wolves took after him, thinking they found an easy meal. The battle that had now begun showed all the signs of being a heroic event. The outcome of this conflict depended on which side showed the most courage and strength.

Way up in the tree, Davie paid close attention to the action down below. He saw that some of the wolves were trying to jump on Bear's back and take him down. Wasting no time, Davie quickly climbed down the tree. Reaching the ground, Davie found an old tree limb that was just the right size to use as a club. Swinging that old limb wildly, Davie struck one of the wolves in the head. He next jabbed the end of that stick into the side of another attacking wolf. That old wolf let out a loud groan of pain and then slumped to the ground. Davie fought his way up to Bear. He got behind him and covered his back. Together this fighting team took on all challengers as the wolves tried to overpower and outflank their opponents. Bear and Davie held their ground. If a wolf tried to attack from the side, Davie and Bear met that challenge by swinging around to meet that attacker. It was simply awesome how the fighting team of Davie and Bear kept the wolves back. Despite their success, Davie and Bear began to tire. For these brave fighters, quitting was not an option. The real question that remained was if there was enough strength in them to finish the fight.

Meanwhile, Floppy took action that could save the day. He led the three wolves chasing him on a wild race.

Just as one of the wolves was about to reach him, this clever rascal darted back in a new direction. This wild action of outrunning the wolves went on for a long time. Finally, our friend planned a more practical and misleading strategy. Seeing a hollowed-out log ahead, that cagy rabbit shot right through and came out the other side. Next Floppy ducked under some thorny bushes that had long branches reaching clear to the ground. It took the wolves a long time to figure out where that rabbit went. Why, those silly hounds just pawed at the entrance to the old log. Seeing Floppy's hiding place, those wolves wanted nothing to do with those sharp barbs on those bushes. The wolves barked and growled for a long time but chose to quit their chase. After waiting a short while, Floppy came out from underneath the thorn bush. Dusting himself off, he took off to find Mr. Owl. For you see, Floppy thought that wise old owl could help in the fight. He quickly found the owl and encouraged him to join with them. With Mr. Owl helping in the struggle, things began to look better for our little band of warriors.

While Floppy made his way back to Davie and Bear, Mr. Owl took to the night skies to do battle with the enemy. He found our two warriors locked in deadly combat with the wolves. Joining the fight, Mr. Owl dove down on those blasted wolves. Why, that brave old bird used his beak and razor-sharp claws to inflict great punishment on the pack. In fact, before the wolves could respond to their attacker, Mr. Owl quickly flew away. In the meantime, Floppy ran in and distracted the wolves by running toward them. When the wolf turned to see Floppy coming, that brief pause was all Davie and Bear need to inflict additional pain on their attackers. Bear used his massive paws with sharp claws to rip at the confused wolves while Dave took his club and hit his attackers with great strength. After considerable effort, the wolves began withdrawing from the battlefield. As it turned out, our two heroes, with the help of Floppy and Mr. Owl, had met and defeated some of the most skillful hunters in the forest. They had won the battle and fought the good fight. For the moment, our little army rested and reflected on their victory.

After sitting for a while, Bear broke the silence and asked Davie why he had left home in the middle of the night. Davie had no reply for his friend because he was sorry for what he had done. Finally, after great urging, Davie poured out his feelings concerning his present state of life and the events that developed since Ida May's death. Davie said these words to his friends: "You know, since Ida May passed, I've not been myself. Things are simply not the same anymore. No matter what I do, the joy of life seems to have left me. I miss my mom terribly. And to make things worse, I am now an orphan without a mom or dad." At this moment, Davie hung his head down in sorrow.

Then Floppy seizing the moment, spoke to Davie in a profound way, "Well, Davie, how about Aunt Mimi and your cousins Jackie and Big Dave?"

Davie replied, "You know, my aunt and cousins are great people, but it's not the same as before. For one thing, the farmhouse is a lot more crowded than usual. And secondly, it's really hard for us to get along together."

Now Bear, sensing Davie's frustration, made these statements: "You know, Davie, life is about meeting challenges and learning to deal with change. No matter how hard we want to keep things just the way they always have been, well, someone or some force comes along and messes everything up. But you know, Davie, change is not always bad. In addition, struggle and suffering are not always bad for us either. You see, Davie, by struggling in life, our inner strength is built up so that when the next crisis comes, we can better handle the pain."

Then Bear went on further by saying, "If we learn from the lessons life teaches us, then in the long run, we come away as better persons. It's like this: In life a person has many battles. Our response to those battles and life's difficulties can go either one of two ways. For our part, we can become either cold and unpleasant, always angry about our losses, or we can have the courage to become stronger and more giving." Bear and Floppy continued to talk with Davie over the meaning of life and death, but it was obvious to his pals that their young friend had many questions that remained unanswered.

As the night lingered on, Floppy and Bear carried on their talks with Davie over the question of death and why this fate awaits all leaving creatures. In their little chat, Davie asked Bear this question: "How could a loving Creator allow pain, suffering, and death to exist in a world that is so beautiful? And why did Ida May die in the fullness of her life?" Davie then asked Bear why a person so good and kind had to die.

Bear's response to Davie is worth noting. It was this: "Life moves through cycles. It's just the way things work. This is part of the natural order or law that governs the universe. Now some folks believe that this natural order is determined and run by the Creator, and others believe that natural laws happen either by chance or physical laws alone. But the truth is that life here on earth is temporary and ends at some point."

When Bear had finished talking to Davie, Davie said loudly, "It's simply unfair that Ida May had to die way before her time." At this point Floppy jumped into the conversation.

"Davie, learn from the forest around you." He went on to say, "When a ground fire sweeps through the forest, most of the time, it's the younger growth of trees that the fire consumes first. The younger trees are consumed by the fire more quickly because they lack the heavy bark or coverings to protect themselves like the older trees. This whole process is called regeneration. But you know, Davie, something really amazing takes place after a fire.

In some species of acorns, rebirth begins almost imme-diately after a fire has devoured an entire forest. You see, these tiny acorns lie dormant for years, just lying in the rich forest soil. Davie, you know, it's the great heat from the fire that opens up these little pods so they can begin to grow."

Floppy really drove home his argument by saying, "Davie, you have a choice before you. You can stay in a state of fear and anger toward life, like the blackened forest after the fire, or you can accept what has happened to you and grow like one of those little seed pods that sprouts and gives new life." Davie knew this too. "Ida May died so that her spirit could rise like one of those tiny acorn seeds." Now as the night wore on, Davie took to heart what his pals had said. But this young man still had many doubts that remained unanswered. However, something huge was about to happen.

Davie's thoughts turned to many things as he sat atop an old log next to Floppy and Bear that night in the forest. Then without warning and out of the blue, Davie asked his pals if they believed in a creator. You see, Davie had many doubts about whether a creator really existed after his sadness from Ida May's passing. Bear spoke first and made these kind remarks: "You know, Davie, the reason why some people do not accept the Creator into their lives is that they simply feel that no one has the power to tell them what to do. But you know, when you truly love someone, it's never a problem to give up a little bit of yourself. Your mom, Ida May, was one that always gave. Why, she was willing to give everything for you and the people of her community. In totally giving to others, Ida May reached a new height in her life. What she gained was more than personal satisfaction."

Then Bear went on to say, "From a realistic view, it's hard to believe that the universe is not shaped and controlled by someone or something greater than ourselves. Now for energies and forces that govern all things in the physical world, it just seems that there's a logic that governs and limits all of this. Now for example, take that old tractor you have on the farm. A machine like that never came about on its own. That machine is complicated with many moving parts. You know, whoever created that machine was one smart person. And still further, you and Ida May kept that machine working just like something keeps the universe on track. Why, I used to see you guys always out working and fine-tuning that old tractor. Well, in many ways, that old tractor is like the universe, but on a smaller scale. Our universe is held together like that old tractor by a series of powers like gravity, chemical bounds, and atomic structures that maintain a time, a beat, and a life force that is not a mistake. Just like that old tractor that you guys kept running, there is a power or force that keeps an overly complicated universe operating. Aristotle refers to this power as the Unmoved Mover. Likewise, in Neo-Platonic theory, all composites have causes. Therefore, Davie its unreasonable to believe that something less is driving our universe and the rest of the cosmos. It's completely unreasonable to believe in anything else.

"Davie, my facts are true and here is why. The complexity of the universe indicates that there are controls and laws that govern the physical world. This means that some sort of authority exists that regulates our ecosystem and universe that is beyond complete human understanding. Things don't exist in a void, and neither does the universe. Then if authority and structure exist, then we know that an intelligence is present that is capable of making, changing, and governing its entire creation. In turn, intelligence, in this case, means higher thought and a logic that is indicative of knowledge and wisdom on a grander scale. Along with this capability is the power to act independently. Therefore, higher intelligence brought together within the structures in an infinite universe leads to only one conclusion—that a life force exists that is capable of creating and forming and molding structures and life itself. With these facts present, Dave, there is no doubt. A loving and all-knowing life presence and energy is around us and with us. That person is our Creator, the Father of us all."

Then Bear went on to say, "It's no accident that when forces or structures are altered because of outside force or natural or disturbance, they usually come back together in the same way or adapt into new forms. These new physical compounds and complex configurations take on new atomic structures. Furthermore, under the laws of physics, it's impossible to keep things permanently suspended in a state of continual motion. Nevertheless, somehow the universe keeps moving and refueling itself either through the paradox of the matter/antimatter theorem, which is no more than a relational arrangement of energy, or through a supernatural association. It is far more plausible to believe in the Creator since he is physical, pure spirit and energy, and completely one and powerful throughout our universe. This accounts for a universe that is constantly changing and structures that progress for a higher purpose. Conflating these properties together with an order that is unmeasurable, a supreme intelligence, a structure and algorithms that are undefinable in human terms, plus a complexity that is unfathomable, and you have a formula for he that is. Therefore, one can draw only this conclusion, that a driving and intelligent force exists and governs all. This theory is far more plausible than believing in randomness of creation based on assumptions that lack unity and authority. Thus, Davie, there is no doubt that a loving Creator keeps and holds the cosmos firmly in his hands."

Then Davie asked Bear these questions: "If the Creator controls the universe, then how come natural disasters such as floods, hurricanes, and volcanic explosions occur in our world? And how come asteroids hit the earth, and diseases strike down people in the prime of the lives? And, Bear, why do people hurt and kill others?"

After hearing these questions, Bear knew that Davie was still mad and saddened over the loss of his mother.

Bear then gave our young man this remarkable similarity: "It is like this, Davie. The world we live in is like a big orchestra. Why, you play the trumpet in the in the school band, so you're going to understand what I am going to tell you. The orchestra has a leader called a conductor. The conductor follows the sheet music in front of him known as the musical score. The individual instruments have the same music arranged for their individual parts.

"The conductor then tries to get absolute perfection from each player in the orchestra. The conductor wants the music to sound its very best. But you know, Davie, from the time the conductor taps his baton on the music stand, small imperfections creep into the performance. No matter how hard the players try, some form of mistake occurs. One or more of the players may skip a rest, hold a note a millisecond to long, or play the wrong note entirely. Now to the audience, they probably won't even hear anything out of the normal. But you know the conductor always hears those small errors. However, the real beauty of the orchestra is the unity of the instruments blending together to bring harmony and joy to the work. Small mistakes are covered over by the greater good of those executing their parts correctly. In this way, the good and the imperfect form a unity, a purpose."

Bear went on to explain, "Well, Davie, the universe, with all its separate parts, is like an orchestra. The players are like the different parts of the solar system and the life forces that make everything up. And, my friend, the conductor is like the Creator. No matter how hard the Creator tries for perfect harmony, some imperfections occur because of the resistance to his authority plus a lack of commitment by some of the players. Now, Davie, what you want is a perfect world, and let me tell you, a perfect world does not exist and never will."

After Bear's explanation of how good and evil exist in the world, Davie brought this question to Bear: "My friend, is the Creator perfect in every way?"

"Well, Davie, you know he is."

"Then, Bear, if the Creator is perfect, shouldn't all that he has made and controls be perfect too?"

"Well, Davie," Bear said, "I just knew you were going to ask that question. Try to look at this question from the Creator's view. The Creator gives freedom because without freedom, there is no love. You see, complete, absolute obedience is not love at all but, simply put, a fear of authority. The Creator wants people to react to him not out of fear of punishment but instead out of fondness and acceptance. The Creator wants folks that will love him, not humans that act like programed machines.

"Regarding the Father, for him, living alone and without others is as lonely and difficult as it is for us to live in a world without family or friends. The Creator gives freedom to individuals so that they are not compelled to accept him but simply choose to love him. After all, love is a decision, not something forced upon a person. Now, Davie, I know that you loved Ida May very deeply. I also know that the two of you had your fights and squabbles as well. Both of you made the decision to love each other. Therefore, strife existed at your house from time to time despite your love. In the same way, Davie, strife exists in the universe as people struggle to live their lives perfectly in an imperfect world."

Then Davie asked Bear this important question: "If the Creator is all good and powerful, just why does he allow children to die?"

"Well, Davie, that's a tough question, but here's the reason why. The Creator is omnipresent, which means he can see both the past, present, and future at the same time. He can also look deeply into the hearts of all men. For the creator, calling someone home to him is very personal. He may love a child in a deeper way than the parents of that child can ever imagine. The Creator gives life and sometimes allows children to die so that they can live with him in a more complete and loving way.

"You see, Davie, a child just doesn't belong to the parents, and the life of the child is a gift from the Creator. The Creator knows what is going to happen to all of us before it ever becomes reality. He is not bound by time and space like mankind. Therefore, the Creator may act in some cases to save an individual and society from harm.

Let me give you a case that may help you understand better. For an example, if a child really loves the Creator with all his or her heart but later in life would turn away and become detached and wicked, then it's possible that the Creator may take the individual into his glory before he or she reaches adulthood. Why the Creator allows this to happen in some cases and not in others has more to do with his will and plan for each of us."

Bear went on to say, "Since sin has continued to increase over the years, his grace is not accepted. Thus, bad things, including the death of children, continue to happen. The state of sin in the world allows failings to flourish while the Creator's kindness goes unused. Likewise, man himself is responsible for some of the suffering children undergo. You see, by man's pollution of streams and fields, many harmful substances are ingested from our food chain. These substances bring with them dieses and cancers that affect little bodies in a deep way. In addition, the number of children experiencing neglect from their parents is on the rise. Children that suffer neglect suffer more than those who live in loving homes. What this all boils down to, Davie, is that as a group and as individuals, our actions count and affect others. And yet, the Creator allows good and evil to live side by side. A child, after reaching a certain age, has the decision to either accept or reject the love shown by the Father. The final outlook of all children is in the loving hands of the Creator, who knows, without doubt or delay, what is truly the best and most just for each of his kids."

Now after all this time, our friend Floppy jumped in the conversation. He said, "Regarding your earlier conversation concerning the existence of the Creator, let me give you some useful facts. From a mathematical view, there exists a single number that seems to have greater meaning than all other numbers. In essence that number has unique properties. You see, the number one is the first in the series of whole numbers. We count by saying one, two, three, and so on. Now, Davie, have you studied the use of the number line with positive and negative integers?"

Then Davie replied by saying, "Well, Floppy, we went over that material last semester."

"You see, Davie, the first number on the positive side of the number line is one. When you take the number one and add any number to one on the positive side of the number line, you always get that number plus one. For example, 'seven plus one equals eight' represents seven units plus one unit. In this case, adding the one makes the total larger by one and closer to infinity. Likewise, a life without the one is alone and without meaning. From a personal standpoint, we always need the one to make us increase both inside and outside ourselves.

"Opposite the positive part of the number line is the world of negative numbers. Using the same value for positive one, we find that any number on the left side of the number line plus or minus positive one is either zero or a *negative number*. For example, one plus negative one equals zero, or one plus negative eight equals negative seven. Using this example, we see that a life on the negative side of the number line with only the positive one always leads us partially to the positive side. In addition, if we end up in the world of negative numbers, we are further away from the true life and light of a positive infinity. Likewise, we can take a larger whole positive number and add or subtract any negative number of similar placement and get a higher value. For example, three plus negative five equals negative two, or negative five plus three equals negative two. In this example, the sum value is increased, but like in life, a life with many negatives is unfilled. If our life has too many negatives, we end up further from the whole number one and closer to a negative infinity. To have lasting meaning, we must always strive for the positive side of the equation and closer to a positive infinity." Now after this little talk, Davie seemed a little bit confused to the true meaning of the one, so Floppy went on to explain its importance.

Floppy then said to Davie, "Here is another set of facts concerning number lines. Number lines have more than a single dimension. In fact, they can be three dimensional in their overall makeup with three distinct axis: X, Y, and Z. The layout and construction of a three-dimensional number line indicates both a height and depth not indicated with a singular plane or axis model. When taking a step further, the observer notices a connectivity between the numbers on either side of the axis. Similarly, our own planet Earth has both negative and positive forces at the poles and a round geometric shape, so the number line has points on an axis that when connected form a direct sphere. For example: the-1 and 1 connect each other on the X, Y, and Z axis, forming a semicircle on each side of the axis. Together these structure form completed circles when connected through the axis on the other side. This entire process extends outward with each number group. The Riemann Sphere is an example of the spherical number line. Additionally, in atomic structures, we find similarities with number line math. In these structures' protons are positively charged and electrons negatively charged. These physical characteristics form a circular mass with round orbits that shows some parallels to the spherical number line.

"Davie, like planetary groupings that extend out to the outer reaches of their galaxies, the spherical number line extends all the way out to positive and negative infinity. Though composed of many circular parts in this case, the total unity of components forms a unique structure, a spherical shape that is united to itself through the power of the number 1. Each new circle along the number line is increased by the power of 1 or-1 and the whole structure is united to its core and first circle, 1, 0,-1 through its axis. The total spherical structure denotes a singularity and unity of one mass. Therefore, the blueprint of 3D spherical number lines indicates an authority that is one built on increments of one but a design that is both simple but complete. These properties of the spherical number line show a vastness that extends forever but a unity that ties back to its source. The structure of this example denotes cause and action, the principle and strength of a round, circular shape with a purpose that reaches beyond physical boundaries. Therefore, it is imperative to know that the relationships imposed in spherical number line math illustrates an inspiration and creativity that can only come from a higher presence, binding the power of numbers to a higher dimension.

"You see, Davie, the power of the number one has even more meaning. Let me explain. One is the number that represents unity. When we say we are one, it means that a group stands in agreement, without doubt or hesitation. In essence that's the way the Creator loves us. His love is without limits, and he takes us to himself because he is the one true one. In addition, throughout many languages, the symbol one stands for a power higher than man. Did you know, Davie, that one is sometimes referred to the First Person, that being the Creator? Some people refer to him as the Absolute One, who is totally united with all his creation, permanent, outstanding, unmatched, essential, and nonworldly. Still, others call him the Father, the first person of the trinity who controls all of heaven and earth. And you know, Davie, what this all means is that the Creator, the one who is above everyone, loves his handiwork. You know he loves us so much and wants each of his creatures to love him back. But with that being said, he gives freedom on a one-to-one basis so that each person can decide for himself or herself whether to love and serve the true one or simply reject the one that gives all life. As for you, young man, the time has come for a decision. Which one will you choose?"

After listening to Floppy for a considerable time, Bear spoke and offered Davie some wisdom on the question of life after death.

"Davie, I know you have been pondering the meaning of death. For practical purposes, let us say that death is like a transformation. While we live on earth, we walk and exist primarily in the physical. When we die, our presence shifts to a spiritual, which is not the end of life but is the start of a new beginning. You see, Davie, Ida May no longer has earthly existence, but she continues to live in real time and space. But you know what, Davie? She lives now through you and is part of a greater community of spirits that help to support and encourage the entire world."

Then Bear went on to say, "As you see, Davie, the time will soon come when you must release the love you had for your mom and share it with all of mankind. And by letting go of Ida May now, you're preserving her memory inside you while passing on to others the spirit of giving and hospitality that Ida May shared with her own community and neighbors. Davie, it's no longer just about your loss but about continuing Ida May's legacy for many years to come."

With those words, Davie turned to Bear and said, "My dear and noble friend, I've never heard such a finer statement before. What you've said is true and just. I assure you that throughout my life, Ida May's memory will live on forever." With that, Bear and Floppy rushed over and held him in their arms. For Davie, this night of darkness was soon to pass. And for the first time since Ida May's death, he had begun the difficult process of personal healing.

Just about that time, Davie, Floppy, and Bear looked off in the distance and witnessed an image of a man approaching. The man carried a bow and had a quiver of arrows resting on his back. This splendid figure of a man wore an Indian headdress with a deerskin shirt and pants and wrapped himself in a buffalo coat. Surrounding this mysterious figure were animals that no longer roam the earth. These creatures followed the man wherever he went. For a long time, Davie and his pals just looked at the man with great amazement. Then suddenly the man spoke to Davie in a firm and sure voice. He said, "My name is Wahkoowah, which in English means Charging Bear. I am from the Lakota people, who lived in the lands were the tall grass grew and the buffalo numbered greater than all the stars in the sky. Many years ago, I was a great chief for my people. Young Davie, I see by your actions that you are a great warrior. You and your friends fought the wolves you encountered tonight with great bravery and without fear.

"For your bravery, the Creator has asked me to lead you on a spiritual journey. I am going to show you mysteries that few mortals know. Young man, I also present to you a bear-claw necklace. Keep it as a symbol of your newfound freedom you earned this night." With that statement, the great chief placed the necklace around Davie's neck. "From this day forward, you have a new name, Little Bear. My friend, use what you're going to learn today for the betterment of your fellow man and the natural surroundings you live in." With that Charging Bear took Davie, and they went to the clearing. The chief took his right hand and extended it across the night sky. The clouds and fog that had covered the earth like a blanket, without warning, simply disappeared. For now, Davie was about to enter a new doorway into things that seemed almost impossible a short time before.

As both Charging Bear and Little Bear gazed into the night sky, the wonder of the universe was keenly displayed. Looking at Charging Bear, Davie asked the great chief these important questions: "How can I know for sure that the Creator exists, and where can you find him? You see, my good friends Floppy and Bear have made a convincing argument for the Creator's presence, but I still have many doubts concerning this question."

Then turning toward Davie, Charging Bear made this unusual response to Davie's quest for knowledge. The great chief said, "Little Bear, look back into the night sky, and you will find your answers."

Then Charging Bear made this profound set of statements to Davie.

"You see, Little Bear, the Creator is like the sun the moon and the stars all rolled into one. His light is stronger than any constellation and brighter than the heavens themselves. His voice is like the roar of the ocean and the whispering of the wind through the trees. He is also like an arrow shooting across the night sky, not knowing where it's going or where it came from. The Creator has a love deeper than the depths of the oceans and longer than time itself. His eyes are like stars in the sky, and his heart is like a million points of light, always there for humanity but always calling and drawing man back to himself. His authority is like the power and majesty of all the kings and leaders of the world, ten, one hundred, a thousandfold and more. His beauty is like a million sunrises and sunsets all rolled into one. And his simplicity is like a smile on a child's face or a cool breeze on a warm summer's evening. All this, my friend, points only to one conclusion: he is the one who is the all of all, the one who is the great I am."

As Davie continued to fix his sight on the night sky, he saw a meteorite stream across the heavens in all its brilliance. This was the first time in his life that he felt something stirring deep within his soul. You see, the sky that evening appeared extra bright, and the stars seemed so near and bright that their presence was almost felt within reach. After considerable time, Davie experienced the presence of Ida May and his father, who had died when he was quite small. (Davie also heard Ida May trying to communicate with him. Her voice seemed far off; he heard his name being called out, and it echoed through the night air. At first hearing his mom's voice seemed almost frightening, but as time passed, he felt an encouragement and comfort in her presence.) Although he heard Ida May speak his name, the two communicated through the language of love. Now as the evening wore on, Davie felt a presence of peace in his heart that he had never felt before. Something incredibly special happened that night, a lifting of Davie's spirit, a reawakening of his humanity, and a putting forth of something special and true was taking place. As the dawn broke further that morning, the darkness from Davie's life faded away.

Then Charging Bear said to Davie, "Before I go, let me depart to you this special knowledge and wisdom. Beware in this world. There are good and evil spirits. Some spirits are evil both in presence and mind. These spirits seek out the destruction of mankind. They cloak themselves in the presence of light. Therefore, Little Bear, always observe and determine who and what these spirits are. Always trust the inner light given to you by the Great One. The Creator always gives an understanding and guidance to each person who is willing to listen and follow his truth. My son, trust, in the Creator's light, for he only wants what's good for you. Also, Little Bear, trust your deep inner feelings, for the Creator has placed in each individual a sense of justice and a pathway that leads to joy and oneness with him. Use what I have taught you today to fulfill and complete your life. After all, that's only what your parents and the Creator want for you."

With that said, Charging Bear slowly began to fade away. As Davie turned around, he discovered that Charging Bear had left behind the bow and the quiver of arrows he had carried. Then Davie thought to himself, What does this gift from this great chief symbolize? Then suddenly, the meaning of the bow and arrows came to him. When arrows are placed together in a quiver, they are both strong and stand for unity of purpose. The bow is an ancient symbol of power and truth. The arrow is sharp and direct, used for protection against the evil in the world and beyond. Now Davie went over and picked up the bow and the quiver of arrows left behind by Charging Bear. He placed the quiver over his shoulder and pulled the bow over his arm. From that point forward and throughout his life, Davie became an excellent marksman and never forgot the lessons learned in the forest that night.

As the rays of sunlight came over the hills and forest of the area, Davie felt as if a terrible burden had lifted from his shoulders. He had sought out the truth and the meaning of life and came away fulfilled and justified. Many of his question were in fact answered, and he felt a great joy inside himself. He no longer feared death and knew that his future looked brighter and more promising. As for Ida May, he knew that she was at peace and always with him in his life. Finally, after a long a terrible night, the birds in the forest announced the start of a new day. At that moment, Mr. Owl flew in with a frantic voice and said, "Davie, Floppy, and Bear, there is a search party coming over the hills just a few miles back. They got search dogs and are headed this way."

With that Davie said to his friends, "I've got to get home fast." Davie took off in a mad dash, and Bear and Floppy took off in a wild chase behind him. Mr. Owl took to the sky and announced to the other animals the triumphant return of their native son and brother in the forest. What was to follow that morning would confound and delight the residents of Wakefield for many years to come.

Finding a trail, Davie took off toward home. With each step, he got faster and faster. For Davie it was like he weighed twenty pounds lighter. The landmarks that were obscure the night before popped up and gave Davie a new sense of direction. Why, that young man covered ground like a streak of lightning. He jumped over big logs and rocks in his way and splashed through small streams and just kept on going. As Davie kept running, the last bit of darkness disappeared before him. Floppy and Bear kept pace for a short time but had to drop back because of Floppy's inability to stay on Bear's back. However, it did not take long for our duo to get back in the chase.

Reaching the clearing near the farm, Davie noticed that other animals were coming out of the forest to cheer him on toward home. Up beside him popped a pair of bobcats, deer, and moose. Several eagles swooped down as well as Mr. Owl and his family. Also, other bears and a pair of red foxes joined in the welcome home. For Davie it looked as if the entire forest had come out to run with him. My, it was quite a sight as Davie diverted a short distance and started up the front drive and ran toward the house. As it turned out, animals of every shape and description had covered both sides of the driveway. This huge group shouted for joy as Davie used his final bit of energy to reach the front gate. What happened next was even more amazing.

After hearing a big uproar coming up the drive, Aunt Mimi, Big Dave, and Jackie went out on the front porch of the farmhouse and were totally taken aback with what they saw. They all were in a state of shock as they caught sight of Davie. You see, Davie looked a complete mess. His clothes were torn and dirty, and he was covered with leaves and twigs and grass. He also had scratches, bruises, and cuts on his face and hands from falling down several times and from his encounter with the wolves. In addition, his hair was dirty and stood up in places. In fact, you might say that Davie looked like a warrior just off a raiding party, with his quiver of arrows and bow and the bear-claw necklace.

Now standing before his aunt and cousins, Davie had no clue what to tell them. However, before a single word was exchanged, the animals grabbed Davie and formed a ring around him. The animals worked themselves into a complete fever, swaying from side to side, shouting, and howling. Finally, they began singing a deep song from their hearts. You see, this was their song, the song of the forest, a song of life and joy. For the animals, a son had returned, and they began celebrating. Davie took part in the action by beginning to dance in the circle. He began the dance slowly and deliberately and then picked up speed. You see, for Davie this was his victory dance; he had survived the long night of terror and darkness and had won the good fight.

After dancing at a fast pace for a considerable time, Davie felt his body giving way to sheer exhaustion. When he thought he had come to an end, his animal pals and friends grabbed him and began tossing him into the air. The animals continued their wild celebration and began chanting a new and different song. In fact, the song deeply expressed their great joy for their friend. As they threw Davie up toward the sky, they sang, "Our son has returned. He's saved by the One. Our son has returned. He's redeemed by the One." They repeated these words over and over. They expressed their joy because their friend had overcome a great struggle in his life, thus coming out on top.

The animals now believed that Davie was in fact ready to move forward with his life with more power and certainty. In fact, he was saved from possible destruction by his own actions and by the wolves that sought his end. Davie's coming-of-age experience that night in the forest brought him into a keener awareness of his own relationship with others and an awareness of a power greater than himself. He also learned that he needed relationships, especially friends and family, to help him navigate the many obstacles that were certain in life. His experience was life changing. From this point, Davie's focus centered not only on the past but on what lay ahead.

The final climax for Davie took place as suddenly as events had begun the night before. Now looking up, Davie experienced the sun warm his face. The morning light blinded his eyes for a short time, and he felt a warmness and love as never before. He lifted his hands toward the sky as if to touch the sun. At the same time, he felt the cool whisper of the wind touch him as if to say, "Always reach inside yourself and listen for my voice. I am always here to help you through life's journey. Trust the new-found skills you've been given. Plus always do right to others, and respect the earth you live in."

With everything completed, Davie felt a pulling sensation on his shoulders and arms. The sun faded away, and he saw Aunt Mimi, Jackie, and Big Dave looking rather strangely at him. All the animals that had greeted him on his return home had disappeared back to the forest. As for Davie, his recent experience seemed to have given him a new warmth and glow. This newfound joy on the part of Davie was something of a mystery to his relatives. However, for now, Aunt Mimi had the job of sorting all this out and keeping the family together. She immediately took charge of her nephew but wondered what had really taken place the evening before.

The transition back home was not difficult for Davie but proved somewhat mystifying for Aunt Mimi. Mimi saw to it that Davie took a bath and put on his pajamas. She bandaged his cuts and put an antibacterial solution on his cuts and scrapes. Next, she fixed some breakfast for her nephew and put him to bed. Because of Davie's long and exhausting ordeal, Aunt Mimi thought it best that she just let him sleep. Davie slept all that day until late that night. In the meantime, Aunt Mimi thought she would do a little investigating on the items Davie had brought home with him. She examined the bow, the quiver of arrows, and the bear-claw necklace very carefully.

Now as it turned out, Aunt Mimi had considerable background in Native American artifacts from an internship she completed at the University of Oklahoma. Taking one of the arrows from the quiver, she closely observed the excellent craftsmanship and the fine details. Aunt Mimi realized right off that the dyes used on the arrow were from plant substances. In addition, the arrowhead was handmade from a substance resembling flint or soft stone. She also noticed that the fletching (which is the feather-like material in the back of an arrow) was in fact made from real bird feathers. Examining the arrow more closely, Aunt Mimi was somewhat at a loss. The arrow she held in her hand looked and felt like the artifacts she worked with at the university.

To get to the mystery of the Indian artifacts, Aunt Mimi called her old professors back in Oklahoma. Dr. Lopez was delighted to hear from one of his former students and referred her to an expert in her area. Paul Frantz, a US Forest Service ranger, was stationed not too far from the farm. In fact, that very afternoon, he planned to be in the area, so he agreed to stop over and look at the objects in question. Now as Aunt Mimi was about to find out, bringing in an expert sometimes only resulted in raising more questions.

Paul Frantz came over that afternoon and went straight to work examining the items Davie had brought home with him. The forest ranger scratched his head and said to Aunt Mimi, "These artifacts are from the Lakota Indian Nation. Their detailing is correct in every measure, and they represent the highest degree of workmanship that I've ever seen. However, what's really surprising is how these artifacts showed up in this part of the country and in perfect condition. You see, the Lakota tribe occupied the area to the west of us in the Dakotas. They were a vast nation with hunting parties traveling for hundreds of miles. On the other hand, the area where we live in northwestern Michigan was in fact occupied by the Chippewa Nation. The real mystery then is how these artifacts suddenly showed up here in this part of the country."

Now the conundrum concerning the items Davie brought home got even deeper. Ranger Frantz told Aunt Mimi this startling development.

"The period for these artifacts goes back over two hundred years. If your nephew had found these items in the forest, only the arrowheads would have withstood the elements for this length of time. The fact that these items are complete and correct is a real mystery." Then Aunt Mimi asked Ranger Frantz if these items were purchased and given to her nephew. To that question, he replied, "These are not commercially produced products. All of the objects here were produced by a master craftsman. Today this type of workmanship is practically nonexistent. You know, only a few individuals are capable of crafting these items, but their workmanship reflects a much earlier period. I am afraid to say we have a real unknown on our hands. When your nephew wakes up, maybe he can shed some light on this question." Ranger Frantz then left the farm. His appearance solved some questions for Mimi but had opened a far greater riddle. Deep down Aunt Mimi wondered what all this meant for Davie and the family.

As the last rays of the sun showed themselves over the tops of the fir trees near the house, Davie woke up in his room and thought about the many events that had happened the night before. He thought to himself how in the world to explain what happened without sounding like an insane person. He also thought, *Nobody is going to believe me if I tell them everything.* Well, just at that moment, Aunt Mimi came in to check on Davie and noticed he had woken. Aunt Mimi went back into the kitchen and prepared a tray of food for her nephew, bringing it into the bedroom and placed it on the bed.

"I thought you might like something to eat." Davie looked over the plate and noticed it had many of his favorites. Why, there was roast beef, mashed potatoes with brown gravy, cooked baby carrots with butter and parsley, and homemade Dutch apple pie. That boy wasted no time and dug right into his supper. At that point, Aunt Mimi thought it best to let Davie finish his supper and rest more. She thought to herself, *Tomorrow there is ample time to ask questions and get to the bottom of things.*

When Davie awoke the next morning, he was still at a loss to tell Aunt Mimi, Jackie, and Big Dave what had really happened to him several nights before. He thought, *They will never believe me.* Just as he was contemplating his problem, Davie remembered what Ida May had always taught him, that in the end, the truth always comes out. She always told Davie that the truth may hurt at times, but honesty was always the best policy. With that, Davie got out of bed and went into the kitchen, for you see, he was going to put his faith to the test, trusting in what was right. Looking at his new family, he said, "Could you come back with me to my room? I have something important to tell you." They all went back with Davie and sat on his bed as he described the events that occurred the previous evening. For Davie it was hard to tell everything, but he stuck to his belief that the light of truth would always win out. As he began to retell his story, Davie sensed from the body language of his relatives he was going to have an uphill battle to prove his case. Nevertheless, Davie kept to the straight and narrow, hoping that his family members trusted his word.

After telling his account of what happened, Big Dave broke the silence first. He said, "Dave, you've had it really hard the last few weeks, losing you mom and everything. But really, your account of the events last night just doesn't add up. This business of fighting off wolves and meeting this mysterious Indian chief called Charging Bear sounds a little far-fetched to me." Big Dave went on to say, "Now, Davie, tell us really what happened."

However, despite the urging of his relative to change his story, Davie stuck to his version of events. In fact, nothing budged Davie from his position. Finally, after considerable talking, Aunt Mimi and Jackie came to Davie's defense. Aunt Mimi spoke first, saying, "Davie, I know something very special happened to you out in the forest that night. To my way of thinking, you must have had some form of supernatural encounter with unknown forces."

Then Jackie said, "The arrows and artifact you came home with are not explainable. This leads me to a conclusion that Davie's statements are in fact partially true."

Then Big Dave jumped back into the conversation, saying, "I still think this all a bunch of hooey, but you know what, Davie? I stand beside you 100 percent. After all, we are family, and family members stand up for each other."

With their conversation completed, Aunt Mimi, Jackie, and Big Dave, reached across the bed and hugged Davie. They all began to laugh together because regardless if they believed in Davie's story, love was more important to them. Then Aunt Mimi made a wise statement: "As a family, sometimes we just must learn to disagree with each other. However, that doesn't mean we respect and honor the other person any less." From that day forward, Davie's new family referred little to his incident in the Michigan woods; their newfound love for one another outweighed any notion of which party was either right or wrong.

After things had quieted down, Aunt Mimi called old Doc Wilson and had him come over to the farm to talk with Davie.

"You know, Davie," said Doc, "I am not surprised with your account of the events the other night. You know I've lived in this area my entire life, and I've known firsthand that many strange occurrences have taken place in these woods at night. This whole area seems under some ghostly power. Don't feel alone. You're not the first one to have sightings with Native American images at night. So, Davie, listen to me very carefully. What you experienced the other night is in fact quite normal for this area. You're not strange or losing your mind because of your experience."

With Doc's reassurance, Davie breathed a sigh of relief. He said, "Thanks, Doc. That takes a lot off my mind. You know what, Doc, I began to have doubts about my own sanity. Why, people in town must have thought I'd lost all my marbles." Then old Doc Wilson spoke up and said to Davie, "Davie, I set everybody in town straight on what really happened. I told them that you had an encounter not unlike others in our area. I also told them that you were in fact a typical boy in every way and completely normal. So you have nothing to fear. Just act like you always do, a fun-loving boy who enjoys the farm and the outdoors."

With Doc's visit, Davie felt a lot better. Why, it was not long before he was back with his old pals, exploring, fishing, and enjoying the beauty of the forest and meadows. Unlike before, Davie had two new playmates to take with him on his outings. With Davie's help, Jackie and Big Dave took to their new surroundings with some difficulties. These two kids eventually overcame their city lifestyles and learned the true joy of country living. This transformation helped unify the family for the challenges that lay ahead.

Now as it turned out, having that encounter with Charging Bear proved both helpful and successful to the family. In fact, Davie's hunting skills kept the family in fresh meat from the forest and fish from the stream that ran through the farm. As you see, without previous skill, this unskilled farm boy became a seasoned hunter. The bow and arrows given to him from Wahkoowha seemed to find a target straight on. Davie became almost an expert with hand fishing, and he acquired a keen knowledge of the healing properties of plants from the forest. On one occasion, he killed a five-point deer and processed the meat and hide from the animal. Davie's love for the forest grew as his other skills in survival increased. In fact, he only took from the forest what he needed for himself and his family, never killing just for sport or the excitement of the hunt. As time went on, he seemed to appreciate his new background and culture. In many ways, the influences of Charging Bear stayed with Davie throughout his lifetime. However, the acceptance of the Native American culture and values brought Davie squarely up against prejudice and hatred.

One Sunday afternoon, Jackie came right out and asked Davie if there was anything from his previous experience that might help others going through the same emotional stress.

"Losing someone so close to you must hurt bad. What can a person do to get through the grief and not loose joy for life?

Turning to Jackie, Davie made these statements: "You see, Jackie, when you lose someone really close to you, why, it's like falling into darkness. You know, after that happens, the pain just engulfs you both physically and mentally. No matter how hard you try, the loss eats at you. Having family and friends around helps, but still you're going to go through some painful moments. One thing I've learned after losing Ida May is that loss is certain. People, and most certainly the ones we love, will come in and out of our lives. The challenge for everyone is to love and appreciate the time we share with others.

"The other thing to remember, Jackie, is that pain can bring growth in our lives. Sorrow can help strengthen us by building our inner charter. What this means is that by inwardly searching, we arrive at a new place freer and less dependent. By going through the grieving process, we have the opportunity to examine past behaviors and make course corrections if necessary. We can then either turn inwardly or change our outlook towards helping others. If we choose to reach out to others, then our love is given out but comes back to us in increasing amounts. Our sorrow is then replaced with joy, and our giving reaps a love that never dies. We also further strengthen ourselves by becoming free of the emotional frictions and rivalries that can characterize relationships. And then we become more like our Creator, whose love is unequalled and above human understanding."

WHAT SHOULD WE LEARN FROM CHAPTER 6?

We should not fear death. Death is a transformation that moves people from the physical to the spiritual world. Death can bring about a healing, too, for those left behind. At the time of our loss, we feel intense physical and emotional pain. However, the pain we experience is simply unavoidable and part of the life experience. If we learn and grow from our loss, then we become stronger and more capable individuals. On the other hand, if we never let go of our departed loved ones, then we focus only on ourselves, our loss, our memories, our relationship. But by sharing and letting go of our loved ones we share them with the world. Our departed ones become free, not held down by regret, worry, and self-blame. They join the ranks of those able to reap the fruits of a life well spent.

Two important examples come to mind that clearly show how we can grow from the simple act of surrendering and accepting pain in our life. The first is that of a diamond in the rough. A diamond cutter takes a rough rock and removes many of the imperfections that surround the stone. Cutting and polishing the stone will reveal the beauty of the diamond, and the light shines through the stone, giving amazing brilliance and color. In the same way, our struggles chip away at our own self-ishness and pride and bring us to a better place. Then our inner light shines for the whole world to see.

The second example that comes to mind is revealed by the vine dresser. The vine dresser removes much of the old growth from the previous season and some of the new growth that appears in the spring. For a successful harvest in late summer and early fall, the life-giving sap that flows through the vines needs to go into the grapes rather than supporting additional vine growth. Like the vines, if we are pruned, then we become strengthened and can nour-ish others in a new and powerful way. Learning through these examples allows you to have a life that is empow-ered and committed toward ministry.

After a loss, a person sometimes questions the exis-tence of a higher authority in the world. That person may think, How could a loving father allow terrible tragedies to occur and children to die? The answer to this ques-tion is quite simple. From the beginning of creation, the Creator wants individuals that love him with their whole hearts. The Creator allows bad to coexist with good, in the same way we have light and darkness in the world and opposite poles on the earth. The other thing to remember is that caring for the sick and taking care of a disabled family member creates humility in us. Having to do the simplest of mundane tasks for others is a blessing at times because it allows us to show compassion to another person and thus enrich ourselves. In this way, the caregiver reaps the blessing and learns to love in a more profound way.

We must always remember that darkness and light coexist in each of us too. We also have external and internal forces that oppose each other within us. Therefore, darkness, disease, and strife will never triumph within us if we are part of the light. And the light will always suppress darkness, bringing forth truth, love, knowledge, and forgiveness. For this reason, we must understand that good and evil and light and darkness exist for a higher purpose. That purpose is to draw humans outside themselves into perfect freedom. Thus, humans become in tune with the harmony of the world around them and the light of the Creator that illuminates and nourishes us all.

David Swindell

7

Aunt Mimi to the Rescue

After going through his recent trials and difficulties, Davie found himself in a new place emotionally. The many doubts and fears from his past just disappeared, and he clearly saw a new direction for his future. Striking up a conversation with Aunt Mimi one afternoon, Davie said, "I've come to a decision concerning the farm and what's needed for my upcoming years. You know, Aunt Mimi, this land holds a special place in my heart. My ties to the farm are so strong that living someplace other than here seems so unreal to me. Now if

your offer still stands, I am ready for you and your children, Jackie and Big Dave, to also make this your home."

Looking at Davie, Aunt Mimi began to smile, for
you see she knew deep down that staying on the farm
was the best decision for everybody. After giving Davie a
big hug, Aunt Mimi said, "You know, Davie, making this
decision will require some sacrifice on your part."

Davie replied, "Yes, this is true, but the positives of
sharing my life with a new family outweigh any of the
difficulties of living together in a small house. As for my
plans beyond the present, they include someday receiving a degree in agribusiness management from Michigan
State University. You see, I just want to develop the farm
commercially, using conservation practices that will
honor the land and the legacy Ida May started." With
Davie's road map firmly in place, it was now time for him
and his new family to move forward and face the many
challenges that lay ahead.

Transforming from city to country dwellers took
some time for Mimi and her kids. For one thing, both
Jackie and Big Dave had to do chores. You see, back
in Kansas, where the three of them had lived, they all
resided in town. Why, the only thing these kids had to do
was keep their rooms clean and do their homework from
school. However, now that they lived on the farm, things
changed quite drastically for our little trio. You see, now
the kids had to get up early, feed and water the animals,
milk cows, and check the nesting boxes for eggs left by

the chickens. All this took place before breakfast and the rush down the drive to catch the school bus. Aunt Mimi had to prepare breakfast for herself and the kids and pack school lunches. During the day, while the kids were at school, Aunt Mimi did the laundry and housework and prepared the evening meal. She also scooped oats for the horses and cleaned their stalls.

After the kids got home, each one went to assigned tasks, bringing in wood, feeding the chickens, and milking the cows a second time. All the kids took turns doing the evening dishes. Then it was time to do homework and get ready for bed. As you see, from the list of things required on the farm, that leisure time is greatly treasured. It is no wonder that it took a big adjustment on the part of our little band of newcomers. But you know, the three of them, with Davie's help, turned into respectable countryfolk.

One rather interesting event took place right after Aunt Mimi and the kids arrived on the farm. One evening after they had eaten, Aunt Mimi instructed Big Dave to go out and help Davie clean the barn. Well, when you milk cows, you have to bring them into the barn, then place them in a stall and hook up the automatic milking machine on each animal. Unfortunately, these cows poop on the floor during the process. When the boys went into the barn, they put on some rubber boots to keep their feet dry. Davie started by telling Big Dave the process involved in keeping everything clean.

"Dave, it is like this. We start by scooping up all the manure on the floor and putting it in the wheelbarrow over in the corner. Next, we wash down the concrete floors with a high-pressure water hose. We then must wash and sterilize the milking equipment to rid it of bacteria. This is to prevent the milk from making people sick." Then turning towards Big Dave, Davie said, "Here's the shovel. Get started." Big Dave looked at Davie and began to turn red.

Now the prospect of doing farm chores seemed out of the question for Big Dave. He ran into the house and told his mom, "You've got to be kidding. I am not going to scoop up poop here or any other place."

It was then that Aunt Mimi gave out some of her soundest advice concerning the virtue of work. She said to Big Dave, "You know, son, all work, no matter how difficult, is very meaningful to mankind. Take the example of cleaning the barn. If we do not keep it clean, then we cannot sell our cream and milk to our buyer, and someone may pay a higher price for the product. In fact, the United States Department of Agriculture, or USDA and state agencies sets the standards for the industry, they can come on the farm and shut down the entire operation. Why, son, if that happens, then our entire livelihood will disappear and us along with it. You see, son, we don't want to hurt others because we failed to follow good food and beverage practices." Well, Mimi's little talk with Big Dave helped adjust his thoughts concerning farmwork.

From that point onward, he never complained again about doing chores.

Another funny event that happened on the farm concerned Aunt Mimi and the tractor. Ida May had purchased an old Farmall tractor made in 1956. She found and bought the machine at an estate sale right after Davie was born. Now let me tell you, that old tractor really did a lot of work for the family. But even with that said, at times that tractor acted unpredictably. In fact, that machine had many bad habits that simply tested a person's worth. Dave had shown Aunt Mimi how to run that old tractor, but being a greenhorn, she really struggled with getting the hang of things.

David Swindell

One morning after the kids had gone to school, Aunt Mimi thought she would go down and fetch a few bales of hay to feed the horses with. On her return trip back to the barn, she lost control after the tractor suddenly backfired. Trying to shut the ignition off, she became rattled and pressed down on the gas pedal instead of the brake. The resulting action propelled the tractor right through the barn doors. She crashed through some of the stalls and equipment before coming to a complete stop. Poor Aunt Mimi was shaken but not hurt. She dusted off her clothes and went in and called some neighbors for help.

Now one thing you learn when you live in the country is that neighbors are usually willing to drop whatever they're doing to help a friend in need. This was the case when Aunt Mimi called the Olsons for assistance. The Olsons came right over and immediately pitched right in. Mr. Olson fired up the tractor and drove it out of the barn. Mrs. Olson and Mimi began picking up broken wood and straightening up things inside. Other neighbors arrived with hammers and saws and immediately began work on the barn. Everyone pitched in, and Aunt Mimi prepared a wonderful lunch for the workers. By the time Davie and the kids got home, why, it looked like a beehive on a clear summer's day.

Davie was upset with his aunt after the accident, but he knew she would eventually learn the ropes of farm equipment. At first, he did not say anything to his aunt and let his feelings cool down.

It looks like you and the barn had a good fight. I think you knocked it out in round five," Davie then said to Aunt Mimi in a comical way, using a boxing expression. Davie went on to say, "We'll work on your driving skills a little more. You'll get the hang of driving that old tractor soon enough." And that she did; from that moment on, Aunt Mimi was determined to master the use the machinery on the farm. After a short time, she picked everything up as if she had been born on the farm. Why, throughout the years, regardless of the weather, you would see her fly like the wind on that tractor. In fact, she got almost as good as Ida May. In the meantime, the barn got rebuilt, but another more frightening challenge lay ahead.

One late fall afternoon, a strange encounter happened on the farm. A very fancy car drove up the lane to the farmhouse. It was a Saturday, so Davie, Jackie, and Big Dave were home alone since Aunt Mimi had gone for groceries. Getting out of the car were two older ladies in their late forties or so. Along with the ladies was a smartly dressed gentleman around the same age. The ladies were dressed in fancy dresses, and both had mink coats. Looking at Jackie and Big Dave, one of the women whispered to the other, "Why, those are those bratty kids of Mimi's." Then they turned their attention to Davie. "Why, that's Davie, Ida May's poor little orphan boy." With that the women began to laugh out loud. Taking the first step, Davie introduced himself along with his cousins. Then the gentleman in the suit said he was an attorney and real estate investor. He gave Davie his business card and asked to see Aunt Mimi. The kids informed the trio that their aunt left but planned on returning later that day.

Next the attorney asked permission for himself and the two ladies to look around the farm. Before either Davie or Big Dave could say anything, Jackie spoke up and asked what their purpose was in coming and looking at the property. You see, Jackie always had an inquisitive nature, and well, quite frankly, she sensed something wrong with this whole situation. When Jackie asked for an explanation from the visitors, the attorney fired right back and told her it was none of her business. At this point, Davie knew that action was needed, so he called out to his old buddy Bear. Bear, being not far away, came strolling up to the house. Davie gave Bear his secret hand signal. With that Bear stood up on his back legs and let out a huge roar. After seeing this, the visitors who had come so uninvited to the farm left in great haste.

As the group of visitors left the farm in their car, the attorney stuck his clinched fist out the window and shouted, "You have not seen the last of me, son." The kids were relieved that these pushy folks had left. But for now, the kids felt deep down that something was wrong. In the next few weeks, they found out what these visitors were up to.

When Aunt Mimi returned from shopping, she helped the kids figure out who the mysterious visitors were. Aunt Mimi asked the kids to describe the individuals who came to the farm that day. Jackie spoke up right away and gave complete details of what these folks looked like and what they were wearing, including the kind of car they drove. It did not take long for Aunt Mimi to solve the riddle of the pushy visitors.

After hearing more from the kids, Aunt Mimi smiled and said, "Let me tell you about our family. The people that came to visit are my two oldest sisters and their greedy attorney, Mr. Cornelius P. Rothschild. Well, kids, it is like this. There were four of us in our family, all girls. The oldest children were Rhonda and Gladys. The two youngest children were Ida May and me. As far as temperament and morals, my two older sisters have values that center around two things, that being money and pleasure. My attitude towards my older siblings has never changed through the years. Love is always present in our relationship, but trust between is always guarded. If Rhonda and Gladys showed up here, it only means one thing—they're out to get something for themselves."

Well, it did not take long for Mimi and the kids to get their answer. A registered letter showed up a few days later, stating that the sisters intended to challenge grandfathers Will at the upcoming probate hearing that were coming up soon. (By the way, a will is a legal document that describes how you intend to leave money and property to family and friends after your passing. And a probate hearing is a legal hearing that decides how an estate is divided or dissolved.) At the news of the upcoming hearing, Davie became very worried because he knew his future and the future of the farm were at stake. However, Aunt Mimi assured Davie that his present situation was not something to fear. For you see, that very day, Aunt Mimi took Davie into Wakefield and hired the best lawyer in town. As the probate hearing approached, Aunt Mimi and the kids felt confident of their chances for success. Nevertheless, a real battle was beginning to brew that pitted family members against family members.

When the day of the hearing finally came, the whole family was nervous. The ride to the courthouse seemed to take forever. Entering the courtroom, Mr. Gladstone, the attorney Aunt Mimi had hired, greeted the family. He reassured them all that their chances were in fact better than normal for successfully winning their case. However, Mr. Gladstone did express a word of caution, stating that in these types of cases, sometimes things go the other way depending on how the judge interprets the evidence. Now the one thing that helped the family's case was his grandfather's second will leaving everything to Davie after his passing.

The main sticking point in the case involved a previous will written by Grandfather, dividing the farm into four equal parts, a quarter interest for each sister. Ida May was placed as the administrator of Grandfather's affairs. Now if the judge ruled in favor of the previous document, then the farmland and everything owned by Grandfather was then available for division between the four sisters. If the court ruled in this way, then Davie stood to lose the most, only receiving a quarter share, Ida May's share of the property. Now the real issue in this case involved which will or legal document the court was going to accept and use. Davie's future hung in the balance. Davie could only wait with anxious expectation as others decided his fate, or so he thought.

The hearing opened with Mr. Rothschild immediately challenging the second will. This document gave the farm to Davie. If Davie was under eighteen, then a guardian was necessary. You see, after Davie was born, his grandfather had his attorney write a new will before his death. The real question at play during these proceedings was whether Grandfather changed his will with a sound mind and with clear intentions.

Mr. Rothschild addressed the judge with these statements: "It is my goal to prove that my client's Ms. Rhonda and Ms. Gladys's claim is more legally sound, since their father was not physically and mentally of a sound mind at the time of the new will." ("Not being of sound mind" means that a person is incapable of exercising good judgment. If this was proven, it would abolish the validity of the second document.) "Furthermore, I intend to prove that Ida May used her position as caregiver of her father to unduly pressure and persuade him in favoring her own son rather than staying with the conditions of the original agreement."

With that statement, Davie came out of his seat, but before he could say anything, Aunt Mimi grabbed him and pulled him back down. She leaned over and whispered in Davie's ear, "Don't worry. He's just blowing a lot of hot air."

In reply to Mr. Rothschild's statements, Mr. Gladstone jumped up and spoke loudly, "Your Honor, I object to the second part of Mr. Rothschild's statement. I object because Mr. Rothschild's statement is groundless and unproven.

The judge then looked at Mr. Gladstone and said, "Overruled." ("Overruled" means Mr. Gladstone's protest is rejected.) The judge then said, "It's the purpose of this proceeding to get at the truth. You will have adequate time to dispel this claim later, but for now we need to explore all possible motives in this case." As the proceedings rolled on, it became clear to Mimi and the kids that they had a tough fight on their hands. Deep down they all had their doubts as to which outcome to expect.

Next Mr. Rothschild called to the court a host of friends and family who testified as to the weakness and overall bad health of the grandfather in the last days of his life. Calling Mr. and Mrs. Olson to the stand, Mr. Rothschild asked each one if they ever witnessed any arguments between Grandfather and Ida May. Mrs. Olson said that on one occasion, there was a disagreement over eating his supper. You see, Ida May knew that Grandfather was weakening and needed to eat better. Mrs. Olson went on to say that Ida May had a constant challenge getting Grandfather to eat. She also stated that this was an ongoing problem and often upset the household. In addition, Mr. Rothschild brought in others to testify that Ida May was not a true and loving caregiver but took care of Grandfather strictly for her own advantage. In fact, Mr. Rothschild painted a deep and deceptive picture of Ida May, trying to discredit both her reputation and honesty in the community. For Davie this was almost too much to handle. Aunt Mimi stood by his side through the entire proceedings. Aunt Mimi, Davie, Jackie, and Big Dave watched as the case took many twists and turns.

Now the first major break in the case came when Mr. Rothschild called Doc Wilson to the stand. Mr. Rothschild believed that the doctor's position in the case reflected his own opinion. Starting with a series of questions, Mr. Rothschild probed for information that showed Grandfather's failing mental health and his over-all condition during the signing of the second will. To the great surprise of this attorney, Doc Wilson offered a different interpretation of how events had unfolded. For Doc Wilson, the real issue was about justice rather than proper legal rights. For you see, old Doc Wilson had known Grandfather for many years, knowing full well his real intentions. Grandfather, with all his heart, wanted the farm to continue as a family business and be handed down to the next generation. But since there were no male children to carry on his work, he decided to split it up between his four daughters. When Davie was born, why, this changed everything.

As the doctor continued his testimony, the real problem he faced was how to balance the facts with the overall actual intentions of grandfather. In fact, Doc knew that Grandfather's capacity for making clear legal decisions was somewhat lessened at the time of the second will. But you know what? Doc always took pride in his ability to judge character and the true grit on the people he served. With that Doc Wilson had no problem stating to the court he believed that Grandfather was capable and mentally sound during the signing of the second will. Then Doc went on to say, "Grandfather's attorney agrees with my professional opinion." With this discovered in the case, Mr. Rothschild asked for an adjournment. What was to come next surprised even Aunt Mimi and the kids.

When Davie and his new family came into the courtroom the next day, they were quickly greeted by Mr. Gladstone. He looked at Aunt Mimi first than glanced over at Davie.

"Something for you folks to consider—Doc Wilson's testimony yesterday really helped our case. Nevertheless, we still have a long way to go in persuading the judge. What we need is something to prove that Ida May acted for the best interests of her father and not herself. To do this, we need someone who knew her very well. What I am asking will require some sacrifice and courage."

Then Mr. Gladstone had these words to say: "Let's not beat around the bush. I need Davie to testify on his mother's behalf. Ida May's character has taken such a beating the last couple of days. We need someone to build it back up and to prove that her intentions were honorable. Davie, are you ready to make a commitment to testify?"

With that Davie said, "That Mr. Rothschild is a real bully in the court, and you want me to testify." Aunt Mimi and the kids reassured Davie that everything was okay. In fact, they all said that Mr. Rothschild was more show than anything else. After considerable encouragement, Davie agreed to come forward and do the right thing. The coming days in Davie's life proved troubling for this young man, but somehow Davie found the inner strength to move forward.

The next day in court, Mr. Gladstone called Davie forward to testify. They brought him up, had him put his right hand on the Bible, and said, "Repeat after me. Do you swear to tell the whole truth and nothing but the truth, so help you God?"

Davie replied, "I do." At that point, he took his seat in the witness stand. As the questioning began, Davie felt the weight of the world on his shoulders. It was not an understatement to say that the star witness was somewhat nervous. After all, this was Davie's first time in court, and he always showed some fear in the past when public speaking was concerned. Regardless of what happened earlier, Davie knew that today counted. Somehow, he had to find the courage to come out with strength and calmness. For today his future and the future of the farm were all on the line.

Mr. Gladstone led off with these questions: "Davie, tell us in your own words about your mom and how she cared for your grandfather in his last days."

Without hesitation Davie said right off, "Grandfather received the best care possible. Why, my mom fed and clothed him and saw to his needs without complaint for over eight years. In fact, almost all our neighbors complemented Ida May on the job she did in taking care of Grandfather."

Then Mr. Gladstone asked Davie, "Did Ida May use her position as care giver to influence Grandfather in his decision to leave the farm to you?"

"Well, Mr. Gladstone, it is like this: She wanted me to have the farm—that much is certain. But she never went out of her way to force that decision directly with Grandfather. Then one day when we were talking, Grandfather asked me these questions: 'Son, do you respect the land we live on and want the farm to grow?' I replied yes."

Then Mr. Gladstone said, "Davie, let me ask this question of you. Did Grandfather ever talk or show an indication that the farm would someday be yours?"

Then Davie sat straight up in his seat and said, "Why yes, in an indirect sort of way. You see, Grandfather always taught me about agriculture, what to plant and how to take care of the land and manage milk cows. In my mind, he always indicated that someday everything he owned was to be mine. He was always encouraging me to be a farmer. In fact, on my seventh birthday, he bought me a pedal tractor. It seems that he was always getting me some kind of farm toy."

While on the stand, Mr. Gladstone asked Davie a whole series of questions concerning his relationship with his grandfather and how the farm was run and managed. Then Mr. Gladstone turned to the judge and said his questioning was complete. It was now time for Mr. Rothschild to cross-examine (which means to ask questions from the opposite side.) Davie braced himself for the long series of questions to come. However, he was steadfast in his newfound courage to do what was right and protect the great gift given him.

Mr. Rothschild then asked a series of questions to Davie. Looking straight at Davie, he said, "Tell me, Davie, how you came to know Grandfather's intentions concerning the final division of his property. Did Grandfather ever tell you the farm was yours at some point?"

Looking back at Mr. Rothschild, Davie told the court that Grandfather never came right out and said that the land was his to keep.

"Then the answer is no, Davie?"

"That is right, sir," Davie replied.

Then suddenly without warning, Mr. Rothschild asked Davie this question: "Grandfather never intended for you to have the entire farm, did he?"

With that question came Davie's first opportunity to win an important point. Davie's answer came quick and like a bolt of lightning: "You see, Grandfather wanted me to have the farm because he wanted his own work to continue after he was gone. He also wanted all his children and grandchildren to have a love and respect for the land as he did. Furthermore, to my memory, he never talked about splitting the farm up. I learned about this later from my mom. Sir, Grandfather never had to come out and say the farm was mine because everybody already knew it. You see, everybody in town and all our neighbors knew the farm was going to me. If you don't believe me, ask any of them." With this response, Mr. Rothschild was taken aback a bit.

Sensing that things were not going as expected, Mr. Rothschild tried a different approach to his questioning. He said, "Davie, is it true that your mom was rough with Grandfather and used her position as caregiver to get the old man's money and property for herself and you? Didn't she have constant fights with him, and didn't she always shove and push him around out of frustration and anger? After those statements, Davie began to boil over in the witness stand. The judge stopped the hearing to give Davie a moment to regain his self-control.

As the hearing resumed, Davie told his and Ida May's side of the story.

"Mr. Rothschild, Judge, and members of the community, the only reason there were any arguments between Grandfather and Ida May centered on these facts and these facts only. As Grandfather got older, we moved in with him. His level of pain shot up because of his increasing illness. It's just that simple. Pain make us crankier and harder to live with. In addition, Grandfather's decreased appetite came about through the many medications he was taking. As time progressed, he was less interested in food. Thus, struggles over food and his appetite became a regular part of family conversations. Now let me say one other thing. Before this legal proceeding, Ida May was one of the finest people in and around Wakefield. Her love in caring towards others is second to none. Her record stands for itself." With that said. Mr. Rothschild tried to trip Davie up, but you know what? His efforts always came up short. In the end, the probate proceedings did not come out the way Mr. Rothschild and Rhonda and Gladys wanted.

The hearing resumed the very next day. After the final argument by both sides, the judge took a short recess in his chamber to consider the merits of the case. When he returned to the courtroom, everyone stood up. The judge started by thanking everyone who had come out for the hearing. Then getting down to the details of the case, the judge made these comments: "It's always difficult when you have two wills to deal with in probate. In this case, Mr. Rothschild and his clients have not proven their case. They did not bring conclusive evidence that the grandfather's memory and mental capacity were compromised during the creation of the second will. In reaching this decision, the evidence presented by Doc Wilson and Davie were most helpful. Therefore, the second will stands as a valid document. Thus, Davie becomes the sole receiver of all properties and assets of the farm on his eighteenth birthday." With that the judge gaveled the case closed. Upon hearing the news, the whole family breathed a sigh of relief. Aunt Mimi began to cry while Jackie and Big Dave gave Davie high fives. With this going on, many of their friends and neighbors came rushing forward to congratulate the group. As for Davie and his new family, this turned into one of the happiest days of their lives.

Upon exiting the courthouse, the family ran into Mr. Rothschild and his legal secretary. Mr. Rothschild was pleasant in his greetings to everyone. But though things seemed okay on the surface, well, you could tell that this attorney was smoldering with anger underneath. As they all got on the elevator to head down to the main lobby of the courthouse, Mr. Rothschild spoke to Davie in a very rough manner. He said, "Thanks to you, young man, I've lost my first case in three years. That veterinarian friend of yours and others in the community told a big bunch of lies. You've cheated my clients out of their inheritance and their share of the estate. Why, poor Rhonda and Gladys will simply not have the means to enjoy life in the manner they're accustomed to. Furthermore, we intend to fight this decision to the fullest. As for you, young man, after all this, I don't know how you can live with yourself."

Looking at Mr. Rothschild, Davie expressed these words: "Well, sir, I was only standing up for what was right. You see, deep in his heart, Grandfather wanted the farming tradition to continue in our family. By standing up for myself, know I am doing what's right and just for everyone. In essence this decision helps the family tradition as farmers live on."

At about that time, Aunt Mimi jumped into the conversation.

"Mr. Rothschild, I can't believe you'd talk to my nephew in this way. Let me tell you a thing or two. As for poor Rhonda and Gladys, I know that each of them has considerable money. In addition, this much I know about my sisters. These poor, delicate creatures you describe are as greedy as they come. If there's a buck to be gotten, then my sisters are the first in line with their hands held out. Don't get me wrong. I love my sisters but, at the same time, acknowledge their faults. As to the matter of taking this case to a higher court, just go right ahead, but remember this, I've got a lot of money, so don't mess with me. I can fight you at every level financially. Mr. Rothschild, if you're going ahead with this case, it will only cost you precious time and money."

With that the elevator doors opened into the lobby. Then Aunt Mimi said in a raised voice to Mr. Rothschild, "If you ever decide to harass my nephew in any way, then be aware that I will personally take every step towards having you disbarred." By the way, *disbarred* means "never to practice law again." With that brief exchange, the parties went their separate ways. As for Mr. Rothschild's threat to take further legal action, well, that was only a trick to scare the family.

Regarding Mimi and her sisters, the matter about the farm took a little longer to resolve. After some time, both Rhonda and Gladys understood that keeping the family farm together was in fact the best decision. Aunt Mimi also reassured her sisters that she had lost her own share of the property to Davie as well. After several years, the family was able to put aside the property issue and support one another in a more loving way.

That night Aunt Mimi cooked up a big supper to celebrate their victory in court. Doc Wilson was invited along with the Olsons and other friends and neighbors. Everybody loved Aunt Mimi's cooking as she set out country fried chicken, corn on the cob, freshly baked rolls, and mashed potatoes with delicious chicken gravy. Mimi followed this all up with homemade cherry pie with big scoops of vanilla ice cream. Everyone that night ate with a true passion because they knew that a burden was off their shoulders, and they breathed easier knowing that the farm was in good hands.

Justice was served in a most profound way that day, allowing another family farm to stay together. For you see, family farms are the soul of American agriculture. These tiny units of production usually put out a better product because of the love and attention shown by their owners.

These noble caretakers of the land carefully strike a balance between man and nature. Those living and working on small farms love the soil and want to do what is right in the long term to save the land from the large corporate farms that place profits above conservation. The victory secured by Davie and his family helped, in a small way, hold back the forces of greed that wanted to sell the land for immediate gain rather than keep the sacred tradition of tilling the land in a careful manner. By winning their case, our little family continued honing the spirit of the land while feeding multitudes with food for their tables.

If the issue of the probate hearing was not enough, another turbulent event crept up on the farm. Let me tell you what happened. Now let us go back in time to see what happened. When it came to growing crops, Ida May was a pioneer. After receiving sound advice not to plant a cherry orchard from her county extension officer, that woman forged ahead anyway. The county man told her that the growing conditions were not right, and she was too far north for the trees to do well. But you know that Ida May always had a sense of how to tackle problems and grow the most beautiful flowers, fruits, and vegetables.

Vanya Cimino

The secret that Ida May knew centered on a prime piece of real estate that the family owned, nestled in a valley right next to a beautiful lake. The valley provided protection from the winds in winter, and the lake helped keep temperatures from becoming extreme. Now keeping this in mind, let us jump ahead a few years to the current situation. That spring Aunt Mimi and the kids faced a crisis, when colder-than-normal temperatures set-tled in the area. With the family having over twenty acres of cherries in blossom, immediate action was the only solution to save their crop.

Aunt Mimi got the kids up early one morning for something important. She had already prepared breakfast for the kids. After they had eaten and got dressed, Aunt Mimi pulled Davie aside and said to him, "It doesn't look good for the cherry crop. You and the kids better move fast. The temperature is dropping like a rock. It's only going to reach a high of twenty-nine degrees today, and if it goes that low, it will wipe out our entire crop."

Then Aunt Mimi called the whole family together and said, "Davie, I want you to go out and start up the tractor and hitch up the trailer. Next load up those con-tainers of heavy oil sitting in the back of the barn along with the burners. Have Big Dave help you load because they're quite heavy. Next, she told Jackie to fix lunches for the entire family plus some extras. Aunt Mimi phoned the school and told the principal that the kids were not coming in for a few days. In the meantime, she gathered up some extra blankets and supplies and took the cof-fee pot and the makings for hot chocolate. They all put on their heavy coats and headed for the door. However, before leaving she phoned their good neighbors, the Olsons, and some other friends. Aunt Mimi, Jackie, and Big Dave jumped into the trailer, which had sideboards, and Davie drove them all off for the orchard. What hap-

pened next helped instill in this new family the importance of teamwork and cooperation.

A frosty tinge in the air seemed to linger over their
cherry orchard that day, possibly changing the future of
the family. The morning sun broke through with only
a slight breeze. As they arrived at the orchard, everyone
went straight to work. Aunt Mimi had the boys set out
the smudge pots (a heating pot that burns oil or other
heavy fuels). Spacing the pots in a row down between the
rows of trees, the boys set up a warming zone. The warming zone helped keep the frost from forming on the trees
and damaging or killing the crop. In the meantime, Aunt
Mimi and Jackie set up a base camp by lighting a fire
and heating up water and some soup. After Big Dave and
Davie filled the smudge pots with oil, the girls came after
and lit them up. It took the better part of the morning to
set everything up. When everything was finally in place,
they all took a brief break. They were exhausted from their
work. At this point, the only thing that remained was
checking and refueling the pots and waiting on Mother
Nature to see if they had a crop.

One of the nice things of living in a small, tight-
knit rural setting is the feeling of community that occurs
when someone needs help. By gosh, that's what happened
when the citizens of Wakefield found out that Aunt Mimi
and the kids needed assistance. Why, people from town
and their rural neighbors brought out food and offered
to help keep watch over the orchard until the cooler

weather passed. Old Doc Wilson even brought out his travel trailer with a propane heater so Aunt Mimi and the kids remained warm. The kid's teachers brought out their homework assignments along with some of their favorite books to help pass the time. Even the local Rabbi, Mr. Steinman from the local synagogue came out and offered a blessing for the orchard.

As the sun came over and through the valley on the third day, temperatures slowly began to rise. The frost disappeared, and everybody held their breath to see how much damage, if any, had occurred. Aunt Mimi and the kids, along with the whole community, wondered if their efforts were enough to stop the tide. Well, on the fourth day, they got their answer. The sun came out in a glorious array of color, and the temperature climbed into the low forties. On that day, the cherry blossoms put on a full array of color and beauty. The blossoms stayed on the tree, and there were no signs of browning or damage to the leaves or any parts of the trees. At this point, the family and the whole community knew that the danger had passed. With the help of their friends and sheer determination, they had beaten back nature.

Realizing the full weight of what had happened, the whole family and their friends gathered at the orchard and said a prayer of thanksgiving. Then everyone celebrated the remarkable turnaround that had taken place over the previous days. Our little band had won the day through hard work, the help of friends and neighbors, and an unseen force that guided them all.

As the days grew longer and spring turned to summer, the anticipation of the upcoming harvest grew with each passing day. The cherries were extremely plentiful and bright as they took on a deep red color and swelled in size to a roundness not seen in most years. Everything pointed to a good harvest. For Mimi and the kids, this was their first full harvest since Ida May had planted the orchard many years earlier. Then suddenly, a real bombshell hit the family and the farm. As a grower, Ida May had joined a local cooperative to get higher prices for her cherries.

One day a letter came from the growers' cooperative stating that the Cherry Board for Michigan was only allowing each producer to harvest and market 50 percent of its crop. The other part of the crop simply had to rot on the trees. Now the Cherry Board set an amount each grower could sell based on the expected price and size of the overall crop. In this way, the grower would net a higher price but with a lower volume. If the harvest was too big in any given year, then the price of cherries dropped, thus leaving little or no profit for the grower. For Mimi and the kids, this news was especially bad. You see, for a new grower such as themselves, start-up costs eat away at the business for the first few years. With no previous profits to rely on, a blow like this can mean shutting down a start-up business. After receiving this bad news,

Aunt Mimi told the kids not to worry. Meanwhile, the cherries were getting riper every day, and the family had to find a solution fast before the crops came in and the bills piled up.

That evening after supper, Aunt Mimi took out the contract that Ida May had signed with the growers' cooperative. After looking over the document for several hours, Aunt Mimi came to a quick solution concerning the contract and the legal consequences for breaking their agreement with the cooperative. Under the agreement, the grower was not to sell or distribute any of its products to outside parties. However, Davie and the family were not obligated to follow the contract since Ida May had died. No one from the growers' cooperative had issued a new contract, an error on their part.

Looking over their legal situation with the cooperative, Aunt Mimi announced to the family that they were going to sell the allotted amount to the cooperative as required and market the rest directly to the public. Now Davie asked Aunt Mimi if this was right to do as commercial owners. She replied by stating, "Davie, as a matter of fairness, no one has the right to force you out of business." Then Mimi further stated, "I believe it's not ethical to let product rot on the tree just to get higher prices when scarcity always exists in many quarters of or population."

Then putting her hand on her nephew's shoulder, Mimi made this impactful statement: "If you were an established grower, losses like this are considered normal. For a grower, the profitable years absorb the lean years." Then she went on to say, "For you, young man, the objective is to ride out this bump in the road and get to tomorrow. And furthermore, by us selling a few boxes of cherries, there's little impact on the overall market price." With that said, the family now had a plan to keep their business afloat. To accomplish their goal, hard work and determination were necessary.

When the harvest came in, Aunt Mimi had everything lined up and ready to go. The pickers came and harvested the cherries on the front part of the orchard. The trees in the back were left without harvesting. Meanwhile, Aunt Mimi bought several large chest-type freezers and boxes of canning jars. She also purchased a small portable generator and some large canners. Canners are large containers used to cook and can preserve fruits and vegetables. The whole family went into the field and began harvesting the cherries on the tress left by pickers. The work was hard and long. Finally, they had enough cherries to start processing. The boys stayed out in the orchard while the Aunt Mimi and Jackie prepared the fruit. The Olsons came over to help, with Mr. Olson helping the boys pick the cherries while Mrs. Olson helped Jackie and Mimi with the processing. With their hard work and the help of their neighbors, our little group put together a huge amount of product. Why, they had over two hundred quarts of canned cherries and had three huge freezers full of sour pie cherries in two-pound freezer bags. They were also planning to sell fresh cherries in the box. The next thing to do was to load this all up and head over to the farmers market.

That Saturday they all headed over to the farmers' market in Marquette, Michigan. They loaded one of the freezers into the back of the pickup truck, put the boxes of cherries next to the sidewall of the pickup, and carefully loaded the boxes of canned cherries. Next came the generator and sun umbrella plus lunches and an ice cooler full of assorted beverages. Pulling into the location of the market, they found their space and immediately set up their product for display. After the market opened, it did not take long for the customers to come rolling in. Aunt Mimi prepared some delicious samples for the customers to try, even making some pastries with the cherry filling she had fixed. And you know, what even amazed Mimi was the speed folks bought up those cherries. Why, by noon they had run out of frozen cherries and had to send Mr. Olson back to the farm to fetch more product. By the end of the day, they had sold over seven hundred dollars' worth of cherries. This whole process of harvesting, preparing, and selling went on for three weeks. By the time it was all said and done, Aunt Mimi had cleared close to two thousand dollars. The family's hard work had prevented the business from going under. Furthermore, by taking this action, they kept alive Ida May's dream of a valley committed to experimental agriculture. This, in turn, helped growers like Davie and his family to provide a valuable and wholesome food for his community, state, and nation.

Davie's newfound family came to a better place after many trials. They had beaten back those who wanted the farm primarily for their own gain. They stood up to the raw forces of nature and kept their cherry crop intact. The family also wrestled with the economic reality of the agricultural business. This included production limits and market forces that threatened their livelihood and very way of life. The family, with Aunt Mimi's help, underwent a transformation. All members of the family now thought beyond simply satisfying their own needs. From separate individuals, they emerged into a unit filled with courage and determination. The family's new character, brought on by growth and persistence, forged a new identity. The future now looked bright for Aunt Mimi and the kids. Nevertheless, many storm clouds were developing off in the distance. New tests and obstacles awaited each member of the family. Only inner strength and a determined spirit guided our little group on its new path.

WHAT SHOULD WE LEARN FROM CHAPTER 7?

Let us face it—life is a real struggle. We must never give up. To keep active and alive, people need to rediscover the inner strength that resides within them. We must use or own intelligence to search and look for answers outside our own experience. By taking this step, we become searchers that always look for the truth. And then when we reach the end of human understanding, we must recognize that something outside the human experience holds and secures us. And finally, we must know that the only way to beat back self-doubt in our lives is to rely on a community of friends and family and a faith that sustains us. A true family will respect us for who we are and encourage us to go beyond our own fears. In this way, we will fight the good fight and carry with us a love that moves us forward.

In life, we are always presented with choices. The choices we make can make or break us as a person. Sometimes in life, we must take risks to push ahead. However, we must never make stupid mistakes that go beyond sound judgment and core beliefs. To be effective, in life we must manage risk and learn from our mistakes and the mistakes of others. And next, never underestimate your own abilities. Lastly, never fear being a pioneer and pushing beyond current boundaries. After all, Ida May took this risk when she planted a cherry orchard way to the north.

At times in life, we experience darkness. In these circumstances, we need the help of our families to help us navigate the many pitfalls and dangers that come our way. If a family is truly positive, they will affirm and love us in a way that lifts our spirits and pulls us out of darkness. Because darkness will, in the long run, always drag us down. In cases where one has no real family or has a broken family, the challenge then is to create your own. By befriending others in a way that is unconditional, it shows that you are willing to lay down your life for friends. In this case, your friendships become stronger than mere blood ties. By taking this step, you will create a circle of new friends that become your family. Contrary to popular belief, joining a gang is no substitute for a real family. The reason for this is the destructive behavior the gang engages in. Selling drugs, destroying property, and hurting others only harms yourself and the community you live in. A true family will never build itself up at the expense of somebody else. By engaging in this type of activity, you only tear down others and do a great harm to yourself.

Lastly, we need to know that all work is useful and benefits mankind. The "lesser" jobs in society are just as important as the higher-paying and glamorous positions. The person that cleans the restroom or sweeps out a classroom is doing a service that is needed and essential to our health and safety. A world where no one cleans up has huge pitfalls by allowing rats, mice, bacteria, and germs a foothold either at home or in public places. Also, living in a world where no one drives a bus to take kids to school means that parents and guardians are delayed from reaching their own jobs, thus affecting their own worker productivity and performance. In a world where no one wants to be a nurse, who then would look after the sick? From a practical standpoint, we are dependent on one another for our needs and services. In fact, all workers are worthy of the same respect regardless of their positions. Of course, those with higher levels of education and experience can command a higher salary, but people who work in lower positions also deserve a livable wage to support themselves and their families. In addition, no one has the right to feel superior and hold their noses up at workers preforming less complicated tasks. Today, as in the past, society needs to recognize the value of all work and those who tirelessly look after our needs.

Kristina Paukshtite

8

New Friends

Learning to live with each other proved a challenge for Aunt Mimi and the kids. For one thing, the farmhouse had only two bedrooms. Big Dave slept on the couch while Davie had a small room to himself. Mimi and Jackie shared the other room. With one bathroom, you can see why this adjustment posed problems. For one thing, Davie was used to having a lot of space to himself without competition. In addition, Davie had to share his time with Aunt Mimi for affection and the special help he needed with his homework. Davie suffered from a learning disability called dyslexia. This condition slowed down his learning process and made school harder. At times, the many changes the family had to endure made tempers flare up, making the transition even more difficult. Conflicts flared up at times within the group as Aunt Mimi had to play the role of peacemaker. It required a lot of hard work for this new family to sort out their feelings, but they did so and became unified.

When it came to the living arrangements with his cousins, the situation was not ideal for Davie. The main reason for this difficulty had more to do with the backgrounds and interests of his cousins. Jackie and Big Dave were city kids and really did not care for farm life. Jackie liked to read, especially fiction and murder mysteries. Big Dave loved his comic books and TV. Davie's interests included hunting and fishing and being in the great outdoors. He also loved being with his pals Floppy and Bear and sports of all kind. As you can see from the variety of these activities, finding things that bonded them all together was hard. Nevertheless, despite their differences, this family united. Their respect for one another grew as they began to genuinely love the other person for who he or she was.

One thing about being a kid is the special interaction and rivalries that shape the growing years. Let us face it— kids love to compete. When a group of kids get together for a game of hoops or a baseball game, the first thing they do is choose up sides. In the heat of the competition, it does not take long for things to get tense as the two teams lock in battle for the final victory. During the ensuing game, the better side of sportsmanship and fair play can emerge. However, in some cases, the darker side of human emotions and winning at all costs enters the picture. On occasions like these, self-control takes a back seat to trash talk and human anger. It is under this kind of circumstances that we find Big Dave, Jackie, and Davie as they headed over to the park for a baseball game with their friends.

That Saturday Afternoon, the sun was high in the sky, and the wind blew gently across the field. Fred Thomas and Tommy Frazier were picked as the captains for the game. Fred picked first, making sure he got the best player in the lot, Stevie Sherman. Now Stevie had a cannon for an arm and lightning-fast speed and reflexes. Stevie also had an ego and temperament to match his other talents. As the selection process continued, Davie, Jackie, and Big Dave were all chosen last and ended up on the Frazier team. What these three lacked in skills was offset by their spirit and passion for the sport. For this reason, that afternoon's baseball game shaped up as a remarkable contest.

In the first three innings of this epic baseball game, Fred Thomas's team pulled away with a big lead. From the onset, it looked as if it was an uphill fight for the Frazier team. But you know what? Baseball is a funny game, and the momentum can sometimes swing to the other team in a heartbeat. And to their credit, the Frazier kids never gave up. It all started with Davie getting on base with a walk. Jackie then got up and hit a long ball in the gap between the right and center fielders. With another hit from the Frazer team, Big Dave came to the plate. On the first pitch, he sent that ball sailing over the left field fence for a grand-slam homerun. The rest of the kids on the Frazier team joined in the hitting fest, and the score was changed from a 0 to 10 deficit to 7 to 10 in a single inning. As it turned out, a real sleeper of a game had now become exciting.

Gaining a big shot of confidence, the Frazier kids stepped up their defensive play. They cut down Stevie Sherman as he tried to take home from second base on a center field hit. Now Stevie was madder than a wet hornet and pleaded with the other kids that he had got under the tag. But you know what? Davie had caught the ball in his glove and slapped it across Stevie's feet seconds before he slid across home plate. A big argument ensued at home plate with all the kids involved. However, despite Stevie's grumbling, Davie was having no part of his argument. Davie then told Stevie in a loud voice, "You are out and that all there is to that!"

Finally, after a few choice words from both sides, one of the kids from the Thomas team said, "Hey, Stevie, you were tagged out, so forget about it. Let's get on with the game." With that statement, the contest resumed but with even greater intensity and purpose.

By the time the game got to the eighth inning, things turned against the Thomas team. At this point, it was all tied up at 10 apiece. In the bottom of the eighth inning, Stevie Sherman came up first and hit a slap single between the left and center fielders. Running with blazing speed, Stevie tried to stretch a single into a double as the center fielder scooped up the ball and threw to Jackie at second base. Rounding first base, this firebolt on energy never slowed down. Jackie caught the ball at second, but it came out of her glove just as Stevie plowed into her with his cleats aimed high. Seeing the collision, Davie ran out and confronted Stevie, saying, "Hey, knucklehead, everyone knows that sliding is all part of the game, but for God's sake, must you try and kill someone?"

At this point, Jackie was hobbling around, and her leg was bleeding. Davie then got up in Stevie's face, and the two of them were just about to fight. Before push came to shove, Jackie grabbed Davie and pulled him back. Yelling at her cousin, Jackie said, "Davie, let it go. I am okay. Let's speak with our bats next inning." As it turned out that inning, Stevie's double went for naught as his teammates popped out and hit into a double play. Events were now set for the final showdown between these super giants of the baseball field.

In the top of the ninth inning, the Frazier team really got down to business. They scored three quick runs starting off with Jackie's shot down the left field line. By the time the fielder got to the ball next to the fence, Jackie had already passed second base. She slid headfirst into third base just before the ball arrived. She got in safely and stood on third base, clapping her hands with great excitement. Jackie's actions inspired the rest of her teammates as they drove her in and scored two more runs. The score was now 13 to 10 in favor of the Frazier team. Despite the Frazer advantage, it was still anybody's ballgame.

As they went into the bottom of the ninth inning, the Thomas team had their backs up against a wall. However, their situation improved as Eddie Russell hit a deep ball into center field. Big Dave played center and dove for the ball and came up short. The ball rolled to the fence as Eddie turned on the speed. The throw-in from the outfield was not even close as Eddie defiantly slid into the home plate. It was now 11 to 13. The Thomas team got one more run after a triple and a single down the right field side. With a score of 12 to 13 and a runner on first, the next batter hit a ground ball to Jackie, who turned the double play by tagging the runner between first and second and throwing the ball to the first basemen just before the runner crossed. With two outs and a slim one-run lead, Jim Simpson the best long ball hitter, for the

Thomas team stepped in the batter's box. This hitter represented the tying run for Thomas. What happened next is what legends are made of.

The stage was now set for the final play of the game. Jim Simpson waited for the right pitch to tie the score and start a winning rally. Looking out into the outfield, Jim focused on the center fielder, Big Dave. Now Jim thought to himself, *Placing a hard-hit ball to center field will greatly enhance our chances for victory.* Then on the third pitch, Jim got a fastball right down the middle of the plate. He leaned back in the batter's box and swung at the ball with all he had. As he made contact, the ball took off faster than a lightning bolt in a thunderstorm. The ball started to descend as it neared the warning track in left-center field. What happened next surprised everybody, setting into motion an epic finish.

Seeing the ball headed his way, Big Dave sprang into action. This kid from the city normally found it difficult to run at top speed. Now for some reason that day, his reflexes became lightning fast. Taking off, Big Dave became one with the speed and direction of the ball. He zeroed in on that projectile like a heat-seeking missile. The sweat came flying off his body as his muscular contractions showed great effort and force. Normally, because of his weight and size, Big Dave found it most difficult to jump higher than twelve inches off the ground. However, on this occasion, something was different. Running like a gazelle, this young man took to the air like a bird in flight.

He thrust his glove out into the air while his body was still moving. Arriving at the right time and place, Dave made one last effort to make the play. The ball seemed to know where to go. It hit the leather of the glove and made a snapping noise that broke the silence of the moment. Big Dave, holding on to the ball, came crashing down on to the top railing of the outfield fence. His teammates came running out to meet Big Dave, shouting, "You did it, you did it." That amazing catch by Big Dave helped the Frazier kids win the game that day. It also gave Big Dave, Jackie, and Davie a shot of confidence that they desperately needed. After that day, these kids held their heads high.

When the Frazier team came in from the outfield, the situation was tense. Stevie came out to meet the Frazier kids. His body language told the whole story about the outcome of the game. Clearing his throat, Stevie spoke with a great deal of agitation, "You guys were just lucky today, and that all there is to that. Why, we outplayed you in every aspect of the game."

Then Davie replied, "Hey, Stevie, every aspect of the game except one, that being the final score."

Stevie got even more upset and pushed up into Davie's face. Saying some real choice words, Stevie told the entire group, "Don't think for a minute that I am going to forget about what happened today." Then in a burst of energy, he stomped off the field.

Then Jackie, in her usual coy manner, said, "His problem is that some of his ego just got deflated. However, the real thing to remember today is that we won and defeated a better team than ourselves." With that they all headed for home. The joy of their victory was sweet, but something more happened that day.

Now before Big Dave, Jackie, and Davie got home from the ballgame, Aunt Mimi got a phone call from one of the other moms in town. She learned about the Frazier team victory and how Big Dave had made the game winning stop. For those of you who have never lived in a small town, let me emphasize this point. News travels extremely fast in a tiny community. After hearing the good news, Mimi paused for a few seconds before considering a course of action. She thought, *This victory deserves a special homecoming dinner.* Mimi went straight to work. She got some meat out of the freezer and prepared her special smothered steak recipe. She whipped up some mashed potatoes and sliced up some fresh tomatoes. She also opened a jar of corn relish that Ida May had put up the year before. Aunt Mimi fixed a feast fit for a king. When the kids got home, they were taken back by the preparations, especially the white linen tablecloth and napkins. Mimi had put out the best china, and everything looked great. Davie knew what was up, immediately saying to his aunt, "How did you know we won the game?"

Aunt Mimi smiled back at her nephew, saying, "Can't reveal my sources. And don't you know, news moves pretty fast in a town like Wakefield?"

A few days later, Jackie, Davie, and Big Dave decided to make a trip over to Mr. McGregor's store. Going over to the store was always a special outing, usually walking many miles to reach their objective. Fortunately, Davie knew all the shortcuts through the many trails running toward town. On that day, they arrived at Mr. McGregor's by midmorning. As they entered the store through its massive double doors, they heard in the background the whirling of the ceiling fans and felt a gentle breeze. A moment later, the front doors opened with a slam, and Stevie Sherman entered. As it turned out, his arrival proved most unfortunate for our trio that day. The events that took place later in the store resounded throughout the town.

Being an outsider in a new community is always difficult regardless of who you are. For Jackie and Big Dave, the change to small-town life was full of many ups and downs. For the local townspeople, learning to trust in someone whom you have not grown up with is even more difficult. It takes time and understanding to reach acceptance. For Jackie and Big Dave, the steps toward respect and tolerance from their peers and the town was going to take some time. Nevertheless, the event that happened in Mr. McGregor's that lazy summer's day forever altered the perception and attitudes the townsfolk had of these two young people.

As each kid was picking out the treats they wanted to buy from the store, something very strange and bizarre happened. Seeing an opportunity to get revenge for the loss of the baseball game, Stevie Sherman took a candy bar from the candy display. He next sneaked up behind Jackie as she waited in line to pay and carefully placed it in her jacket pocket. Then Stevie went over and stood by Mr. McGregor, who was just behind the counter. Stevie announced to the entire store that Jackie had stolen a candy bar with no intention of paying for it. Stevie's accusation of a possible shoplifting incident got Mr. McGregor's attention right off. The accusation by Stevie caused quite a stir at the store and proved most embarrassing for Jackie. Now let us see what happens next.

Maintaining her innocence, Jackie told Mr. McGregor that Stevie's charge was false. Mr. McGregor took a dim view of shoplifting since he lost money every month from these thefts. Mr. McGregor then said to Jackie, "Young lady, since you claim innocence, you will have no problem in complying with my request. Please empty the contents of your pockets out on the counter."

Jackie reached deep into her left jacket pocket and placed its contents out for everyone to see. She pulled the pocket liner out and stuck her tongue out at Stevie, saying, "You're nothing but a big liar."

Then Mr. McGregor told Jackie, "Let's see what's in the other pocket." Reaching into her right pocket, Jackie felt the edge of a candy bar wrapper. Pushing her fingers down, Jackie traced a long, slender object. At this point, her facial expressions of joy turned into complete embarrassment. She turned a bright red as she gently pulled out the candy bar from her coat pocket and placed it on the counter.

Upon seeing what had taken place, Mr. McGregor's smile changed into a deep scowl. Looking directly at Jackie, he said, "Young lady, there's nothing worse than a thief. You see, this deprives me of my livelihood and takes money away from my own family. As for you, young lady, you must pay for the candy bar and cannot come back into this store for two months." Now Jackie began to cry and continued to plead her innocence. Even Davie stuck up for his cousin, but it did not help. At this moment, everything seemed so dark and hopeless for Jackie. However, something extraordinary happened that changed everything.

Hearing a commotion from the back of the store, Jimmy Anderson stuck his head out from the stockroom door. Jimmy was an employee of Mr. McGregor's and had seen the kids while he stocked the shelves. As it turned out that day, Jimmy had witnessed Stevie getting a candy bar from the snack section in the store. He also noticed that the candy bar was not with him standing up by the counter. Then Tommy pulled Mr. McGregor aside and spoke privately. Upon returning, Mr. McGregor asked Stevie if he took a candy bar from the shelf. Stevie replied in a loud voice, "Absolutely not."

As it turned out, at about that time, Mrs. Bennet, an important local citizen, pulled up to the checkout counter with her cart. She had overheard the conversation and said to Stevie, "Stevie, you know better than that. You took that candy bar and you know it." Then Jimmy jumped back in the conversation and reassured Mrs. Bennet that it happened just as she described. Mr. McGregor looked at Jackie and apologized for judging her wrongly. Then all the attention in the store turned toward Stevie.

Now Mr. McGregor had Stevie on the spot and was not going let him get away with his actions. Addressing Stevie, Mr. McGregor asked Stevie how two separate people in the store witnessed him taking the candy bar and why the candy bar was not with the other items he had at checkout. Confronted with this evidence, Stevie held to his story and continued to blame Jackie. At this point in the conversation, Jimmy Anderson said to Stevie, "Just stop lying, Stevie." Then Jimmy went on to say, "From my vantage point, it became clear to me that you had a motive for placing that candy bar in Jackie's jacket pocket."

Stevie then turned to Jimmy and called him a few choice words and a snitch. Then Mr. McGregor spoke to Stevie and said, "Since it was clearly you who were responsible for this entire incident, the burden of shame rests on your shoulders. Stevie, I am requesting that you buy this candy bar and restrict yourself from this store for the next two months. And by the way, this same restriction goes for anyone else caught stealing." With that said, Stevie paid for his items, including the candy bar, and left the store without making a big deal.

When the kids got home that day, they all reflected on what had happened at the store. Sitting around the kitchen table, they talked about the wrong and consequences of stealing. Then Big Dave and Jackie told their cousin that they needed to make a promise, agreeing to always stick up for one another. Then Jackie said it best: "We're a family now, drawn together both by blood and an undying commitment for the other. In fact, we must strive always to help each other and look out for others less fortunate than us." Now placing their hands together in the center of the table, they repeated the words "We are family. Yes, we are family." From that day forward, these three kids acted in more true unity. The fussing and fighting that had characterized their earlier days now came to an end. They also began the process of respecting and loving one another in a more profound way. The craving for attention and the me-first attitudes of these kids melted into one common purpose and a love for the other, a love that withstood the test of time and anything the world threw at them.

WHAT SHOULD WE LEARN FROM CHAPTER 8?

Sometimes in life, we are forced into circumstances that require us to meet new people. This usually takes place at work or at school or in the social clubs and activities we engage in. At our first meeting, the situation proves either exciting or difficult. Depending on your perspective, new social opportunities provide a way to reach out to others and stimulate new friendships or prejudge and withdraw from people. If you make the latter decision, you miss a golden opportunity to expand your social circle. It is often said, most people form impressions of others quickly, usually after meeting for the first time. This hurried judgment offers little into the true depth of a person. Therefore, it is imperative that you reserve your feelings about someone until you know him or her better. If we choose this positive approach in meeting new people, then the possibility of making new friends is much greater. The rewards of friendship are lasting and are one of the greatest gifts given us.

Unfortunately, we run across those who limit their friends. For little or no reason, they reject others. In many cases, their judgment is based on trivial reasons, such as how a person dresses or looks. In some cases, people pre-judge others because of their religious faith or the color of their skin, while some judge on how much money the family has or the amount of material things they own. When someone acts this way, it is unfortunate. The real loser in this situation is the one who does the rejecting, for he or she has failed to see the true value of another human being. All people have worth; sometimes it just takes a bit of time to reveal the hidden qualities below the surface. One additional thing to remember is that when you reach out to someone, there's always a risk of rejec-tion. However, the risk is always worth the joy when you find a really good and true friend. Having a true friend is like receiving a great gift. For you see, no possession, money, or group approval equals a friend.

Seeking revenge against another always backfires in the long run. The person who intentionally hurts others through speech or physical acts damages his or her own soul. The reason for this is that when we hurt others, even if we feel justified, a bit of ourselves dies with that deed. Likewise, if we do not forgive others, we then take on the same bitterness and frustrations that usually comes from the other person. Additionally, grudges and hatred only make relationships worse. The transformation away from love always leads the individual toward self-centeredness and mistrust. This person then becomes more critical of the actions of others and is less able to see his or her own faults and shortcomings. So you see, it is always best not to let hurts overtake you. Leave punishment and judgment to others, and take the higher road to forgiveness and healing.

9

Davie's Awakening

At a certain point in life, you pass through a new doorway. Old things are put aside for the reality of new experiences. Such is the process that happens when a young person goes from childhood into maturity. For the most part, puberty occurs both gradually and at times in huge leaps. For teens this is a time when their emotions and bodies change. And in addition, they discover their sexuality and begin the process of finding a future mate or seeking a committed single life. This time of reflection is either viewed quietly or with great excitement and confidence. In either case, the ever-increasing awareness of the meaning of intimacy brings the teen to a new reality concerning relationships. They also become aware of what a life of service requires and what their future role as a partner and parent entails. And along the way, they must struggle with the how to balance their inward desire for sexual pleasure with their individual value-system and religious beliefs. It is under these circumstances that we find Davie as he searches out his own future.

For Davie it all began one summer when he turned twelve. Over the course of several months, he hit a huge growth spurt. Other physical qualities became apparent and prevalent as well. His voice deepened, and his body hair increased. He needed more sleep than usual, and his overall physical frame increased and got stronger. It was during this time that his interest in the opposite sex increased, and he liked to show off his strength to the girls. Despite Davie's outward appearance, the changes that were taking place inside him seemed mystifying and frightening at times. As a young man, he had many questions that needed answering. It was at this point in our story that a chance encounter with a friendly creature helped bring some important issues into focus.

On one glorious day, Davie took a long walk through the forest. Coming upon a small stream, Davie heard the unmistakable sound of a bull frog calling out. It sounded like *rivet, rivet, rivet.* Following the sound, this visitor to the forest found a large green frog perched on a rock. Looking at his newfound friend, Davie said, "Hi there, so you're the one making all that noise." The frog stopped calling and then looked up at Davie. He then began to speak.

"Young man, what brings you out to my neck of the woods on such a fine and glorious day?"

Davie then replied with great astonishment, "Why, you can speak."

"Why yes," said the frog, "and even more, my powers of wisdom and perception go beyond mortal understanding." Now after hearing these amazing statements from a lowly frog, Davie was more than curious about what he stumbled upon.

The conversation between the frog and Davie began like this: "Let me introduce myself. My name is Frankie, and I have lived in these parts for many years. Davie responded by telling Frankie all about himself. This important conversation opened an important dialogue between the two of them. After a while, Davie began to trust in Frankie and confide his most important thoughts and feelings. This important conversation made it easier for Davie to understand and take in what Frankie was about to tell him. Frankie, for his part, did not sugarcoat the difficult realities that face an individual of his age.

Frankie then said to Davie, "Young man, I believe that you have many unanswered questions that are disturbing your peace. Judging from your age, it's certain that you have entered that golden time in everyone's life when a huge transformation is taking place inside you physically and emotionally. Rest assured that what's going on deep inside of you is preparing you to pass on life and bring offspring into the world or the inner calling to a higher life. It's also important to note that you are only at the beginning of this process."

Young man known this too. "Living just for yourself and your own personal pleasure, weakens you through selfishness. It also reduces society through declining values and downgrading of moral authority, the true underpinning of any culture." Now Davie was somewhat taken aback by Frankie's directness, but he found truth and solace in his words. For the two of them, this was the beginning of an important conversation.

Then Frankie went on to say, "Young man, I am going to show you a symbol that will help you grow. This symbol is important to your entire species. Now, Davie, go over to that pile of rocks over by the large oak tree. Look sharply for a special heart-shaped stone." Davie looked high and low, and his efforts proved unsuccessful. Finally, after much effort, Frankie said, "Son, search with your mind and spirit, not just by sight. Trust your inner self. It will show you the way." Then after concentrating for a short time, Davie pictured a ray of light pointing to a place within a pile of rocks on the ground. The witnessing of this remarkable event made Davie step back in complete amazement. From this point forward, he was sure that something very strange and mystical had just occurred. He was uncertain on how to proceed.

After considerable silence, Frankie said to Davie, "Look forward, not back. Just trust me." Frankie then pointed to the pile of rocks. Davie saw before him a small rock unique in texture and appearance. He reached for the rock, but before touching it, a surge of electrical energy shot throughout his entire body. Then finding the strength to go on, Davie pushed through the invisible force that held him back. He reached down and pulled from the pile of rocks a stone of exceptional beauty and brightness. As he held the stone up, it turned a bright ruby red. In fact, the stone even pulsated, giving off large amounts of light that turned the whole area into a very red cast. Then looking down into the place where the stone had rested, Davie spotted a large gold coin and removed it from its secret hiding place. Finding that coin proved to be a confounding mystery for this young man. However, Frankie was now ready to reveal the riddle behind the coin.

Frankie made this rather remarkable comment concerning the coin: "What appears on the surface of the coin?"

Then turning the coin over several times, Davie made this observation: "Engraved on one side of the coin is a tree with its roots exposed. On the other side, there's a steep rock cliff with snakes at the base." Turning to Frankie, our young seeker of knowledge asked the meaning of these images.

Pausing before he spoke for what seemed like hours, this sage of wisdom made these profound statements.

"The tree side of the coin represents the virtue tree. The tree stands for self-discipline, honor, and love, to name only a few of its qualities. The tree is shown with its root system fully exposed. What this means is that, in order to have a purposeful life, you must have roots. Being rooted with the proper values allows you to grow and reach full maturity physically and mentally. Then like the tree, you can take in the deep waters that nourish and support you and strengthen you when the storms of life try and rip you apart. However, if you are not fully rooted and live just for your own enjoyment, then you will come to something less than your true potential. The secret, then, is to have balance between your pleasures in life and to remain true to yourself and those around you."

Then Frankie told Davie, "Let me explain the other side of the coin for you. The cliff represents man's dangerous position on earth. Man finds himself perched between two opposing forces. The forces of goodness and light are very much at odds with the forces of evil and darkness. People who side with the forces of evil and darkness will fall from the cliff and thus face being eaten by the snakes of pleasure, pride, and greed. On the other hand, those that choose goodness and light in their lives remain on the cliff, subject to the sun, wind, and unpleasant elements. These individuals must undergo a test of their strength. They must also remain committed to principles that stand for something greater than themselves. Know this as well: only a handful of people reach the summit of the cliff. Therefore, make the right decisions, living a life that truly makes a difference. Then you will find true happiness and reach the top considering the vastness and splendor of the world below."

Not sure of what to think next, Davie took the heart-shaped stone out of his pocket. He asked Frankie to explain its importance. Frankie then told Davie the secret of the stone.

"The red ruby stone is a symbol of goodness and power. The heart shape indicates the richness of the completeness of the Creator's love for all of mankind. Keep the stone as a reminder of his great power and your purpose for upright living. Know this too: by your very birth you, are a descendant of a king. Use his power to enrich your own life and bring hope and healing to your fellow man." Taking all Frankie had said into his heart, Davie prepared himself for the challenges that lay ahead.

On the way home, Davie decided to go the long way. Upon entering a clearing, he stumbled upon a buck running after a doe. Davie paused for a moment to watch the mating ritual unfold. For our young traveler, seeing the beginning of life unfold had special meaning. He thought and wondered what to expect when it came his turn to pass on life. For now, waiting was his only option. However, Davie quickly learned that finding and taking on a permanent union required more than just emotions and good intentions. It required a maturity and responsibility that he had not achieved. In fact, he was soon to discover that feelings alone can sweep you away long before you are ready.

As time passed, Davie looked for opportunities to meet girls at his school. As a matter of fact, there was a girl named Sally that he found most attractive and pleasant. One day after class, Davie found the courage to talk with Sally. From that moment forward, whenever they met, these two felt a surge in emotions. As for Sally, she was glad Davie had come over and spoken that day. After all, she found Davie attractive and hoped he would pay more attention to her. When the spring dance came around, these two found themselves together and were the life of the party. With their involvement growing, their attitudes and outlook toward each other changed as well. With the passage of time, their bond became deeper. The real question was whether they were now ready to pay the price and bear the responsibility for this level of closeness.

The peak of Sally and Davie's early relationship happened one night as both were invited to a party at a neighboring farm. It was still in late spring, so their host built a huge fire to keep everyone warm and roast hot dogs. All the young people and adults enjoyed the other goodies, including potato chips, baked beans, and chocolate brownies. As the evening wore on, the adults that were chaperoning the party slowly went up to the house and left the kids alone. Well, with this development, it did not take long for things to get out of hand. Some of the older couples wasted no time and slipped away to the woods for some passionate lovemaking. Then without warning, Sally took Davie by the hand and said, "It's time for us. Let's go into the woods with the other couples." Now Davie was not surprised with this development since he and Sally were already kissing and involved in heavy petting. For Davie, this moment was something he wanted for quite some time. However, despite his urge to please Sally and his own inner desires, something held him back from this opportunity. What he told Sally next came straight from his heart.

Looking at Sally straight in the eyes and smiling, Davie poured out his love for the one person in his life that made him complete.

"Sally, I am honored that you have chosen me above all others for your partner in life. My love for you is so strong, but this is not the right time for this to happen. You and I have grown so much together, and our love for each other is something very special. Our love goes to a deeper level beyond the physical. Our spirits have collided and become one with ourselves and the one who loves all mankind so deeply. Therefore, it's important that we honor and uphold ourselves in a way that strengthens our calling to a higher dimension. We must revere and respect the spirits of our ancestors and follow the light of the true spirit. We must also keep our pride through decency and personal honor. Sally, also know this—the hour will come for us to form a union together. Let's wait tell it's time." As it turned out, Sally was not disappointed with what Davie had said. She also knew that sometimes it takes more courage to say no than quietly go along with something you know is wrong. With the passage of time, their love for each other grew and matured. As their relationship developed, so did their trust.

Later that week, Aunt Mimi noticed that Davie was unusually quiet and, from her motherly instinct, knew something was wrong. Knocking on his door one evening, she came straight to the point.

"Davie, I sense that something is out of place with you. You've not been yourself lately." With that encouragement from Aunt Mimi, Davie wasted little time in telling about his experience from the party a few nights earlier. Mimi's reaction to Davie's story was direct but loving. She gave this incredible response to her nephew.

"There's something you need to know regarding sexuality. It's way too early for you kids to engage in this activity. For one thing, you're not yet capable of being able to nurture and provide for the new life should Sally conceive a child. And secondly, sexually transmitted diseases are running high around the country at this particular moment. The next thing you need to know is that using protective devices and pills does not always achieve results. Therefore, let me make this perfectly clear to you, Davie. The person who gets hurt the worst in sex before marriage is you. The reason for this goes deep into the human purpose. When people want gratification above everything else, it's because they don't respect themselves and the partner they're with. When they're not willing to make a commitment before others, then it means it's all about them. They place self-satisfaction in their relationships higher than anything else. And in the end, they fail miserably. Davie, therefore, today we have so many couples that can't get their act together. They either live together uncommitted or got married for all the wrong reasons. These relationships won't stand the test of time because they have no depth. Everything is based on the superficial, the attractiveness and personality of the individual, how much money they make, etc. And to make things worse, couples are carrying these same mistakes and baggage from one relationship to the next as the weight of life settles in on them. Now, son, it's because of these reasons that things need to slow down between you and Sally. I love you both and have your best interest at heart."

Aunt Mimi went on to say, "Davie, for now it's important that we set some limits on your involvement with Sally. Son, you must understand that I am not taking these actions to hurt you or overly restrict your freedom. Simply put, I am doing this for your own protection and to uphold your own dignity as a person. In the future, you are to only go out with Sally in a group or to an official school dance or activity. And no more parties when you're not properly chaperoned." When Aunt Mimi had finished talking with Davie, he showed his approval by giving her a big smile. You see, deep down, he knew his aunt was right. Then Mimi gave her nephew a big hug and said to him, "I am so proud of you for not giving in to Sally. It took a lot of courage on your part to say no while your classmates followed a different course. Just remember this—the choices you make today determine who you became tomorrow. In other words, we carry with us both our own virtues and wrongdoings." As time went on, Dave came to appreciate what Aunt Mimi had done for him. The real question for Sally and Davie was whether they had the patience and trust in a higher ideal before becoming one.

Then Mimi said to Davie, "While we're discussing the subject of sex, let us talk about masturbation. I have noticed that you're spending a lot more time in the bathroom these days. Now I know that teenage boys and girls are obsessed with their appearance and grooming. However, this is also the time when people of your age discover their sexuality. They begin experimenting and find that sexual stimulus is very enjoyable. Now, Davie, let's face it. Sex is all part of the human experience. However, as you go from boyhood to manhood, there's certain dangers that can lead you into a life of addiction and shame. If you engage in a lifestyle that is primarily about pornography and self-pleasure, then your fulfillment is a selfish existence." Upon hearing these words from his aunt, Davie was both concerned and embarrassed. But despite his shyness, he had many unanswered questions about this matter.

To explain human sexuality to Davie even further, his aunt jumped into the discussion of the beginning of human existence.

"Some people believe that we are descendants from primates and thus come by our sexual practices from the animals. These same people claim that we have little control over our desire for sex since it is encoded through biological processes and human genetics. If this were completely true, then humans' sexual patterns would reflect instinctive behaviors rather than human freedom. Humans have intellect and have broken the bonds that govern mating practices that govern the lower animal species. Therefore, Davie, humans can choose their own time for sex within the limits of a loving relationship. Likewise, they have control over sexual urges and can channel them to a higher purpose, that of finding a suitable lifetime mate and producing a stable home with offspring."

Aunt Mimi wasted no time and gave Davie more to think about.

"The whole process of sexual addiction begins innocently enough. Usually it starts with pictures and movies and videos of naked women and men. Then the telling of dirty jokes comes in. From there people graduate to mental imagery of sexual intercourse and finally to watching performers at a strip club. At that point, it does not take long for the pressure to build inside them, and they seek relief in the form of sexual support with a partner or alone through masturbation. Now some people think this kind of activity is okay. But let me tell you the truth. These sorts of deeds are immoral and drive a person down to the lowest level of human existence."

Now before she finished her little chat with Davie, Aunt Mimi brought up some examples of people she knew who had a serious sexual addiction and how this affected their lives.

"The first person is a man who worked at the same manufacturing plant I interned in one summer. This individual got started on the wrong foot by viewing pornographic materials. Sadly, his life became consumed in this trash as time went on. It didn't take long before these images no longer satisfied him. He then took to visiting prostitutes in the neighboring town. After a while, the only thing this man cared about was having sex, and it dominated his entire life. What made this tragedy worse was that he never found a true love in his life. He had become eaten away with his passion, and no self-respecting woman ever gave him any consideration."

The second person Aunt Mimi brought up was a woman, a person who was a good worker and someone who cared only for the moment.

"From the time of her puberty she became very sexually active. She took on multiple partners in sex. From the very start of her adulthood, she found it difficult to establish a committed relationship with someone of the opposite sex. This woman never got the consideration from the potential mate she wanted. In fact, men only thought of her as a good-time girl. Their only objective was to have sex with her. Finally, after many assorted affairs, this young woman contracted HIV and the herpes simplex virus, and everyone immediately shunned her. She never found that special someone in her life and now lives alone, with few friends ever coming to visit." Then Aunt Mimi went on to say, "This tragedy illustrates the dangers of uncontrolled sexual pleasure. A lot of people think that something like this can never happen to them. Well, Davie, think hard on what I've told you."

Urged on by their conversation, Davie asked Aunt Mimi this important question: "Why is sex so wrong when it is so pleasurable? And why is it okay for married couples to have sex while for singles it is viewed as wrong?"

Then Mimi said to Davie, "The complexities of life are sometimes hard to understand. In the first place, married couples have made a deep and lasting commitment towards each other. They have agreed to accept children and raise and nurture them. Therefore, sex is a natural outpouring of their love and acceptance of each other. In their relationship, no one person is above the other, and they both hold bonds of mutual respect. Now regarding sex before marriage, listen carefully to what I am going to say. As a male, you carry the capacity within you to begin human life with your partner. This is an awesome responsibility. This action of producing life requires more than a casual moment of physical attraction and fun. Therefore, you are required under the laws of humans and common morality to defend your mate and the life you've created. Doing anything less only brings shame upon you as a person." With Aunt Mimi's explanation, Davie did a lot of soul-searching. From this point forward, he was better able to understand his own role as an individual and future father.

To strengthen and stress the importance of personal responsibility in relationships, Aunt Mimi had these additional words to Davie: "A man needs to provide for his family providing financial and emotional support to the mother and his children. He must help her share the burden of raising their kids so all the responsibility doesn't fall totally on her. For you see, Davie, a father who refuses to help with his own child—well, let's call it really what it is—he's not a man at all. He's somebody that wants to play without any of the costs. When this situation occurs, it has lasting effects. If a father refuses to do the right thing, the responsibility for raising and bringing up that child shifts back to society. This means that a single parent, grandparents, or the state must step forward and do somebody else's job. Then often the child suffers through being denied the resources, love, and support needed for success." Then looking directly at her nephew, Aunt Mimi said, "Do you understand what I have explained to you?" Then Davie nodded in agreement. For the first time in his life, Davie came to a fuller awareness of what the adult world was all about.

As their conversation continued about sex, Davie asked his aunt these relevant questions: "Mimi, a lot of the kids in my class talk about having safe sex. They think as long as you don't get a girl pregnant or come down with an STD, it's okay and nobody gets hurt."

Then Aunt Mimi smiled at her nephew and said, "Davie, I've always told you the complete truth, so listen to me now. Condoms, diaphragms, spermicides, and the pill all achieve the same thing: they stop potential life but hurt society in other ways. Likewise, thinking that your actions affect only yourself and your partner is a false narrative. We do not live in a vacuum. We are interconnected as a group through norms and laws that unite mankind toward harmony and morality. One of the great virtues that is often overlooked today is self-control. When a group is highly irresponsible regarding sex, the entire society suffers. We find this reality through the devaluing of relationships. Today there are fewer committed bonds as a greater number of individuals shift from partner to partner. At the same time, people carry with them even greater amounts of guilt and baggage as they try to find happiness through casual relationships. Today uncommitted sex has hurt relationships, especially for children, through emotional and physical neglect. In addition, the number of people living alone is on the rise, and single parents often struggle emotionally and financially. All these factors listed above, contribute to ills that drive down community and do nothing to raise up hope and stability.

"Davie, regarding abortion and birth control, these facts never seem to come out into the open. By removing and keeping life from forming, these methods only weaken the gene pool of humanity. A decrease in genetic diversity places man more at a disadvantage as outside forces such as droughts, diseases, and plagues hit the world. Human intervention through pollution has put strain on the entire ecosystem, degrading our environment and making an impact on reproduction. To make things even worse, the high number of abortions throughout the world has eliminated large numbers of potential individuals from the upper groups of the intelligence quotient. In some ways, this has produced a brain drain just at a time when the world is faced with huge problems such as epidemics, climate change, and huge financial instabilities.

"Davie, let me tell you one thing for certain. Two wrongs never make a right. It's simply wrong to stop life before completion, and it's just not right for couples to engage in something that's going to hurt them and society in general. For a lot of people, they say they need birth control because they're weak and can't resist the temptation of sex. However, the main reason for reliance on birth control products is simple enough—the person has low self-esteem or has never experienced the dignity of a higher calling.

"You and your classmates are better than you think. You don't need birth control because of your higher calling and intellect. You have intelligence and can control your lives through drive and a higher purpose. Davie, humans are called into nobility, a state of life that is above the lower species and inwardly strives for goodness and greatness. From the beginning of dawn, humans have embarked on a quest to find out who they are, where they came from, and where they're going. Therefore, all of you must use your inheritance to move forward and strengthen the greater world. Be true to yourselves and your calling, and never believe the doubters who say your less of a person."

Before they closed the subject of sex, Aunt Mimi gave Davie some more to think about. She said, "Davie, you can take the higher road concerning sexual intimacy if you choose to. The first thing to remember is that in a relationship there is more than just the physical. To keep a relationship together, you need a truth and a love that places the other person first above your own needs. In addition, both of you need to exercise self-control until you are able to formally pledge your love and are willing to serve and protect each other. You must also be able to provide for the life that comes from your coupling of your minds, body, and souls, bringing a love to the child that is without equal." Then Aunt Mimi placed Davie in her arms and said, "I am so proud of you for standing up to what was right. Davie, you kept your emotions and inner cravings under control, and, son, that takes courage. Instead of following what was quick and easy, you chose a better path. For that decision, your inner self is clear and free to pursue a relationship that will endure more than time itself.

"Son, from time immemorial, people have pressured other to have sex. It was true in my time as it is today. These folks want everybody to follow after them and are usually the ones with the lowest morals. They want all in your class to do as they do so they're more comfortable with their own misdeeds. In fact, in most schools, there's always the popular set who are very sexually active. This group is usually exclusive to those who will do the deed. Therefore, to become one of these elites, you must lower your own morals and have the right physical features for consideration. These are the so-called beautiful people, and you can find them at any school. This same elite group will ridicule anyone who doesn't fit in with them.

Anyone who is overweight or has a disability or who looks or acts differently is open to special scorn. They will call those who don't date or engage in sexual relationships gay, homosexuals, or lesbians. For this reason, most kids today will do anything to fit in with their peers. They do not want the label of virgin, freak, or oddball. Davie, it's important not to leave behind your principles for the satisfaction of the present. Don't fall into the trap of being accepted and giving away all your honor. This is a price too high to pay."

WHAT SHOULD WE LEARN FROM CHAPTER 9?

In today's society, living hard and fast is held up to you. You see it constantly in the images presented on television and in the motion picture industry. As pre-teens and teens, you are bombarded with sexually explicit lyrics from the rap and popular music industries. With the expansion of the internet, more porn has spread throughout the world with its many addictive influences. Promoters of sexually explicit materials and suggestive language in songs claim creative freedom. However, what is packaged to you is confusion and discouragement that is directed at lowering your morality. The evidence in this assertion is all around you. From the rise of teenage suicide and the increase in drug and alcohol abuse, this trend is threatening your generation. Likewise, a sexual identity crisis plus same-sex relations is hanging over many of your classmates. The reality of all these explosive factors is that some in society are trying to sell you a misleading story—a narrative that leads to darkness. Stay true to yourself and follow the light.

Some individuals struggle with their own sexual identity. These persons claim they are transgender in their sexual orientation. As Christians we need to show the upmost in respect for these human beings because, after all, they are children of the King too. Therefore, it is imperative that we uphold the dignity of all individuals despite differences in our beliefs and traditions. One thing we can do to help these people now is to show them love and pray for them. By taking this first step, we can help these individuals grow closer to Christ.

From a practical and Christian perspectives, this we know: Our loving Creator gave to each man and woman a unique template that is designed for beauty and creativity. This template contains elements that are feminine and masculine. The two elements work together to combine qualities that can provide strength and protection along with caring and nurturing. The example of a father lovingly raising his kids alone shows the feminine side of the male figure. Likewise, the fact that all adults produce estrogen and testosterone shows how these two chemicals are present in every individual. Both males and females share these hormones internally. The problem comes when you have imbalances that skew higher levels of estrogen in males and higher levels of testosterone in females. For the answer to this question, we must refer to the Creator.

Although many males and females have chemical and psychological variables in their sexual makeup, they nevertheless fall within a unique gender. Our design accounts for characteristics or values from the other gender, but each of us has a calling given to us in formation and at birth. Additionally, our makeup is a gift, not a decision. Therefore, we should not reject our own uniqueness, knowing that individual variables within us are part of a master plan that completes all of creation. The reality of who we are transcends emotions and personal circumstance or preference. In total essence, the reason we were created is not a mystery. Profoundly, we are all pieces in a huge puzzle. That puzzle contains many parts and variables. He then mixes the parts together to form a beautiful mosaic that shows his intent for all. Simply put, he wants us to receive his love and pass it on to others.

Furthermore, in certain circles today, its implied that you are not a full man or woman until you have had sex with a partner. In response to this idea, let me set the record straight. Showing you can have sex does not make you a mature man or woman. You can conceive a child in your early teens, but doing so does not make you a complete adult. Adulthood requires much more. Making a deep sacrifice and pledge to your partner, family, and community denotes true maturity. Reaching an age of physical intimacy only marks the beginning of a stage in your life. True maturity comes not just from having the capacity for sex but from taking actions that display wisdom and living a life that shows positive action through worthwhile values.

By keeping good moral practices and values, people achieve a dignity and power that will carry them through the many hardships that come their way. On the other hand, if you have no substance in your life, then when troubles come, there is nothing to support you and carry you through. Those that have little substance in their lives usually end up bitter and negative when things get tough, showing frustration and anger. For this reason, it is important to remember that your choices in life really do matter. Who you associate with and what you permit to enter your mind and bodies defines who you are. If you make the right decisions concerning sexuality and what is viewed on the internet, then you become more upright and confident individual. You will become less bogged down with the clutter of degrading morals and unsuccessful relationships. With a right and virtuous life, greater fulfillment will occur.

10

A Bully Moves to Town

For Davie, riding the school bus was usually a pleasant experience. Through the years, he had made a few friends on the bus, but recently some of his friends had moved away. Making new friends now seemed more difficult after Ida May's passing. As time moved on, Davie retreated into his own little world. In fact, many of the things that seemed so important in the past had less meaning now. At the end of the day, the thing of greatest importance for Davie was just to get off that bus and go home. Each afternoon when that school bus doors opened, it was like a huge burden was lifted off Davie's shoulders. At last he felt freedom and safety and away from the constant teasing from some of his classmates.

Then one afternoon, Mr. Bernard, the school principal, brought a new boy on to Davie's school bus. Mr. Bernard introduced everyone to James, the new student. Many of the kids greeted James with a smile and a handshake while others patted him on the back as a welcome gesture. James immediately spotted Davie and proceeded to sit directly across from him. Now it did not take long for James to start in on Davie. He immediately said, "The folks in town pointed you out to me. Why, everybody talks about you. You know what? I think you look like a freaking Indian. And you know what? There's nothing I hate worse than an Indian." Then before Davie even opened his mouth, James went on to say, "You're nothing but a squaw boy," and began laughing in his face. In fact, as the ride continued, the other students joined in with more insults. By the end of his school bus ride, he thought practically everybody on the bus turned against him. For Davie, this was the beginning of a very painful journey.

As time progressed, the bullying at school and on the bus continued with greater force and strength. Big Dave and Jackie were the only ones to speak to their cousin except for staff members and teachers at the school. For

Davie, this entire experience felt like he was trapped on a desert island with no real friends of his own. It was during this time that he withdrew further from those around him and began spending more time in his beloved woods and with the animals he loved so dearly.

Then one day, Aunt Mimi noticed a big change in Davie. He began spending more time in in his room than usual. He also withdrew from family activities despite the urging of his cousins. Davie did not even want to participate in afterschool activities. Using her motherly perception and observation, Aunt Mimi decided to try and help Davie by getting to the bottom of his depression and withdrawal from the family and the things he loved at school. That evening Aunt Mimi told Jackie and Big Dave to go outside for a while. She sat Davie down in the living room. What proceeded in the conversation helped open the way for Davie to lay his problems before someone who really cared for him.

Aunt Mimi was never a person to beat around the bush with casual conversation. She came straight to the point and said, "What's up with you lately?" Davie at first became very defensive to Aunt Mimi's inquiry but realized this woman was not going to take no for an answer. Davie then told what had happened and relayed his entire experience with James and his other classmates both on the bus and at school. After Davie was finished talking, Mimi said to her nephew, "Is that all that's bothering you? Most folks think that the only way to handle this problem is to fight the bully. Let me tell you, there's a better way. Sometimes in life you have to outsmart your rival." At that point, the two of them laid out a strategy for Davie to deal with James and restore some of the friendships he had earlier with his classmates.

To improve Davie's standing with his peers and reduce the harassment, Aunt Mimi devised a two-part strategy. She first contacted Davie's school and informed them of what had happened. Next, she devised a way to isolate James and reduce his negative impact on Davie and the other students he bullied. To accomplish this goal, Aunt Mimi helped her nephew form alliances with the other students and build a group of students that totally stood with him. To bring about this end, Aunt Mimi hosted a series of lavish parties out on the farm. At first very few students came out, but soon the number picked up because of her good food and the fun they had. Why, she had Big Dave barbeque up some ground meat from a steer they had just butchered. Likewise, Mimi had Davie bring in from the woods both Floppy and Bear, and they really delighted their guests. They brought out their Farmall tractor and hitched up the trailer to take the students on hayrack rides. These parties slowly did the trick as some members of Davie's class began to unite around him. He began the difficult process of restoring old friendships and building new ones.

Evan as Davie's friendship situation began to change, the constant humiliation and degrading by James and some of the other students took a toll on him. When the weather was nice, he chose to walk the five miles or more to the farmhouse rather than endure the hardship of riding the bus. Riding the bus one rainy afternoon, Davie thought of a terrific idea.

Maybe, just maybe, there is a way to outrun the bus and beat it to his stop. By me doing this, my speed and swiftness will impress my classmates and prove ounce and for all that I am a person worthy of their respect. So it began. Almost every afternoon, Davie waited for the bus to leave the school. Knowing the countryside very well, he took every shortcut and trail over land possible. Since the bus had to take the roads, it gave Davie an advantage by taking a more direct route. On most days, Davie was waiting at his stop while the bus brought the other students on their journey home. With great delight, he waved to the other students and James as they shouted insults out the bus windows at Davie. In reply, he just stood there and yelled back, saying, "Have a good day, and the same to you." Although racing the bus did little to improve his situation with James and his friends, it did, however, lift Davie's spirits and help him handle the stress better.

One Saturday afternoon, when the weather was perfect, Davie decided to go in the forest and see his old buddies Floppy and Bear. The three of them went on a brief stroll through the deep woods. Pausing by a big rock, Davie said, "Guys, let go over to Hanson's Meadow, where we all fought the wolves that fateful night." They all agreed and started down the trail toward the clearing. Coming out of the woods into the meadow, they all paused for a moment as they recalled the events that had taken place there. You see, this location was sacred to the three because they had all undergone a great testing of their will and character during that fateful evening some months before. What happened next both startled and affected our visitors to the meadow for the rest of their lives.

Now looking out the corner of his eye, Davie caught the image of a man standing on a rock. The man was as brilliant as the sun, with clothing that sparkled like pure gold. His hair was black and appeared darker than the deepest depth of the ocean. This strange visitor to the meadow carried a horn. The man then took the horn and placed it to his lips. The sound that came from the horn shook the entire land and carried forth for many miles in all directions. All the creatures of the forest and plains became silent. The wind stopped, and it was like the earth stood still. At that instant, Davie recognized the mysterious figure before him. It was Wahkoowah, Charging Bear.

Wahkoowah paused for a short time before speaking. It was like he was completely absorbed in a far-off place. Then turning to Davie, the great Indian chieftain spoke these profound words to Davie: "My friend, in life when you find a mountain that's too high to climb, you have two choices. You can either go back the way you came, surrendering to defeat, or you can find a new path around the obstacle in your way. My son, you have come up against the hatred and sorrows my people have endured for many generations. Therefore, Little Bear, you will suffer the same sorrow and pain that all Indian boys must undergo. The challenge for you, Little Bear, is to take sadness from life and let it make you stronger. You must not retreat but instead soar like the eagle to new heights."

Then taking something long and curved from his shoulder, Wahkoowah presented Davie with the horn he carried. This piece of detailed artwork had carvings and a band of pure gold that encircled the neck. The horn displayed life many years ago with images of buffalo, elk, deer, and bear. The craftsmanship was beautiful, showing the best of carving skills and workmanship.

Taking the horn, Wahkoowah placed it over Davie's head. Then placing his hands on Davie's shoulders, he said these profound words of knowledge: "This is the horn of wisdom and courage. Use it wisely to summon the Creator and all the chosen ancestors who once walked on this earth. They will come to help you and show you the way to a perfect truth and justice. Learn from your ancestors. You are now the guardian of this sacred horn that has great power, so guard it wisely. Now, Little Bear, go back among the people, and show you are a warrior, unafraid." With those profound words, Davie was now ready to go forward and face his difficulties.

The experience with Wahkoowah that day made a lasting impression in Davie's life. In fact, after that day, he never felt alone anymore. In his mind, someone or something greater than himself was watching over him. With a growing confidence, Davie reinserted himself back into the challenges of life. The fear of James lessened. The next time he encountered James on the bus, he held his head up straight and did not look away. The other students picked up on Davie's newfound strength and treated him with more respect. And you know what? Whenever Davie felt down or blue, he would take the horn he received and hold it and hear its golden tone, thus strengthening his very self. Davie's healing and transformation continued in a profound way.

One day on the bus, James tried to pick a fight with Davie. Big Dave got up first and pounded his fist into the seat, saying, "Our cousin is off limits to you." Then Audie and Eddie, two of the students who sat in the back of the bus, got up and put James in his place. They told James, "If you want to get at Davie, you've got to come through us first." After that encounter, James left Davie alone and quit picking on others. Unfortunately for James, his level of hatred and frustration only increased as he could no longer focus his negative energy into hurting his targets.

The situation between James and Davie remained tense. For things to change, something special needed to happen. For James, it was how to channel and handle his anger, and for Davie, it was how to become more confident in himself and overcome his quietness. Each boy had some serious growing to do and needed a shove in the right direction. It was in this situation that Aunt Mimi came to the rescue.

One afternoon Aunt Mimi picked up the phone and called James's mother. After chatting for a bit, Aunt Mimi came straight to the point. She invited James to come out to the farm on the following Saturday. James's mom was delighted at the invitation and accepted for her son straightaway. In fact, she told Mimi that this was her son's first invite to any activity outside of school. At that point in the conversation, James's mom confided in Mimi. She told Mimi about her recent divorce and the family's financial problems. She also said that James was having problems adjusting to his new life in Wakefield. As Aunt Mimi finished her conversation and put down the phone, her feelings told her that something good was about to happen with these two boys.

When Davie got home from school that day, Aunt Mimi sat him down and talked about the events that took place while he was at school. Then Aunt Mimi launched a real bombshell when she told Davie about inviting James over on the next Saturday. Davie became extremely angry and agitated. Raising his voice, Davie said, "For Pete's sake, why, just why did you do such a thing? Don't you know this is the boy that caused me so much grief and heartache? After all, he's the one that mocked and put me down in front of my classmates and teachers. And now do I hear you right, that you want me to host this person on the farm this weekend?"

Then Aunt Mimi reassured and quieted her nephew by saying these kind words: "Davie, this intrusion into your private life is because the sooner you face your fears, the better off you are. You must also learn to trust in those worthy of trust and know they have your best interests at heart. Davie, understand that your family has your back and will not let you down." Now after these kind statements, Davie felt better about his upcoming visit with James. However, as each day drew closer to Saturday, he began to feel uncertain about himself and what lay ahead.

When Saturday came, the day glorified its presence in a beautiful array of light and colors. For Davie, the beauty of the day was overshadowed by the anticipation of James's arrival. After Aunt Mimi had cooked breakfast for the kids, she gave Davie some important instructions.

"Be sure and take James on a tour of the farm. Also take him to all those secret places you go, and introduce him to Floppy and Bear. But remember—come back home for supper at four thirty." Davie nodded his head in agreement as he started out the door to wait for James. He sat down on the side steps of the farmhouse and tried to pass time. At about 10:00 a.m. a dark-colored car appeared in the long road up to the house. In the front seat of the car was an attractive middle-aged woman and a young lad about Davie's age. At that very moment, Davie broke into a cold sweat, and his head pulsed with sudden pain. This was the event he feared all week. Now as things turned out, the upcoming events on the farm served as a new beginning for James and Davie, but before that happened, some tough growing up had to take place for these two.

The arrival of James on the farm began easy enough, but beneath the surface, tension built up the minute James got out of the car. Aunt Mimi, Jackie, and Big Dave all came out of the house as soon as their guests arrived. There were the usual handshakes and greetings as everyone except the boys introduced themselves. Aunt Mimi told James's mom not to worry as the boys had a great day ahead of them. Then without much fanfare, James's mom said goodbye to her son and headed down the driveway in her car. Both Davie and James starred at the car as it slowly disappeared down the lane and on to the road. The boys kept their silence as if no one wanted to speak first. Now for both boys, the prospect of spending the whole day together was just beginning to sink in. Nevertheless, the events that happened next helped form a new friendship between themselves that affected their futures.

Doing as his Aunt Mimi requested, Davie took James on a tour of the farm. He proved a gracious host, taking James deep into the woods. He showed the wonders of nature, from the tiniest of insects to the great majesty of the larger animals that inhabited the northern woods and plains. The weather was especially beautiful that day, with hardly a cloud in the sky. Overall, it was a glorious day with beautiful colors and only a gentle breeze to stir the leaves in the trees. Although everything on the outside seemed perfect, it all was lost with James as he struggled to address his own anger deep inside. For this young man, some new discoveries and deeper lessons about life awaited.

While the boys were wandering around the woods, James paused for a moment to ask Davie this important question: "Half breed, something's eating at my curiosity. Just why did you invite me to spend the day together when it's clear that I don't like you?"

"James, if you really want to know the truth, then here is the answer. I am hosting you today out of respect for my aunt who asked me to do so. I think she wants you to feel welcome in your new town."

Then James said to Davie, "Well, squaw boy, how do you feel being with someone that really dislikes you?"

Keeping his calm, Davie said these words to his classmate: "James, you and I don't see eye to eye on a lot of things, that's for sure. I hope this day allows us to understand each other better. I am hoping that by bringing you out in the woods today, you can learn from the harmony of nature and find deeper meaning for your life."

Then James, in his usual rude manner, said, "You're full of crap, and with statements like that, it proves my belief about you." At that point in their conversation, Davie knew he had an uphill fight to win over James. Finally, after considerable time in conversation, the boys became very hungry. They settled down on some big rocks and ate the lunches Aunt Mimi had prepared. As the afternoon wore on that day, little did the boys know that something was about to test each of their spirits in a deep way.

As the sun became lower in the sky, Davie automatically knew that it was time for them to go home. To save time, Davie chose a shortcut along a narrow trail with many outcroppings of large rocks. For Davie, taking this path home seemed completely safe since he had gone home this way many times without problems. However, on this day, something unusual was about to happen.

Walking along the steep trail that day proved unlucky for the boys. Suddenly disaster struck. From an overhanging rock, a cougar broke free and pounced down on James. James fell to the ground as the weight of the cat inflicted great pain on the boy. Immediately Davie tried to push the cat off James, using a tree branch that lay nearby. He also tried shouting and throwing rocks at the cougar. Then without warning, Davie's good friend Bear showed up and took on the cat. As the battle ensued, James lost his grip and tumbled off the trail, hanging on to the edge in a precarious position. Lying many feet below were sharp rocks and other projectiles. If James fell, it was over for him. James's life hung in the balance as the battle raged overhead. For the first time in his life, this young lad had to rely on the courage and generosity of others to help him through. This was a turning point in his life. Let us see how he handled it.

As Bear fought the big cat, Davie knew he had little time to lose. Climbing down the rock face, Davie positioned himself with one arm around a small bush. In addition, he wedged his feet between rocks. This left Davie with one arm free to reach for James. Unfortunately, Davie was too far away to grab the boy. At that point, Davie shouted at James to reposition himself and make a grab for his arm. At first James was too scared to make any moves. However, James knew he was slowly losing his strength to hold on much longer. Then Davie said to him, "It's the only way. Grab for my hand." With that encouragement, James made a lunge upward toward Davie's hand. James's hand did not connect with Davie as they missed the exchange. For a brief second, James was in a freefall, but Davie managed to grab him by his shirt collar. Then James grabbed Davie's arm with one of his hands. For Davie, the extra weight of James on his arm felt like the weight of the world. His arm felt like it was going to come out of its socket. Then Davie yelled at James to use his feet and find a foothold. With great effort, James got one of his feet into a small split in the rocks. He used his free hand to grab a tree root that had grown on the rocky ledge of the overhang. With considerable effort and determination, the two boys made it up the side of the cliff. For now, they were safe, but deep inside they knew they had escaped serious harm and danger.

Meanwhile, the fight with Bear and the cougar continued. At times Bear got the upper hand in the conflict while at other times the cougar had the advantage. These two enemies were locked in a combat to the death. Just as the conflict reached its peak, Floppy emerged from nowhere. He heard his old buddy was in trouble, so he came to help. Hopping up on a rock nearby, Floppy directed Bear and offered encouragement and support. Bear felt pleased by Floppy's presence since it gave him renewed energy to continue the fight. Finally, after considerable time in combat, Bear's superior size and strength paid off. With one fell swoop from Bear's paw, that old cat flew off the path and slammed into the jagged rocks below. The cougar let out a huge scream as it finally surrendered to its fate. Once again, Bear had come through for his friends. As all of them took a moment to catch their breath, the meaning of what happened began to sink in.

Then James lowered his head. For the first time in his life, James was finally able to trust and confide in someone. He said, "Davie, if it hadn't been for your help, I'd been a goner. Why, falling on those rocks meant certain death for me."

Then Davie reassured James that his gratitude was appreciated. He went on to say, "James, the reason you don't like me is unclear. However, this is certain in my mind—hate has no part in my thought or actions towards you, and despite our many differences, there is still respect for you."

Looking straight at Davie, James made a difficult confession.

"Sometimes my words to others are downright hateful. It's like rage overtakes me. Also, my frustrations build up deep inside me. For some reason, my reaction is to take it out on others. In addition, my mom suffers from depression like me, and she has an addiction to painkillers and alcohol due to an earlier injury. All of this stuff has screwed up our lives. All of our problems spill over and affect other people we interact with." Then Davie responded to James without hesitation.

"You know what, James? Everyone's got problems in life. Your problems are weighing you down right now, but know this—you've got new friends to help you get over this. Aunt Mimi and I will make sure you guys get the help you need." With that said, James and Davie had to find the strength to begin the journey back to the farmhouse.

Getting home proved difficult for the boys. James had injured himself in the fall, so walking was out of the question. Davie's shoulder was in great pain and needed ice to reduce the tremendous swelling. To remedy this situation, Davie had Bear came alongside James. They all managed to push James up on Bear's back for transporting their injured friend. Floppy jumped up on Bear as well, and the quiet procession made its way back to the farm through the forest, meadows, and streams of the surrounding area. Bear carried James with utmost respect and dignity. In fact, Bear made every effort not to bump or disturb James while carrying him. As our little party got closer to home, James fell asleep. For now, at least there was a measure of peace between the two boys. At this juncture, little did either James or Davie know that something had profoundly changed their relationship.

While Davie and James were going through their ordeal with the big cat, Aunt Mimi began to worry when the boys did not show up at 4:30 p.m. By 5:00 p.m. she was even more concerned about their whereabouts. In fact, she had thought about going out and looking for the boys herself, but her unfamiliarity with the area prevented this. Getting lost herself was always a possibility. Davie's ability to find the out-of-the way places also proved troublesome for any searcher trying to locate him. As Aunt Mimi's mind drifted while waiting, she thought up a hundred possible situations that might spell gloom and doom for her nephew and James. Just as her thoughts continued to focus on the dark side, her eyes caught a ray of hope off in the distance. To her amazement, she saw Bear and the boys coming up the tree-lined road to the farm. At this moment, both joy and concern entered her heart. For Mimi, having the boys back safely overpowered her need for immediate questions. Right now, her emotions took hold of her as she ran to meet them with joyful tears.

Wasting no time, Mimi quickly aided the boys. She was totally startled to see the boys in such a condition. She went straight to work like an approaching tornado and put James at the kitchen table, cleaning and dressing his wounded leg. Next she made an ice pack and placed it on Davie's shoulder. She also made a sling out of a bedsheet for him to rest his arm in. After the boys finished supper, Aunt Mimi looked after the many cuts and scrapes the boys had incurred during their encounter with the big cat. For the moment, things were better, but explanations were now in order.

As the boys told their story to Aunt Mimi about their encounter with the cougar, she gasped in total amazement. She said, "You boys are so lucky to have escaped. Why, that old cat might have killed you both. It's a good thing Bear and Floppy came to your rescue. And you know what? It's a true act of love when someone is willing to lay down their own life for you. The next time that old bear comes around, he's going to get a special treat from me. The important thing is that you boys are okay." At about that time, the old clock in the kitchen chimed, and Mimi realized James's mother was coming soon. Everybody in the house pitched in and straightened up the living room and kitchen in a frantic pace. For now, everyone was relieved that the boys' ordeal had ended. For these young lads, the real challenge was whether they learned anything about the true character of the other. This test was about to come.

When James's mom arrived back on the farm that evening, she was somewhat shocked to see her son in such a terrible condition. However, something struck her when she entered the living room of the farmhouse. James and Davie were playing together and getting along quite nicely. There were no long periods of silence or pouting by either boy. For the first time, you heard the boys laugh. This sudden transformation was a sound of joy for James's mom, because for many years, she and her son struggled since their family broke up. As James's mom drove down the lane from the farm that night, Davie stood by the house and waved goodbye. For the first time in his life, he was sad to see James leave. From that day forward, everybody around James and Davie knew that something special had happened to change the relationship between the boys. It was apparent that a new friendship had begun.

On Monday, when the boys were back in school, their classmates immediately sensed something different in their attitudes toward each other. There was no longer the constant hostility and friction between the two. In fact, over time their respect for each other grew. Now James and Davie never became the best of buddies, but they learned to appreciate the other person. In their new relationship, each of the boys trusted the other more completely. With this new outlook, the boys gained more self-confidence and pride. There new attitudes improved conditions at school and in their community. Thus, a new chapter emerged by the new friendship and a lessening conflict. The actions of James and Davie finally put an end to a dark chapter in their lives, thus making Wakefield a better place by the factor of two.

WHAT SHOULD WE LEARN FROM CHAPTER 10?

Bullying is a form of intimidation that hurts not only the person but also society from within. You see, if we allow a single person to undergo needless and unwanted abuse, then we are guilty ourselves of lessening someone's potential and benefit to the whole. Making fun of someone because he or she looks different or has values not shared by us hurts everyone. Likewise, nationally or internationally, when groups or nations put down others, it only shatters the spirit of cooperation and trust that is needed for harmony and survival. However, when people respect others and uphold their dignity, then a bond occurs that is stronger than any single part of the whole. Diversity within a group will never harm society when that diversity is good, celebrating and respecting all life. Furthermore, when all feel equal, their strength and unity will conquer and overcome almost anything that get in their way.

Today we face huge challenges. We need everybody to enter the fight for truth and justice and preserve human dignity. If certain members of our society are weakened and downgraded, then a fractured and broken existence will occur. A state of survival that places individual against individual and group against group occurs. We must have all citizens and nations cooperate and utilize resources together. Whatever talents a person or nation has serves and strengthens the collective. Therefore, no one needs to suffer rejection at the hands of his or her peers or within the community of nations. Everyone needs to feel that they are valued regardless of their status or place.

One thing to remember concerning relationships is that we are all part of humanity and share many of the same struggles. Therefore, let me use a sports analogy to explain how social interaction needs to work. In life, humanity is on the same team. The other team is the explosive side of nature, disease, the dark side of humans, and the unseen spirits of discouragement and lies that continue to batter against us. The beating everyone takes in life can serve as a great equalizer through the knowledge that everyone shares many of the same hardships. Then let me pose this question. If we understand the fight before us, then why do we want to impose additional suffering on our fellow humans? If we are going to learn anything from this narrative, then we need to understand that competing in the great game of life is not just about you; it is always about all of us. As we go through the pain and testing of the present, we must band together as brothers or sisters or face the consequences of failing against an enemy that has no mercy. In other words, do we band together to make our world a better place, or do we simply add to its ugliness?

An additional point we need to remember about bullying is that bullies usually act out of their own internal pain and insecurities. Often the bully faces disconnection from friends and family, frustration, and a broken life through family conflict. Furthermore, if we want people to get help for this condition, then we need to remove the social stigma placed on it. If you are a person that has a condition that makes you hurt others, then get help from someone you trust. A school counselor, your family doctor, a therapist, a minister—all of these are important first steps. These professionals can steer you in the right way. And remember, it is always better to reach out than carry this burden alone. In fact, most people will respect you more if you try to get help.

Secondly, in some cases, bullying goes undetected far too long before anything is done. For those being abused, the pain is real and present. Sometimes the hurt becomes more than people can take, and they attempt or succeed in taking their own life. To avoid this from happening, it is everyone's responsibility to lift and protect their fellow students and coworkers. Being a silent observer to abuse and saying nothing puts part of the blame for bullying on those who keep silent. Now you may argue that it is not your responsibility to report abuse. Or you do not what to get involved. Or perhaps people will not like you knowing you are the one who turned them in. Nevertheless, there are times in life when everyone is obligated to stand up against injustice and ridicule of another person. This solemn responsibility for the protection of others rests with all individuals.

Additionally, offering excuses for letting bullying continue simply do not hold up for this reason. Being popular in school or having your fellow employees think you are the coolest person in the office has no relevance when it comes at someone else's expense. If you want others to look up to you, then show them you are an ethical person who stands up for what is right and just. If you take this action, not everyone will like you, but ultimately most people will respect you. Having both self-respect and consideration for others makes you a complete person. Strive for these higher qualities in your life, and you will become more valuable than acceptance, fame, or gold.

David Swindell

11

Growing Up Together

As the years went by, Davie grew into a man with a strong desire for the land and creatures that inhabited the earth. He kept his word to Aunt Mimi and stayed on the farm. Davie also received a degree in agribusiness from Michigan State University. As he put to work his newfound knowledge, the farm was developed to its full potential. Davie added to his dairy production and increased the cherry orchard Ida May had started. And by the way, Davie did one important thing in his life. Yes, you guessed it—he married Sally, his sweetheart from his youth. The two of them went on to have three children, Shaun, Khloe, and Davie Jr. They all lived and prospered on the farm because they all worked together and had a deep unending love for one another.

Now some of you may want to know what became of Big Dave. Well, let me tell you a little secret. The boy that did not want to scoop up manure on the farm became one of the most successful dairy farmers in the state of Michigan. He, like Davie, married a local girl he met in school and raised up a whole bunch of kids. Big Dave's life turned into quite an irony compared to his early beginnings. From a kid who disliked the farm to an adult who really embraced agriculture, this transformation was quite a turnaround. This sudden change of heart on Big Dave's part only proves that living on the land has a special power in people's lives. Country living really gets to a person after a while.

Regarding Jackie, that young lady really set the world on fire. Like her brother, Big Dave, she had the opportunity to go almost anywhere after she finished school. But you know what? Jackie chose to stay right in Wakefield. That girl really fell in love with her new hometown. And likewise, the townspeople of Wakefield thought Jackie was incredibly special. Why, in no time, she worked her way up through their local farmers' cooperative. She became the general manager and proceeded and set all kinds of sales records. She also became highly active in her local community, and if ever something needed doing or somebody needed help, it always got done with Jackie.

As for Aunt Mimi, she stayed on the farm and raised her two kids along with her nephew. This incredible woman managed the farm until Davie returned home from college. At that point in her life, Mimi returned to her beloved Kansas. When Mimi left town, everybody missed her. Her contribution to the community was huge considering her generous support of local causes. Mimi's bright smile and cheerful demeanor uplifted everybody who met her. Her absence from Wakefield was greatly felt.

Now this brings us to the stars of this book, Floppy and Bear. As Davie grew up, he never completely lost contact with his old buddies. Although Davie took on new responsibilities, he always felt emotionally attached to his friend. Floppy and Bear were always welcomed guest on the farm, and Davie occasionally took his boys and daughter into the forest to meet up with his old pals. Davie always made sure his kids had the opportunity to wrestle with Bear like he had done. In fact, they all got in the act on many occasions. When they all got home, Sally scolded her husband and kids for the way they looked. They were all covered with dirt and grass because of their matches with Bear in the forest. Despite being scolded when they got home, they felt that their encounter with Floppy and Bear always made up for it.

Another thing about Floppy and Bear—well, they became celebrities. They were sought after by an adoring public. Why, sometimes people drove all the way out to the farm in hopes of getting a glimpse of these two. Because of the publicity they generated, people began to pay more attention to the treatment of animals and the welfare of the forest. Floppy and Bear became symbols for saving and preserving the forest. Why, even the Governor of Michigan had the state issue a special commemorative coin with their likeness. The money from the sale of these coins was used for conservation efforts in the state. In the long run, both Floppy and Bear helped people focus on the relationship between humans and the natural world we all live in.

Sometimes in life we are lucky enough to come across a person of extreme inner depth and character. These individuals always seem to lift all those around them in a positive way. Such was the case of old Doc Wilson. His sound advice and profound wisdom helped the people of Wakefield become a better place. Doc led by example and helped others see things through the lens of truth and fairness. The town of Wakefield owed him much for his steadfast service and sacrifice. After many years of service to the animals and people in his community, the good doctor retired. He remained an active voice for good, not afraid to let others know his true feelings. After a struggle with his health, old Doc Wilson left the people he loved and went home to a better place. His loss was keenly felt by everyone who knew him.

The inscription that appears on many tombstones, "Gone but Not Forgotten," is in many ways a true witness to the life and work of Ida May. Her influence for good within and around Wakefield was well-known. Wakefield had the pleasure of knowing this feisty woman from the farm, but through this book, the rest of you will come to know and love her too. A true fighter for what was right, this woman was the voice and conscience of her community. Her passing left a big hole in the hearts of Wakefield's residences. Through this incredible lady's example, everyone was lifted and touched profoundly.

WHAT SHOULD WE LEARN FROM CHAPTER 11?

In the story, the struggles and pain that our characters go through is turned into joy. They all experience a renewal and rebirth that brought hope back into their lives and dramatically reshaped the town they lived in. We can learn so much from Davie, Floppy, Bear, Ida May, and all those represented in this book. If we follow their example, then we can shed some of the unkindness and fear that prevail in our world today. We can also learn from our friends in this book that love always conquers evil and that steadfastness and truth eventually overtake doubt and distrust. I hope this work has helped you find a clearer pathway to fulfillment in your own life.

David Swindell

12

Conclusion and Epilogue

Not the End but a New Beginning
for a Town and Its People

Sometimes in life we are drawn beyond the mere physical and limited range of our own senses. We can experience a calling from within that stirs our very soul. If we carefully discern and follow this inspiration, then great things are possible. Our mission is to follow the light of our creator and to aspire to a higher calling, touching the mysteries that surround us, and reaching into the very hands that hold our very existence. With this new beginning, our understanding of the past, present, and future will take on new meaning. It is in this context that our lives can accelerate and take us faster and wider, past the stars of night and to the very edge of space. Keeping this in mind, we now witness the transformation of Wakefield as it goes through its own metamorphosis as our story unfolds on a cold January day.

Waking up in a cold sweat, Davie immediately knew something was out of the ordinary that morning. It was like somebody had reached down and broke the deep sleep that had overtaken him. He woke Sally and told her about the eerie feeling that plagued him since his awakening. Sally, like her husband, felt the same sensation as Davie. In a dream, they were to take the family to the crest of Summit Hill, the highest point overlooking Foster's Meadow and Sunday Lake. Below was the town of Wakefield, nestled next to the lake and a forest with huge trees covered in snow. The temperature was about ten degrees below zero with an even colder wind chill. There was a strong wind from the north that cut through anything in its path like a knife.

Both Sally and Davie paused to reflect on the revelation of their dream experience. They knew that following this path laid out in the dream required a huge element of sacrifice and danger. Despite the obstacles that may overtake them on such an expedition, they found deep in themselves the courage to overcome their fears. Davie knew he had to take the risk and trust his instincts. Both he and Sally both felt that they were being called to something greater than themselves.

Just at that moment, they all heard a knock on the front door. Davie opened the door in utter astonishment. Standing before him was his devoted aunt, all dressed up like someone on an artic expedition. Now Davie was left completely speechless as he gazed at Aunt Mimi. Looking at her nephew, she said, "May I come in, please." At that point, Davie finally came to his senses and escorted his aunt to the living room, where he helped take off her heavy coat. Before anyone said a thing, Aunt Mimi told her story of how she arrived way up in Michigan in the dead of winter. After Sally gave Aunt Mimi a hot cup of tea, she began her incredible story.

"Five days ago, something came over me that was beyond explanation. It was like someone or something was telling me to get in my car and head up north to you folks. Why, no matter how hard I tried to shake this feeling, it always returned. I am not sure if you were in any trouble or if you needed something. So with that in mind, multiple attempts were made at contacting you by telephone. The people at the telephone company told me that many of the local lines were down because of the heavy snow. In the meantime, the only course of action was to make the long trip. Now let me tell you something—as I was leaving Kansas, it really started to snow. When I reached Nebraska, they started closing the highways behind me. I have been driving and held up in truck stops for the last few days. Adding insult to injury, my car got stuck about a mile from here. It's a good thing I learned how to survive storms way up here in northern Michigan."

Then turning to Sally and Aunt Mimi, Davie said clearly, "Our family is being called out to witness something powerful this morning. We must go despite the brutal temperature and terrible winter conditions."

Then Sally reassured her husband, "It's completely insane to venture out on a morning like this, but deep in my heart, it feels like it's the right thing to do." Then with complete agreement, they all decided to move forward. They all trusted in their calling rather than playing it safe by staying home.

With no time to waste, Sally, Davie, and Aunt Mimi went straight to work and prepared for the journey ahead. Sally got the kids up and had them dress in their snowsuits and heavy boots and gloves. She also had Aunt Mimi bring preparations for hot chocolate and tea and make sandwiches and snacks. In the meantime, Davie loaded his backpack with plenty of dry wood to use as a fire starter. He then made a large torch by ripping up sections of heavy cloth, soaking them in kerosene, and then tightly securing them to the pole. Next, he packed blankets and other supplies for the trip. As they all prepared to step outside that cold winter morning, Davie took the torch he made and ignited it from the fire in Ida May's hearth. This was the same hearth that kept the family warm on many a cold night. The same fire from her hearth was now guiding the family through the darkness. For Davie and Sally, Aunt Mimi, and the kids, this was the start of a great adventure. This was the beginning of a life-changing experience. Davie and his family, along with all the citizens of Wakefield, were about to witness and feel an incredible power and strength in their lives.

As they all stepped out into the winter cold that morning, they felt a sense of hope for the future and the journey ahead. Davie led the way with the torch tightly grasped in his right hand. They took the trail from the farm as it twisted and turned until it reached Summit Road. Summit Road was the back way to the heights that overlooked the lake and the town of Wakefield. It was on this road that the real struggle began. Would Davie and his family have the courage to continue up that hill, or would they sir come to the elements and the forces assembled against them? This was the real question?

Then suddenly, they heard something quite extraordinary approaching. Out of the corner of Davie's eye, he caught the image of a large brown object moving toward him through the whirling snow. As the image got closer, Davie made out his old buddies Bear and Floppy as they raced forward with great speed. Now normally you never see bears out this time of year since it is their hibernation time, and rabbits hardly ever leave their burrows during bad weather. For Davie and the family, this unexpected encounter was quite a shock. Nevertheless, they were all excited to see their dear friends. Well, let me tell you— this was quite a reunion. Bear grabbed Davie and gave him a huge hug while lifting him off the ground, and Floppy tugged at Davie's pant leg until he reached down and picked him up. Floppy showed his affection for Davie by running his soft fur and nuzzling up against his old friend. For Davie's family, this was quite a sight as they rarely got to see their old friends up this close anymore. Then after a short time, they all resumed their journey up Summit Road. Unfortunately, many new challenges lay ahead.

As our little party continued up Summit Road, something strange began to happen. The weather conditions got increasingly worse. The wind kicked up, and the snow got heaver. The snow became harder to walk on, and drifts blocked the way. As they got farther up the steep road, Sally and Davie began to spot many of their neighbors and friends making the same journey as themselves. On stopping and talking with some of these folks, the answer for being out was always the same: "We felt something was calling us out to this place." As they all got farther up the road, they began to see more and more people. Now everyone making this journey wondered what force was pulling and drawing them forward. As the journey continued, one thing was certain—this was not a typical day in the lives of Wakefield and those who resided nearby. Something big was about to happen, and everybody knew it.

The closer they got to the top of Summit Hill, the more difficult the climbing became. In fact, the snow began to swirl around in huge dark clouds. These whirling clouds took on fiendish and ugly facial features. They belted out from their mouths huge quantities of wind, snow, and ice. These gross beings moaned and howled as they tried to instill fear in those moving forward. These monstrous figures began to taunt those below by saying, "It's too cold turn back. You will freeze to death, and no one will ever find you." They also said, "Turn back. Turn back while there's still time." As the people moved forward, these evil forces did everything they knew to prevent folks from reaching the top and secure their appointment with destiny. How the struggle became even greater.

At about that time, something very strange happened. Almost all the animals of the forest came out and joined their human friends as they climbed forward. In addition, a multitude of individuals came out of the woods on either side of the road. This mass of humanity formed a line on either side of the road. These individuals remained silent for the most part, but their smiles and warm gestures only brought peace and comfort to those moving forward. These mysterious visitors raised their hands and pointed to the top of the hill. It was like in a soft and reassuring way that these folks were there to encourage and show support on that cold morning for those coming forward.

As Davie and his family and Aunt Mimi proceeded on their journey, some familiar faces caught their eyes. Looking to his right, Davie caught sight of his old friend Doc Wilson. Now Doc had passed away many years back while he was away at college. Doc waved Davie and his family over to where he was standing. He gave Davie a big hug and patted him on the back. Now Davie was shocked to see his old friend after so many years. He introduced his family to Doc, and after some casual conversation, Davie asked his old friend about the people lining the road. In fact, Davie recognized many of these people as his former friends and neighbors from his youth. Then Doc said to Davie with his sure and steadfast voice, "These are the just ones. Their lives were a living testament to their grace and goodness. They have come out today to provide those making this passage safety and protection." Then without warning, Davie saw Doc just fade away. As they all continued their journey, Davie and his family felt a profound sense of hope for the future.

Danger from the extreme weather was not the only threat facing those destined for the journey. For a brief time, the winds settled down, and a deafening silence came over the forest. Then without warning, Davie and the others heard the loud howling and barking of wolves only a short distance away. The wolves were extremely hungry because of the lack of plentiful game. Sensing an easy meal, these clever hunters of the forest settled in for the kill. Nevertheless, at that very moment, the just ones came to the rescue of the travelers on the road. They placed themselves directly in front of the attackers. Holding their hands out, these noble defenders shot out beams of intense light from their hand and eyes. The light was so intense from these spirits that it caused the wolves to stop dead in their tracks. The wolves moved back and made a hasty retreat. For now, those on the road were safe. A further testing of the will awaited those headed forward.

Looking up to the top of the hill, they all noticed a giant cloud move in front of them. The cloud was large and dark with huge amounts of electrical energy. It shot out lightning bolts with horrible blasts of thunder. Although snowstorms rarely produce these kinds of conditions, it clearly happened that morning. Those present felt that some invisible force was trying to prevent the people gathered from reaching the summit. As the people stopped in front of the cloud, no one knew what to do. At that moment, the just ones came to the front of the column of marchers. They began to chant and sing ancient songs. As they sang, the cloud that had blocked their passage simply lifted away. It was clear to those present that something wonderful and powerful had just occurred.

The people and the animals with them now moved forward with purpose and resolve.

For Davie, on that morning, his faith was rewarded as he saw in the distance the outline of a familiar figure. As he came forward, the appearance of a stately woman came into view. Handing the torch to his oldest son, Shaun, Davie ran up to the woman with every ounce of energy he had. Standing before him was a woman of extreme beauty. She wore a garment woven with pure gold, and her eyes burned like intense fire. Her hair was darker than coal, and her look was reserved and positive.

At that very moment, Davie knew who this woman was. It was his own beloved Ida May.

Not believing his own eyes, Davie looked upon his mother for the first time in many years. He was speechless and did not know what to say to her. Breaking the ice first, Ida May said nothing but instead opened her arms to welcome her son. Holding Davie in her arms, this incredible woman poured out her love. They both cried tears of joy as Sally and the kids were also drawn into the wonder of the moment. Ida May then spoke to Davie and his family with profound wisdom and love. Her special insight and kindness made the entire family feel stronger.

What happened next was even more incredible. Davie introduced Sally and each one of the kids to his mom. Ida May, in her usual manner, embraced each person with a love that goes beyond description. Next, she spotted her sister Mimi, and let me tell you—this was quite a reunion. Then turning back to Davie, Ida May spoke with a clarity and power that is worth noting.

"Davie, when things were difficult after my passing, I was there with you. I walked beside you when you were lost in the forest and when your classmates bullied and mistreated you." I was beside you and shared your joy when you found and married Sally. I was there when each one of your children were born and there when they took their first steps. Son, know this also—despite our separation in the physical world, we were never separated in spirit. Our spirits were united in life and remained so even through my death." With these words from his mom, Davie and his family came to a new understand and reality. From this point forward, they all looked at death in a new light and came to appreciate a fuller meaning of what human existence really is.

Just before dawn, they began to arrive at the hillside overlooking the town of Wakefield. The snow had not stopped, and it was extremely cold. All those who made the journey went straight to work making fires to keep them all alive. Chopping up a dead tree that had fallen, Davie placed the dry kindling underneath then put the chopped branches on top. Taking the torch, he set the dry wood on fire. Slowly the bigger and wetter branches caught on fire as they heard them crackle and snap. Sally made some hot chocolate for the kids and started coffee for the adults. As more people arrived at the summit, Davie helped them make fires for themselves. He passed the torch to others and used hot embers from his fire to light other fires up on the hill. Slowly the hills surrounding Wakefield were dotted with sparkles of orange glowing light. It was ironic that most of these fires were in fact started from the same source, that being Ida May's hearth, in the same way Ida May's fire was bringing warmth and light to all.

The people who made that track up to summit that morning showed no fear. They all had faith that something huge and powerful was about to happen. Something bigger that themselves had summoned them all there, and they were all hanging on as best they could. With worsening conditions, each minute toward first light seemed horrible, yet these incredible people remained. Deep in their hearts, they knew that a new dawn was coming with a better future ahead for themselves and their town. This deep-felt destiny helped the people of Wakefield prepare themselves for their new role and mission as a place of refuge in a world raging with storms.

As the first rays of light appeared over the horizon, a great anticipation fell over those gathered there. The winds quieted down, and it stopped snowing. As the light from the new day danced across the lake, a hush settled on the entire valley. Then without saying a thing, everyone looked at Davie to show them the way. Stepping up to an outcropping of rocks that jetted out from the hillside, Davie took the horn he carried from around his shoulders and placed it to his mouth. Three times his horn let out a powerful and decisive sound that rocked his community below and the forest for miles around.

After the sounding of the horn, there was nothing except the whisper of the wind as it blew through the trees. Then to everyone's surprise, a man appeared out of nowhere. He was strong in appearance and carried himself with great pride. He showed a figure that displayed confidence and wisdom. Now at first everyone wondered who this powerful man was, but Davie recognized him right off. In fact, it was Wahoowah (Charging Bear, the great Lakota chief), his old mentor and teacher.

Wahoowah then addressed the people with these words: "To the people of Wakefield and the lands stretching beyond, you have proven your faithfulness to the Creator. He is well pleased because despite your struggles, you have endured individually and as a people. You have set yourselves apart from your brethren. Therefore, today you will witness the remarkable hand of your father. He will reveal to you his power through his mighty hand, reaching into the four corners of the universe. He will touch your community in a way that is total and absolute." Next, Wahoowah raised his hands into the sky. What happened next shook the people to their very core.

"From this day forward, your city will receive four great columns of stone. Each column represents a virtue that you possess." Pointing out to the North Star, Wahoowah called out to the sky above. He said, "Come forth," and from the north came a long, slender object covered in a beam of light. As it came closer, its intensity appeared to block the morning sun. Finally, the object came so close that everyone gathered felt an intense heat as it passed. The noise from the onrush of this stellar burst became so intense that the town residents covered their ears and sank to their knees. Then the huge object crashed into the northern part of the city. When the dust finally settled, the people of Wakefield were utterly amazed to see before them a column of stone covered with diamonds from top to bottom. The diamonds shone and glistened, putting forth intense light. Above the capitol was a huge star made from sapphires that lit the entire city. When this was completed, Wahoowah told the people, "This gift is presented to you because of the love and respect you have shown to others."

In a similar way, Wahoowah pointed toward Acrux, the brightest star in the Southern Hemisphere. Normally the star is never visible in the Michigan sky, but that morning it shone intensely. From the south came a column even more intense and terrifying as it slammed into Lake Sunday. The column entered the lake with such force that water flew up hundreds of feet in all directions. The column was covered in amber and put off a yellowish light. Atop the column was a huge bowl of fire. The fire represented the virtue of integrity. Wahoowah told the people they were honorable and deserved this distinction because of their honesty and trustworthiness shown to their fellow man.

Wahoowah then told the people to look in the southern sky. As he pointed to the constellation Libra, a huge explosion took place that rocked the very foundation of the earth. Out of the sky came a huge pillar of red light that gave off a creepiness that unsettled everyone present. It also appeared to drag the rest of the galaxy along with it. It slammed into the southern part of the city, throwing up a cloud of dust that covered the whole area. This great pillar from the south was covered in red rubies. Atop the column was a golden scroll with a balance scale on top. This symbol represented the virtue of prudence because the citizens of Wakefield showed the ability to rightly balance their own needs and the needs of others. They also placed a high premium on the truth and social justice.

Next something incredible happened. There was a long pause, if only for a few seconds, but it seemed like hours. The ground beneath them began to shake with violent burst of energy. People wanted to run, but Wahoowah held out his hand and said, "Behold the power of the Creator and the earth below." Then the soil beneath the people began to shift; many assembled began screaming as rocks and trees were toppled, and the earth pushed upward with great force and power. All those who witnessed these events became extremely fearful. Then finally, the earth let out a huge rumble deep inside its core. With that, the fourth column pushed up to the surface as an earthquake shook the ground beneath the people.

As the column rose, the people gathered were spellbound by its presence. The column was shaped completely out of stone and was covered with deep blue gems of cobalt. Atop the column was the symbol of the eagle made from shiny bronze. The eagle symbolized the virtue of strength found within Wakefield. For you see, the people in and around the town have endured many struggles and setbacks through the years. From the dying of the iron ore mines to the closing of businesses, these townspeople endured the loss of jobs and the harshness of Michigan winters. They witnessed the moving away of family and friends, but through it all, they remained steadfast in their values and their ability to embrace charity and compassion for all. With the placement of the fourth column, a huge hand appeared out of the sky. The fingers of the hand extended, and a huge wind blew down bolts of fire. The fire never hurt or consumed the land. The fire burned brightly and was a symbol of the bond between Wakefield and the great one.

To finalize the union between the Creator and the people of Wakefield, a ring of stones surfaced to unite the great columns together. One by one, massive stones emerged from the very depths of the earth. The stones glistened in the new morning light. Then to everyone's surprise, Wahoowah told everyone assembled, "This is the Ring of Justice that now surrounds your city. You were chosen for this honor because you can now extend hope to those around you. The hope you have shown to your fellow man has set you apart. For this reason, you are now elevated to a higher place amongst the cities of the world."

As the sun finally came into full view over the horizon, the people gathered on the hillside knew that a new page had just opened in their lives. As the sun continued to rise in the morning sky, the temperature rose to record highs for mid-January. The ice on the lake began to break up, and trees began to immediately bud. People began pulling off their winter coats and scarves. The events that happened that morning caused a seasonal shift because of the intense heat of the stones descending to earth and the massive geological disturbances. The many flowering trees that dotted the Michigan landscape also went into full bloom. With all these events fully in the back of their minds, the people of Wakefield knew that something incredible had had just occurred.

As they celebrated the amazing power and grace of the Creator's hand, a spirit of gratitude flowed forth from the hearts of the people. Davie stepped up on the outcropping of rocks and sounded his horn with full vigor and force. He then addressed the people, "We have witnessed a display of power and might that few mortals had the privilege of experiencing in their lifetimes. Let us now give thanks to the one who has conferred upon us this great gift." So without anyone saying a word, the people, the animals, and the just ones, all raised their hands toward the sky. They all began to sing a great hymn of joy and thanksgiving. Their voices harmonized into beautiful strains of music heard for miles around. When they had all finished singing, everyone looked around and discovered that all the animals had retreated into the forest, and the just ones disappeared just as quickly as they had appeared. For the people of Wakefield, the last two days of their lives were incredibly meaningful. The struggles and sorrows of winter gave way away to a spring of new hope. Everyone knew that day that something was different. Their hearts were now changed forever.

As they all headed home that morning, everyone reflected on the events that happened. For Davie and his family, a new beginning had just taken place. Davie and Sally held hands as they walked home in silence. The sadness and struggles that had gripped Davie's life for so many years were now over. What had happened to Davie in the past was now his new strength for a more important life in the future. Going forward, he was more able to reach out and touch others in a profound way. Now for the town of Wakefield. They also came to a better place. By their actions they became a portal for goodness and healing. A place of greater respect and love for one another, a place to grow in wisdom and beauty, and to remain in harmony with the natural world around them. Thus, a new relationship came into being between the citizens of this incredible town and the architect and creator, the one that governs with truth and grace.

2014-2015 Auburn Washburn Transportation Dept. Topeka Kansas

13

Readers Guide

This guide contains books and information that reflect the beauty and humanity of Michigan's Upper Peninsula—plus, helpful information concerning human interaction and experience.

The list of books below represents a group of works selected for possible reader review. This collection consists of favorite reading by this author, plus recommendation from friends and other associates. Please use your own careful discernment in considering these titles.

Books on the Upper Peninsula of Michigan

Bullock, Jennifer. *Ghosts of Upper Peninsula (Haunted America)*. Charleston SC: History Press. 2018. ISBN#9781467140133.

Classen, Mikel. *Points North*. Ann Arbor MI. Modern Press. 2019. ISBN# 13: 978-1-61599-490-8.

DuFresne, Jim. *Michigan off the Beaten Path 13th Edition*. Guilford CT: Rowman & Littlefield Group, Inc. 2021.

Merwin, E. *Horror in Michigan*. Minneapolis MN: Bear Port Publishing. 2019. ISBN 13: 978-1642805208.

Tekiela, Stan. *Trees of Michigan Field Guide*. Cambridge MN: Adventure Publications, An Imprint of Adventure Keen. 2002. INBS# 978-1-59193-967-2.

Tekiela, Stan. *Mammals of Michigan Guide*. Cambridge MN: Adventure Publications, An Imprint of Adventure Keen. 2002. ISBN# 10: 1591931118.

Vachon, Paul. *Moon Michigan's Upper Peninsula 7th Edition*. Berkeley CA: Moon Travel. 2018. ISBN# 10: 1640498435.

Novels on the Upper Peninsula of Michigan for Children and Adults

Albom, Mitch. *The First Phone Call from Heaven.* New York NY: Harper Collins Publishers. 2013. ISBN# 978-0-06-247260-1.

Howard, Ellen. *The Log Cabin Christmas.* New York NY: Holiday House. 2000. ISBN# 10: 0823413810.

Miller, Serena. *The Measure of Katie Calloway.* Grand Rapids MI: Revell Baker Publishing Group. 2011. ISBN# 978-0-8007-1998-2.

Miller, Serena. *Under a Blackberry Moon.* Grand Rapids MI: Revell Baker Publishing Group. 2013. ISBN# 978-1-4412-4459-8.

Palacco, Patricia. *Mrs. Mack.* New York NY: Puffin-Penguin Books. 2001. ISBN# 10: 0698118871.

Jenkins, Jerry B. *Though None Go with Me.* Grand Rapids MI: Zandervan. 2000. ISBN# 978-0-310-24305-2.

Warner, Gertrude Chandler. *The Mystery in the Old Attic.* Morton Grove IL: Albert Whitman and Company. 1997. ISBN# 0-8075-5438-3.

Books for Grieving Children

Bergren T. Lisa. *God Gave Us Heaven.* Colorado Springs CO. Water Book Press. 2008. ISBN# 978-1-4000-7446-4.

LewVriethoff, Joanne. *The Invisible String.* New York NY: Hachette Book Group. 2018. ISBN# 978-0-316-48623-1.

Mudlaff, J. Sasha. *A Terrible Thing Happened.* Washington DC: Margination Press. 2000. ISBN# 10: 1557987017.

Books for Grieving Adults

Jasper, J. J. *Losing Cooper.* Chicago: Brett Morgan Publishing, Midpoint. 2014. ISBN# 10: 0578141965.

Kelly, Jill. *Prayers for Those Who Grieve.* Eugene Oregon: Harvest House Publishers. 2210. ISBN# 10:0736929347.

Ross-Kubler, Elisabeth. *On Grief and Grieving.* New York NY: Scribner A Division of Simon & Schuster Inc. 2014. ISBN# 978-1-47677555.

Redfern, Suzanne. *The Grieving Garden.* Newark NJ: Audible Studies. 2008. ISBN# 978-1571745811.

Books on Bullying

Mayrock, Aija. *The Survival Guide to Bullying: Written by a Teen.* New York NY: Scholastic Inc. 2015. ISBN# 978-0-545-86053-6.

Whitson, Signe. *The 8 Keys to End Bullying Activity Book.* New York NY. Norton & Company Inc. 2016. ISBN# 978-0-393-71180-6.

Woytovich, Betsy. *Francie Puts on Courage.* Mira Loma CA: 2020. ISBM# 9780578730493.

Books on Learning Disabilities

Baum, M. Susan Ph.D. *To Be Gifted and Learning Disabled.* Waco TX: Prufrock Press. 2017. ISBN# 13: 978-1-61821-644-1.

Pagnette, Hutchins, Penny. *Learning Disabilities: The Ultimate Guide (Vol 1) (It Happened to me (1).* Lanham Maryland: Scarecrow Press Inc, Rowman & Littlefield Publishing Group. 2003. ISBN# 13-978-0-8108-4261-8.

Nash, Beth Ellen. *Dyslexia Outside the Box.* York PA: Transformation Books. 2017. ISBN# 978-1-945252-27-3.

Power, Kate. *The Big Picture Book of Amazing Dyslexics and the Jobs they Do.* Philadelphia PA: Jessica Kingsley Publishers. 2020. ISBN# 978-1-178592-584-9.

Tomlin, Randy. *Outside Memories.* Meadville PA: Christian Faith Publishing Inc. 2020. ISBN# 10: 1098037057.

Books on Post Traumatic Stress Disorder (PTSD) Stress, Loss & Worry

Krechting, Kathy. *Sky Blue Stones.* Meadville PA: Christian Faith Publishing Inc. 2020. ISBN# 10: 10980026381.

Rozell, A. Matthew. *The Things Our Fathers Saw Vol. V.* Glens Falls NY: 2019. INBS# 10: 0996480080.

Schirald, R. Glenn. *The Post Traumatic Stress Disorder Sourcebook: A Guide to Healing Recovery, and Growth.* Lincolnwood IL: NTC/Contemporary Publishing Group. 2000. ISBN# 10-7373-0265-8.

Schirald, R. Glenn. *World War II Survivors.* 2007. ISBN# 13: 978-1883581237.

Shapiro, Lamb. Jessica. *The Bear Who Lost His Sleep: A Story About Worrying Too Much.* Bohemia NY: Child work/Child play Pub. 2000. ISBN# 10: 158815033X.

Books on Friendship Adult and Children

Brown, Krasny. Lauire. *How to Be a Friend: A guide to making Friends and Keeping Them. Dino Tales: Life Guide for Families)* Little Brown Books for Young Readers. 1998. ISBN# 0-316-10913-4.

DiCamillo, D. Kate. *Because of Winn-Dixie.* Sommerville MA. Candlewick Press. 2000. ISBN# 978-0-7636-1605-2.

Lampos, Cleo. *Riding the Rails to Home: A Newsie Rides the Orphan Train.* Chicago IL: Chi-Town Books. 2019. ISBN# 13: 978-1683149224.

Lee, Harper. *To Kill a Mockingbird.* New York NY: Harpers Collins. 2002. ISBN# 10: 0-06-0935446-4.

Lichfield, David. *The Bear and the Piano.* New York NY: Clarion Books. 2016. ISBN# 13: 9780544674547.

Padgett, Adkison. Eunice. *Homegrown on the Farm.* Meadville PA: Christian Faith Publishing Inc. 2020. ISBN# 13: 978-1098030506.

Sewell, Anna. *Black Beauty.* Blue Bell PA: Kappa Book Publishers. 2017. ISBN# 10: 0766633349.

White, B. E. *Charlotte Web.* New York NY: Harper Trophy, Harper Collins Publishing Inc. 1952. ISBN# 10-06-440055-7.

Books on Dating and Relationships

Eliot, Elisabeth. *Passion and Purity: Learning to Bring Your Love Life Under Christian Control.* Grand Rapids MI: Revell a division of Baker Publishing Group. 2002. ISBN# 978-0-8007-2313-2.

Harris, Joshua, *Boy Meets Girl: Say Hello to Courtship.* Colorado Springs CO: Multnomah Books. 2000 & 2005. ISBN# 978-1-59052-167-0.

Books on Moms and their Sons

Carlson, Melody. *Lost Boys and the Moms Who Love Them: Help and Hope for Dealing With Your Wayward Son.*

Colorado Springs CO: Waterbrook Press. 2002. ISBN# 1-57856-483-2.

Johnson, Rick. *That's My Teenage Son: How Moms Can Influence Their Boys to Become Good Men.* Grand Rapids MI: Fleming H. Revell, Baker Publishing Group. 2005. ISBN# 10: 8007-30771-1.

Helpful Telephone Numbers and Website Information

National Suicide Prevention Hotline
_____1-800-273-8255
Crisis Hot Line_____Texting Talk to 741741
VA PTSD Hotline_____800-827-1000

Resources to Stop Bullying & Helpful Information for Adults Children and Teens
Websites

1. Focus on the Family www.focusonthefamily.com & www.focusonthefamily.ca (Alive to Thrive Prevent Teen Suicide Website & Suicide Prevention Resource List Plus Teen Resources)
2. www.stopbullying.com (Helpful Information on Bullying and Suicide Prevention)
3. www.PACER.org/Bullying
4. www.PACERTeenAgainstBullying.org

5. www.PACERKidsAgainstBullying.org
6. PACER.org (Champions for Children with Disabilities)
7. www.dignityhealth.org (5 Resources for Parents of Children with Learning Disabilities)
8. HospiceAndCommunityCare.org (Grief Resources, Video Library, Reading Lists, Corona Pandemic, Grief Loss Information Websites, Adult, Children & Teens)

A SPECIAL NOTE FROM DAVIE

When my beloved Ida May died, the loss was like someone kicked me in the gut. The pain of her death lingered for many months. For many days after my mom's passing, I heard her voice calling out to me. It was like she was reassuring me and telling me to move forward with my life. During the same period, it felt like my relatives and friends from the past were also urging me on. As I worked through the pain, it became clear to me that others were in fact walking beside me. From that point, I never felt alone. Now looking back at my experience, I am quite sure that their love helped sustain me. For you see, love will always conquer the deepest hurts in our lives. Furthermore, the real key is simply to let others into our lives.

SOME FINAL THOUGHTS FROM THE AUTHOR

Writing this book brought back into my life a new sense of hope and healing. After Ida May's passing, many doubts and fears crept into my life. Although reassured by a faith in a hereafter for Mom, it was still hard to deal with the loneliness and loss of her departure. However, telling her story through this novel lifted some of my grief and made life more bearable for me. It gave more purpose and meaning to my life. Creative storytelling brought many of Ida May's virtues out with amazing clarity. Her story is interwoven into the fabric of this narrative. The deeper meaning and symbolism of this book will take you to a place of freedom and a place to grow. Ida May and all the characters of this work will show you the way to a greater peace and contentment in your heart and life. Just listen and they will speak to your inner self.

BIOGRAPHICAL SKETCHES

Many of the characters and institutions mentioned in this book are based on real-life people, groups, and organizations. Permission was requested and granted for their use. However, any similarities or names not listed in these sketches or by express approval are fictional and are totally coincidental, inserted for the convenience of the author and for the flow of the storyline.

The Character of Davie

Davie is the storyteller in this book. He has two degrees in history and loves children. Currently he is a school bus driver for his hometown in Topeka, Kansas. During his formative years, Davie had the misfortune of being born with dyslexia, a learning disability. This condition affected his life in a big way, especially at school. Having little self-worth, he always thought of himself as dumb and totally devoid of creativity. In fact, he hated who he was and often thought of taking his own life. Furthermore, during these growing years, Davie often let others pick on him. And likewise, Davie took out some of his frustration on his own classmates.

While all this was taking place in Davie's life, his family almost fell completely apart. Davie's father, a good man, suffered from post-traumatic stress disorder from his involvement in World War Two. PTSD is a reaction to physical and mental events in a person's life, in this case, the war. For Davie's father, serving as a hospital medic graphically brought home the reality of combat casualties. Davie's father was absent and hospitalized for almost two years. This situation affected the family in a big way. The family also went through money troubles as they tried to keep their heads above water and pay bills. To make things even worse, fighting between Ida May and her husband, Melvin, occurred quite regularly. During those years, the whole family, including Ken, the oldest child, suffered and struggled with mild depression. It was in those years that our faith in a higher power and a few good friends carried us through.

Just as Davie experienced great sadness and self-doubt while growing up, a tremendous transformation took place in his adult years. After living in fear and with many job failures, Davie reached out and found his true inner self. This transformation in his life took place through an encounter with the Holy Spirit at a weekend seminar. From that moment on, his confidence and talents blossomed, turning him into a more positive individual. He no longer just thought about himself and dedicated his life to the service of others. For this reason, this book is a special gift from him to you. By learning from Davie and his pals, you will experience some of the same inner peace and beauty of a new and committed life.

The Character of Ida May

Ida May was a devoted and loving individual. She held fast to the values of charity and love. Having only an eight-grade education, she showed the world that having tremendous compassion and love is worth more that the trappings of degrees and personal achievements. Ida May was the glue that held our family together through many trying times. Hard work and dedication toward keeping us all going, service to her church, and a true respect for all life were the hallmarks of this incredible woman. Although she was not perfect in any stretch of the imagination, she left something of greater importance. The final gift of her life was not a large monument or an empty inscription but instead a burning passion for charity and doing the right thing even when it was difficult.

The Character of Aunt Mimi

It was my pleasure to meet Mimi over twenty years ago. Mimi was a caring friend and mentor to me for many years. A member of our church, she devoted a great deal of her life in speaking out on pressing social issues and her own ministries. Mimi was a native of Kansas and grew up in Oklahoma. She had a teaching degree from the University of Oklahoma. After teaching in school for a few years, she married and raised two daughters.

Mimi had a special gift for comforting others in their time of need. And in this light, let me mention to you one of her special gifts. Mimi knew that there are times in life that people needed something to hold on to. And in this light, let me describe to you one of Mimi's gifts to those she met. Mimi, through the help of a friend, started a stuffed-animal ministry. This pair delivered many teddy bears and animals of every description to children and adults alike who felt the pain of loss or who needed that special friend in their life. She also ran a fish tank at our church bazaar every winter. Those stuffed animals the children received at that event were the highlight of many a young person.

This special ministry of Mimi's helped Ida May in the last few years of her life. You see, Ida May suffered from the debilitating disease of dementia. This terrible disease robs people of their short-term memory and leaves them confused and quiet. Many of those who suffer from this sickness have what is called sundown syndrome. As the sun goes down, those who have dementia often progress into greater confusion. In the case of Ida May, it was sometimes hard to get her to bed at night.

To show you how important Mimi's teddy bear ministry was in our lives, let me tell you this amazing story. One day a box magically appeared on our doorstep. When we opened it up, inside were a beautiful teddy bear and a stuffed rabbit. Instantly, Mom took to these and always enjoyed their company. From the time of their arrival, these comforting friends always slept with Ida May, and I almost always made sure they awoke her. Holding these two companions close to Ida May, we sang a little song, and with my wrist movements, these two friends danced for their beloved owner. We named these two Floppy and Bear, and they were the inspiration for this story after Mom's passing in 2010.

The Character of Old Doc Wilson

Our family doctor was a general practitioner in Topeka, Kansas, for many years. Doc maintained a huge general practice and performed as a surgeon at St. Frances Hospital in Topeka. Some of the scope of his commitment and activities in the community included being the company doctor for the Goodyear Tire and Rubber plant and being a special friend to Our Lady of Guadalupe Catholic Parish. He also supported other philanthropic activities.

The things that impressed you about Doc was his openness and direct manner and his practical approach to life. At times he was frank with people but never in a rude or unpleasant way. This incredible doctor helped those less fortunate and cared for those on the lowest part of the socioeconomic ladder. He was a faithful friend to our family. In fact, Ida May worked for him for a few years as a cleaning lady, and he always treated her right.

The Characters of Carrie and Mason

In my former school district, there were a few moms and dads who brought their children to work with them. For most of the drivers and staff, these kids represented something special. The interaction between the adults and kids was nurturing and caring. About four years ago, Mason and Carrie began coming to work with their mom, Julee. Right away her kids became rock stars in the drivers' lounge as they interacted with everyone. It did not take long for us to become good friends. Mason and Carrie attended middle school at Auburn Washburn in Topeka, Kansas, and were excellent students. Knowing these kids was a real pleasure. Both Mason and Carrie have a good sense of humor and are not bashful about their opinions. In my estimation, these kids will go far since they have the right values and good parenting to guide their way.

The Character of Charging Bear

John is a driver from Auburn-Washburn in Topeka. Throughout his years of service, John has always shown compassion to his students and his fellow employees. One day while we were sitting in the employee lounge, the discussion of my book came to the forefront of our conversation. John asked me this question point-blank: "How about writing me into your book?" Well, after some hesitation on my part, an agreement was reached. John is a descendant of the Cherokee Nation and proud of his Native American heritage and blood. With John's entry and influence, the book took on a whole new meaning. This work became much deeper and more symbolic. In many ways, John has served as a guide to me, giving me greater insight into the culture and history of native peoples. For his help, I am gratefully indebted.

The Character of Big Dave

I have known Big Dave for many years. The common thread that brought us all together was our friend Mimi. Mimi never liked to dine alone. So it was only natural that a tiny circle of her chosen friends gathered almost every Sunday evening. It was under these circumstances that Mimi introduced us to each other. At times, our group indulged in highly spirited conversations. Mimi always served as the moderator and was never shy in sharing her views. When Ida May was in better health, her presence at the table brought a sense of dignity as she and Mimi asserted a matriarchal presence and grace to our dining. Another thing that was special in these situations was the way the waitstaff treated all of us at the hotel where Mimi stayed at. The staff usually bent over backward to serve our every need. For most of us, this was a special time in our lives as we all bonded into a new family.

Big Dave has many talents. He worked for many years as a cook. His knowledge of the fine art of the culinary trade is astonishing. He has an active interest in history and is well versed in English history and tradition. He especially loves the British monarchs and is familiar with their rise to power and succession. Dave is also blessed with a photographic memory. In fact, his memory is so good that he can recall even the most trivial of matters long after the rest of us have forgotten. Added to all of this, Dave also is a keen collector of comic books and loves all the superheroes. He also loves sports, especially British football, and rugby. Overall, Dave is an extraordinarily gifted individual and trusted friend.

The Character of Frankie the Frog

Frankie mysteriously appeared in the garden at the monastery. Mother Superior and the rest of the sisters conveyed to me how Frankie had arrived one day without warning and stayed near the statue of the Blessed Virgin Mary in the cloister. When we visited my niece at the monastery, the story of Frankie was conveyed to me, and the rest is history. The character of Frankie represents the call to freedom and chastity that all young people need to consider in their lives. Through sacrificing and giving, a person can gain something much greater than pleasure, a relationship that's beyond human understanding and a love that knows no boundaries.

ABOUT THE AUTHOR

It has been a profound pleasure to share *The Wonderful Friendship* with you. This book reflects my own life in a lot of ways. A degree of sadness shadowed my youth. Nevertheless, through the prayers of others and my own faith conversion, I found a way forward. The emptiness of my past life has slowly faded away, overtaken by a new and wonderful light.

As to my own background, two college degrees were added late in my thirties. The degrees are in history from Kansas State University and Emporia State University. My interests include reading, history, antiques, and attending car shows. Currently, I am employed part-time for Kansas Central School Bus Company in Topeka, Kansas. One of the greatest highlights in my life was to volunteer as a big brother in Big Brothers and Big Sisters program for or local affiliate in Topeka. Through my years in the program, two little brothers took up my time. In 1982, the BB organization bestowed upon me the Kansas Big Brother of the Year. Also, I have worked through my church as a Eucharist minister for nursing homes and the homebound.

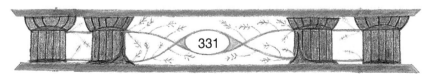

Working as a bus driver over the last eight years has opened my eyes to a lot of the suffering and challenges facing some of our youth. In writing this book, it's my fervent wish that every child in every school district can come to a better life through their commitment to higher principles of caring and service to others. It is through finding a purpose-driven life that a child builds something of great value for themselves, passing on a more just and decent society in the future.

CPSIA information can be obtained
at www.ICGtesting.com
Printed in the USA
JSHW032253070223
37406JS00005B/7

9 781685 701918